WILDE STORIES 2012

WILDE STORIES 2012

The Year's Best Gay Speculative Fiction

edited by

STEVE BERMAN

LETHE PRESS
MAPLE SHADE, NEW JERSEY

Published in 2012 by Lethe Press, Inc.
118 Heritage Avenue • Maple Shade, NJ 08052-3018
www.lethepressbooks.com • lethepress@aol.com
isbn: 1-59021-397-1 / 978-1-59021-397-1 (library binding)
isbn: 1-59021-398-X / 978-1-59021-398-8 (paperback)
isnb: 1-59021-410-2 / 978-1-59021-410-7 (e-book)

Set in Jenson, LemonChicken, Courier New, Helvetica Neue, and Bookman Old Style.
Interior and cover design: Alex Jeffers.
Cover art: Ben Baldwin.

TABLE OF CONTENTS

INTRODUCTION

Lately for another project I have been watching the old Amicus portmanteau/anthology films. *Ayslum. Tales from the Crypt. From Beyond the Grave.* An English film studio, Amicus cast a range of British actors—from genre favorites like Christopher Lee and Peter Cushing to then-unknowns like Tom Baker and Donald Sutherland—to emulate on the silver screen the late Grand Guignol of EC Comics rather than the more subdued yet chilling 1945 masterpiece *Dead of Night* (which is responsible for our fear of ventriloquist dummies).

Why all this talk of cinema in the introduction to a print (and, these days electronic edition) anthology? All my viewing of the Amicus films brought to mind how the editing of an anthology is somewhat similar to those portmanteau films: a brief preamble, then on to the stories, and, one could suppose, the final wrap-up with the reader curious about the "fate of the authors" by glancing over the bio entries.

A stretch? I suppose. These pages do feature genre favorites: Richard Bowes, Joel Lane and Lee Thomas. And there are new voices, such as Mat Joiner, Justin Torres and Stellan Thorne. Yet, this introduction is not truly introducing the authors as if they were doomed characters in some film (I always wondered why the portmanteau style was confined to horror—I suppose *The Twilight Zone* had staked an earlier claim on the weird, the fantastical as well as thought-provoking science-fiction.

Pity.) Or could I? Should I introduce to you *before the stories begin* all the troubled men found in the pages of *Wilde Stories 2012*? Fifteen very different stories offer quite the rogue's gallery.

Or would that diminish the effects, the intent, of the contributors? I think so. Reading is such a different experience than watching film. More intimate. More revealing of the self. More secrets are told, as if the author stands just over your shoulder and bends down to whisper in your ear his tale rather than performing on a set several feet away. I have never liked those introductions where the editor feels he must summarize or bait each and every story before the reader can turn the page and discover for him- or herself. Since these are the best of the gay speculative tales I discovered last year, I feel there is no need to do so. Their elegance and grandeur, mischief and subversiveness, need no preamble.

So let me end here and welcome you to the latest treasure of all that's gay and wondrous, eerie and fey. You could even snack on popcorn while reading. Some of the stories might be better read in the dark than others, but then, that all depends on your fantasies...

Steve Berman
Summer 2012

He would have liked to kiss his man but that would mean doing the ablutions over.

THE ARAB'S PRAYER

Alex Jeffers

Whrrr-click. The door near the top of the white plastic minaret opened and the little plastic mannequin teetered onto the balcony. Its painted beard was black, its turban green, its lips unmoved. *"God is great,"* sang the speaker behind the door, *"God is great!"*

"Time for you to get up," said Yaffe, jostling Mus'ad. "Prayer is better than sleep."

Mus'ad groaned indistinctly. Yawning, he tried to sit up, but his boyfriend's arm had him pinned down.

"I attest," sang the device on the shelf across the room: *"there is no God but God!"*

They struggled for a moment before Yaffe gave in, kissed the back of Mus'ad's neck, and removed his arm. Momentarily saddened by the loss of that weight, Mus'ad blinked gummy eyes and rolled away from Yaffe's sticky warmth to the edge of their bed.

"I attest: Muhammad is the messenger of God!"

"God honor him and give him peace," Mus'ad murmured, lowering his feet to the floor and sitting upright. The only light in the bedroom came from the glowing dome of the miniature mosque on its shelf. The window was so dark he could barely distinguish the tessellations of the mashrabiya through the glass. "How is it," he asked, turning back to Yaffe, a dark shadow on shadowy sheets, "you may be a secular Jew but I not a secular Muslim?"

"It's not *my* alarm clock."

"Come to prayer!"

"It was a gift from my mother!" She'd been amused by it, he assumed—she was a secular Muslim. Assembled in Gaza from Brazilian bioplastics, Turkish and Indonesian electronics, running Egyptian software and catching its time cues from an Israeli satellite, it commented on the world in ways its producers had failed to consider.

"Come to salvation!"

"I honor your mother as my own!"

Mus'ad shook his head. "I know you do. I know she doesn't care two figs. Habit, I guess. Will you kiss me before I brush my teeth?"

"Prayer is better than sleep!" sang the plastic muezzin as Yaffe sat up. They embraced again, nuzzled closed lips to closed lips, and Mus'ad stood. "Go back to sleep if you can, habibi."

"God is great! God is great!" The clock's voice was sampled from a famous Turkish muezzin so its accent was off. *"There is no God but God!"*

Yaffe dropped back to the pillow. "Perhaps." Mus'ad imagined a thoughtful frown.

In the bathroom, he blinked, dazzled by the lamp over the mirror. He brushed his teeth, shaved, showered. After the shower, before drying himself, he ran a trickle of cool water from the tub faucet and crouched to perform the prescribed ablutions.

Dried but damp again for the morning was already hot and humid, still nude, he returned to the bedroom. Yaffe snored. Pulling the white dishdasha off its hook, Mus'ad smiled. He would have liked to kiss his man but that would mean doing the ablutions over. The clock's glow had dimmed. He checked to make sure it wouldn't wake Yaffe with the second call—*he* would do that.

Nakedness covered, he went to fetch his rug, rolled and propped by the flat's front door. It was Pakistani, not an antique, not precious except by being all he had of his father's, a childhood gift. Going through the door, he touched his fingertips to the mezuzah on the frame and kissed them.

On the roof of their building, he spread the rug out below the tallest white-brick malqaf. When they moved in, he had worked out the position of the holy city: from this point the qibla axis projected between two smaller windcatchers, their verticals framing a mihrab in the air. It had seemed to him not quite right to say his prayers in rooms shared with a kafir nor fair to expect the unbeliever to observe them. He was not especially welcome at the most convenient mosque.

Before he began, he stretched and looked out from his height. Five years before, when he first said the fajr prayers on this roof, dawn had been hard to make out, quarrelling with the city's lights. But now, except for aircraft-warning beacons on their spires, the towers of Tel Aviv stood mostly dark, street lamps only blinked on when they sensed a pedestrian, and stars glimmered over the Mediterranean even as the sun's limb rose above the inland horizon. From a minaret's loudspeakers in Yafo, Mus'ad heard a faint voice proclaim the iqama, the second call. He sank to his knees.

Yaffe still slept, still snored, sprawled across half the bed. Mus'ad admired him for a moment, the lushness of his flesh pixellated by thin sunlight through mashrabiya, then went to the kitchen to make coffee. Both of them liked it Ottoman style, a finicky business. When the brass ibrik was balanced on the element, heating toward the first boil, he rooted through the basket by the door for his earpiece. He found Yaffe's first—they were distinguished by Yaffe's having a blue button. Another rummage found the 'piece with a green button. Tapping it into his right ear, he returned to the ibrik, not yet bubbling. The boot-up chime sounded deep in his ear. He waited for the second chord to indicate a connection established.

"Good morning, Mus'ad," the jinni in the cloud said in Hebrew.

They danced the call-and-response of ID verification, jinni and Mus'ad, while he watched the coffee seethe—the foam reached the ibrik's lip and he lifted it off the heat before the jinni was satisfied.

"Messages?" Mus'ad asked. The coffee needed to stew a moment. He turned away from the stove.

"Eleven professional, one personal."

The windows in the flat's main room faced north. No mashrabiya broke up the view. He looked down into the street. Indicators flashing, a van stood at the curb outside the bakery across the way. They might stop for breakfast.

"Personal."

It was Yaffe's mother in West Jerusalem. "My dear, my dear," she sang in her lovely, not quite idiomatic Arabic, "the Knesset votes today. I shall endeavor *not* to say a prayer."

Mus'ad smiled, wondering whether Yehudit had left the same message in English with her son's jinni, or Hebrew. He took two cups from the tray that displayed the painted coffee service he and Yaffe had brought back from their first holiday abroad, Spain—Sfarad. Al-Andalus.

He replaced the ibrik on the element for the second boil. His own mother, fond as she was of Yaffe, would never think to echo Yehudit's hope. Nadiyya was a staunchly modern woman who had divorced Mus'ad's mad father without sentiment. In '18, faced with the choice, she had not hesitated to resign Israeli citizenship—crossed the border only infrequently for coffee and shopping with the Jewish woman she called *sister* or to visit their sons on the coast, a foreigner in the nation of her birth. None of her former husband's actions had surprised, only saddened and angered her. She had no use for marriage.

The coffee smelled good, dark and rich with cardamom, and Mus'ad preferred not to think of his father. He poured it out and carried the two little cups and Yaffe's earpiece to the bedroom.

Yaffe was awake, surly, sitting cross legged on the mattress. The backlight of his slate gilded his face. Smelling the cardamom, he looked up. "I have to go to Cyprus."

"Oh." Mus'ad offered a cup. "Today?"

"Have to be on the dock in three hours. Should be back tomorrow night."

Mus'ad sat beside him. "That's not so bad."

"Unless something goes wrong."

Mus'ad didn't entirely understand Yaffe's job. He seldom had to travel but it was always sudden, while Mus'ad's business trips were meticulously plotted out months in advance. "Three hours—time for a fuck?"

"Come with me, habib." Slinging the slate aside, Yaffe took his boyfriend's free hand. "We'll get married."

Mus'ad met Yaffe's fierce grin with a smile. "Your mother called."

"I know—me too." Yaffe frowned, squeezed Mus'ad's fingers, sipped from his cup. "Drink your coffee, then we'll fuck. The act won't pass, you know. The rabbinate's been calling in favors all month."

"I have to work today. The Arab parties are far from certain, either, even the leftists. If it doesn't pass, I'll catch the night 'foil to Famagusta. I expect it takes a day or two for formalities—we'll spend the weekend."

"That, my love," said Yaffe sweetly, "sounds like a plan."

Mus'ad and his co-workers Yael and Yoel left the office for lunch. "You know," he was saying, "all my favorite Jews have *yod*-names—the two of you, Yaffe, his mom."

Fumbling for her ID, Yael laughed.

"You know," said Yoel, "I feel Vered would find that statement hurtful."

The building's retrofitted low-carbon-debt climate control wasn't overly efficient outside the server cores—the lobby especially, designed in the bad old days, was routinely warmer or chillier than ideal. Low-e glass had only succeeded in making the atmosphere murky. It meant, though, that the transition to outdoor summer heat wasn't quite so shocking. Mus'ad submitted to the retina scan, waved his ID past the sensor, held the antelobby door for his friends. "I adore your wife," he told Yoel, donning his glasses, "but I don't know her well enough to rank her as a favorite."

In turn, Yoel opened the outer door. Mus'ad strode through a moment of brilliant blindness before the glasses compensated.

Yael caught his swinging hand in an anxiously friendly way. "You don't come out with us enough, that's why you don't know Vered or Amir."

"Dinner tonight," said Yoel, hearty, from his other flank. "You and Yaffe. We'll add a *vav* and an *alef* to your favorites list."

"Thanks, but another time. Yaffe's on his way to Cyprus. I'm thinking of joining him."

"That's why you were working so hard!" Yael was a romantic.

They waited at the corner to cross. K-cars and electric runabouts and vans purred past. "What's in Cyprus?" asked Yoel. "Besides Yaffe."

The light changed. In Rabin Square across the street, there appeared to be a demonstration, noisy, parts of it joyful or expectant. "Marriage," Mus'ad muttered, removing his hand from Yael's and stepping into the crosswalk. Maybe they hadn't heard.

Yoel had. "It's that important?"

"It is to *them*."

He didn't mean the crowd in ordinary, everyday clothes listening to an orator on the City Hall steps, though their presence demonstrated its importance, their banners and signs and noisemakers. He meant the unholy alliance of the righteous—the clots and pustules of dog-collared Christian clerics, Arab and European, of robed Muslim imams and their bearded or veiled followers, of angry Torah scholars in crow plumage. He'd never seen so many Haredim at once outside of Jerusalem. He hadn't seen them so angry since the internationalization of the Old City and the holy places, the division of the new between two nations. A distant cousin of Mus'ad's, a little girl, had died in the Jerusalem riots in '17.

He looked away from the demonstrators, those on the side of the angels and those who said they spoke for God—looked up. Looked away from the scaffolding that had served as City Hall's façade for four years.

"Our very first holiday together," he told his friends, "abroad, that is, Yaffe and I went to Spain." They were cutting across the square, well away from demonstrators and counter-demonstrators. "In Granada, I asked him to marry me. Because, you know, we *could*. There. Civilly. Legally." Not unconsciously, he thumbed the ring on his right hand, rotating it around the finger. "I'd bought rings! When we came home, we could register with the Interior Ministry like any couple who married abroad."

Yael took his hand again. "He turned you down."

"He was feeling idealistic. Some politician, I don't remember who, had floated another attempt to instate civil marriage. Yaffe said it was an immoral abridgment of everybody's rights for marriage to be under the thumb of the religious courts. If he was a woman or I was, we still couldn't marry in our own country."

Yoel, who had married within the status quo, laughed. "I doubt the rabbinical courts would permit dear Yaffe to marry a Jewish woman even if he weren't gay. I doubt he'd put up with the rigamarole. I had my rebellious moments—" He laughed again. "But honestly, Mus'ad, why is it important? Vered and I only did it to please our parents. You and Yaffe, Yael and Amir—as common-law spouses you have all the same rights and privileges as me and Vered."

Mus'ad knew Yoel well enough not to be offended—Yoel was a conventional, don't-rock-the-boat young man—only vaguely hurt that Yoel didn't know him.

Yael was less patient. "If I could marry Amir without first convincing a pack of doddering nineteenth-century rabbis I'm a proper Jew, I would."

"Exactly. It's the principle." Mus'ad took a breath. "Also, I hate the term *partners*. I want Yaffe to be my husband."

Their path did not take them near the rebuilt memorial to the martyr Rabin. It did pass through the shadow of the newer monument that honored the seventy-nine civil servants killed in the City Hall bombing twenty-one years later. Yael squeezed Mus'ad's hand, making him cringe, and murmured too low for Yoel to hear, "It's nothing to do with you."

He should never have told her. *I was in Spain,* he thought. *In al-Andalus with my beloved.* Taken into custody at Ben Gurion, right off the plane, taken from Yaffe, interrogated, drugged, the least contents of his mind opened to their view, pawed over. It wouldn't have been appreciably easier for Yaffe to protest if they'd married in Spain. There were no charges, he was released—had known he would be released as well as he'd known they would arrest him. He had had no dealings with his mother's former husband since the divorce, nearly ten years.

He walked faster. He didn't think about it. Everything was better now.

"So you wore him down?" Yoel asked.

"Sorry?"

"Yaffe. Willing to settle for an EU marriage certificate now."

"Knesset wore him down. How many times has an act been floated? How many times have the rabbis and imams and bishops got it shot down? He asked me. Here, if today's vote is successful. Cyprus if not."

"Congratulations! Felicitations!"

"Indeed." Yael was grinning, the '16 memorial forgotten. "Here would be better, in all ways. I should like to be on hand."

"We should—oh." Stopping short, Yoel shook his head, then hurried after. "No, I forgot. I suppose not."

"Yoel, my friend, if you buy a bottle of Champagne, I promise to drink a glass with glad and grateful heart."

He supposed he was tipsy. Not drunk—he had been drunk once. Yoel had insisted on calling Yaffe, speeding across the blue Mediterranean, and standing him a split from the hydrofoil's bar. He, Mus'ad, drank a second glass without noticing—he broke the messenger of God's commandment perhaps twice a year—and then a client's call interrupted the dickering over division of the bill. He waved his friends off, back to the office, ordered coffee, and unrolled his slate: the client was calling from Kuala Lumpur at, for her, a thoroughly inconvenient hour.

The rally and counter-demonstration on Rabin Square had not broken up in the interval. The same speaker or a different one addressed the crowds. The separate religious parties still refused to mix, oil and oil seething atop troubled waters, united only in their anger. Passions might be more elevated, but not in a way that suggested a clear result from Givat Ram in West Jerusalem. He could ask the jinni but he was reacting poorly to the heat and bright sun. And Champagne. He took off his glasses to wipe sweat from his eyes.

"Are you ashamed?" The words were Arabic, the voice unfamiliar. "I know you, ibn Hassan. Your father would be ashamed."

Ashamed? The man who had been his father? That was one explanation. Partial, invalid explanation.

"I have no father." Mus'ad put his glasses back on. "I do not know you, uncle. Let me pass."

The man was not so much older than himself—not old enough to be truly his uncle. In the tired fashion of a decade before, he wore a black-and-white keffiyeh loose around his neck, three days' worth of black stubble on his face. "It was to prevent such abominations—"

"That man, Hassan, was the abomination," said Mus'ad, weary. "Let me pass, uncle. I have work to do and an appointment to keep this evening."

"Filth," the stranger said, flecks of spittle pinging the lenses of Mus'ad's glasses as he crowded closer. "Faggot filth unworthy son of a blessed martyr."

It was not anger, not yet, simply sorrow. "Indeed. I am quite certain the martyr reclines in paradise even now, surrounded by houris whose touch revolts him." Mus'ad stepped back and raised his left hand, spoke deliberately, formally, in Hebrew. "I do not know you, adoni. I do not wish to converse with you. It would be regrettable if I were forced to request assistance of these public servants." With his chin, Mus'ad indicated the armed young woman in IDF uniform on the point of taking an interest, her male partner intent on the restive Haredim.

As much a relic of an ugly past as any stubborn Haredi, the man stepped back. Another man than Mus'ad might find him handsome—the martyr Hassan, perhaps. He spat at Mus'ad's feet. "You will not escape the judgment of God."

"Oh, surely not," Mus'ad murmured under his breath as the man strode away. "Nor will you, my friend." He nodded politely to the IDF woman and walked on, ignoring a change in pitch in the noise of the crowd.

"My dear," said Yehudit through his earpiece, "foolish Haredim are rioting outside the Knesset and you may marry my son."

"Oh?" Mus'ad closed his eyes and flexed his fingers before pushing his slate away, across the desk. "I've been busy, not keeping track." The Kuala Lumpur client's problem was nearly solved. "I'm a little surprised. Have you told Yaffe?"

"He's not accepting calls. Not from me, anyway. I left a message. Are you well, Mus'ad? You sound…weary."

"Work." Mus'ad shook his head. "Going to join Yaffe in Cyprus tonight, have to finish things up." He breathed in, breathed out. "That is excellent news. Thank you for letting me know."

"Every Jewish mother wishes her son happily wed. This Jewish mother has waited years to call you her son."

As often as it was repeated, the claim never failed to make Mus'ad flinch with gratitude. "Yehudit—"

"You should call your mother. Or I will, if you're too busy."

"It will be some years more, I think, before Palestine or Gaza acknowledge such marriages. Yehudit, earlier I was reminded…."

"Yes?"

A lawyer, Yehudit had been his advocate when he went to court to renounce nasab, laqab, nisba, the whole panoply of patronymics and family identifiers that so bewildered non-Arabs, in favor of a simple Israeli-style surname. "When I changed my name—I don't think I've ever thanked you enough. It was a difficult time."

She hissed air through her teeth—he'd seen her do it, many times. "That man. Hardly a man, a sad, broken boy never permitted to grow up or be happy. He and his family lost any claim to share a name with you, Mus'ad, long before he killed himself."

And all the others, but she was too kind to mention them. "Thank you." Mus'ad's voice came thin.

"You paid my bill. Thanks are superfluous. Get back to work, my dear. Give your future husband my love tonight and tell him to call his mother."

Jeffers

Time was short. He needed to be at the dock by 1630. Even with the world at peace, security screening was never swift. Particularly not for an Arab. Another day the Knesset might abolish the requirement that IDs and passports proclaim one's religious affiliation—that one declare an affiliation. Another day.

He had packed for a holiday weekend. Doubtless he'd forgotten something but he and Yaffe had ready funds between them for incidentals, even at EU prices. He glanced around the flat's main room again. He had watered the plants, shut off devices that drained power even when inactive, given the thermostat permission to allow the flat to get warmer than they generally preferred. The rolled prayer rug by the door caught his eye.

"You were nobody's father, nobody's husband. You died unloved."

He shoved aside the low table before the sofa. Its feet screeched across the tiles. When he spread out the rug, he made sure the mihrab woven into its pattern did not line up on the axis to Mecca. It wasn't handsome, the rug, its colors garish, its workmanship not fine—it was small, the table would hide most of it. They should buy a bigger carpet for their home, he and Yaffe. In winter, the tiled floor became uncomfortably chill. He'd heard that artisans in Gaza were weaving interesting carpets—not as cheap as those from Pakistan, not as precious as even new Turkish or Afghan rugs, but interesting. Modern. He lifted the table onto the rug. The pieces of the Spanish coffee service trembled, ringing against each other. He looked around again, went to the bedroom.

On the nightstand by the bed he shared with Yaffe, the photo frame blinked from a snapshot of them in the Alhambra's Court of the Lions, where Mus'ad had asked Yaffe to marry him, to one of them at the Western Wall. The frame's carbon debt was minimal but he reached behind the nightstand to pull its plug from the socket. He twisted the ring on his finger. Now he was just wasting time he didn't really have.

Before unplugging the plastic mosque his mother had given him, he opened its control panel. The buttons were easy enough to figure out. He shut off the voice of the muezzin, saved the action into permanent memory, closed the panel. Deprived of its purpose, the thing was tacky, but a gift from his mother. He pulled the plug.

A Muslim was permitted to marry an unbelieving woman so long as their children were raised within the ummat al-mu'minin, the community of belief. The restrictions on a Jew, he believed, were more stringent. An Israeli had the whole world to choose from.

On his way out, Mus'ad brushed his fingers across the mezuzah on the doorpost, brushed them across his lips. There was sentiment and there was sentiment. Tapping the 'piece in his ear, he asked the jinni to let Yaffe know he was on his way.

And just yesterday we
discovered that Uncle
Gabriel's growing wings, too.

FAIRY TALE

Justin Torres

Father, I'm writing to tell you that Uncle Ramón has grown wings. It happened a couple of years ago, when I was still, in many ways, a child. They grow out of the side of his head, behind his ears. They aren't feathered wings, they're skin wings, like on a bat. He can't make them flap, but he can curl them in on themselves, roll them up like a sleeping bag, and then pop them out again. I remember when they first appeared—I used to follow him around, pulling on his pant legs, begging him to let me see and feel and smell them.

They smelled like cat piss.

"Come on man," I'd say, "give me some wings!"

He'd pretend like he didn't hear me, like he didn't notice me trying to jump up on his back and get a hold of them. He'd just whistle or hum softly to himself, ignoring me, then, all of a sudden he'd stop what he was doing, whip his neck around, bring his face down close to mine, and *bam!* Out would come the wings, so fast they'd make a noise like someone had been smacked in the face.

He hides them now. He's grown his hair, not a far-out seventies deal, but just enough to cover the wings when they're curled down. He wears hats with earflaps. He's fallen in love with some woman named Carissa, or Carmen, or Carmencita—I can't remember which.

"She don't want to be thinking about them when we're out at a restaurant, or on the street, or what have you," he told me the other day, "but when the door's closed, them wings get her juices flowing, if you know what I mean."

I wasn't quite sure then, but now I think I know what he meant.

Turns out, Uncle Miguel grew wings too, tiny ones, like a moth. He tapes them down with bandages because they flutter constantly and the noise of the fluttering so close to his ears gives him headaches and makes him feel crazy. He says it's like a dozen helicopters landing on his head. Thing is, the taped down wings give him headaches too.

"All that pent up longing," he says, "all that desire to flail and flap around. Them wings have needs."

And just yesterday we discovered that Uncle Gabriel's growing wings, too. His are even smaller than Uncle Miguel's, they don't curl or flutter yet, and everyone's saying they hope, for Gabi's sake, that they'll stay small and hidden. But to tell the truth Father, I'm hoping for some big, badass wings, hawk wings, or eagle wings, big enough for Uncle Gabriel to cover his eyes with when he's afraid.

This might disappoint you, but after the whole affair with Uncle Gabriel, I went straight to see Uncle Tito at his place. I didn't tell anyone where I was going, because everybody acts like Tito's some kind of an untouchable, a creep, a black smear of disgrace on the family. But I knew that if all of my other Uncles had wings, then he must have them too, and I was just dying to get my hands on them. I'm hot for wings, Father; I can't get enough.

Uncle Tito's wings were wilder than I hoped for. He couldn't even roll them up they were so huge, and they hung down the sides of his face like a bloodhound. He sat me on his lap and spread them for me with his hands. They were enormous, the size of pillowcases. The skin was thin and pink and translucent. Tiny, red and blue veins crisscrossed underneath the surface.

"Fuck," I thought, "them wings got my juices flowing."

"Watch this," he said, and wrapped them around my face, smothering me. It was warm and sweat-sticky and the stench of cat piss was overwhelming. I tried to pull the wings off me but they were elastic, the skin stretched and pulled like pizza dough. I couldn't breathe, and I couldn't scream, and Uncle Tito just kept pressing down harder and harder, until

I had to slam my knee down into his crotch and get the fuck out of there before he killed me. But I'll tell you, Father, all day I've been smelling that funky, ammonia smell, dreaming about them wings.

The way I see it, your wings should appear anytime now, probably within the next year or so, and I thought I'd give you a heads up. Don't be scared Father, they're beautiful really, and nothing to be ashamed of. When they do arrive, I hope they're strong enough to fly you home, so you can come and see us, after all these years.

Picture it Father, I'll scrub them clean for you, I'll rub them with oils until they shine, and I'll massage them wings, when they're sore. Maybe you'll take me for rides, up and up until we're both dizzy and tired. Maybe I'll grow wings of my own someday and when we walk down the street together, all the old grandfathers will stop to shake our hands and clap us on the shoulders. They'll tell us they see the resemblance, they'll point their chins at me, they'll say, "This one must be yours."

At this distance the buildings were black silhouettes, as though their real selves resided elsewhere and only the shadows they cast on the world could be seen.

THOU EARTH, THOU

K. M. Ferebee

Dunbar set to work at once in the garden. Whilst Mason unpacked boxes, airing the linens and arranging dishes in the narrow kitchen cabinets, Dunbar was on his knees in the knotted foliage, unearthing weeds. It was the principal feature of the house, this garden, and had been the aspect that finally committed them. It was unusually large for a suburban neighbourhood, measuring perhaps four metres by fifteen, and had been ferociously neglected by the former owner. Rosemary ran rampant in great spiny outgrowths; tomato plants towered and drooped their sad, untidy leaves. There were masses of flowers, grown tall and rather savage. The smell that rose out of it was vast and wild and heady, a riot of scent somehow indecipherably green. Dunbar was mad for gardening and had fallen for it instantly. "Just think," he'd said, "by the start of summer I could have it cut back, and we could plant pumpkins and courgettes and runner beans."

"We can buy all of those in a supermarket," Mason had pointed out, but by then it was too late: Dunbar had set his heart on having the garden. And, Mason was forced to admit, there was something pleasantly domestic about looking out the kitchen window and seeing his partner rooting in the sun-drenched greenery. Dunbar was slight and fair and sunburned easily, but he seemed at home in the outdoors in a way that was difficult to explain. Indoors he grew restless. Rooms seemed not quite large enough to contain him. Even in his sleep he moved constantly, shifting and reaching, as though his dreams were a box he longed to escape. In the garden he looked already calm and somehow restful. Mason allowed himself a small and wary smile.

They had left the city because Dunbar found it confining, though he was careful never to say so. This was on account of the fact that Mason thrived amongst the city's coffee shops and bookstores, and amongst its theatres—for Mason was a costumier. It was a trade he had undertaken not because of any particular affection for clothing, but rather out of a consuming passion for the antique. He worked on productions where it was necessary for period wardrobes to be meticulously recreated: waistcoats, farthingales, doublets with slashed sleeves. His work was detailed and exact; he had (he was aware) a reputation as slightly tedious. What satisfied him was his first glimpse of the clothes fitted to the living man or woman. After this moment the man, the woman resumed their prior form as actors and actresses, but for one instant a transformation took place. It was as though some small window had opened across the great distance of time, and Mason alone could press his face to it and see. A slow quiet joy suffused him at these times, which in all his life he had described to no one except Dunbar. The revelation that he loved Dunbar had been coincident with the revelation that Dunbar was capable of comprehending this one thing.

The suburbs had a quality of newness that Mason found disturbing. Their thin layer of civilization sat uneasily on the land. The bookstores were lined with fluorescent lighting; the coffee in the coffee shops tasted of machines. The cars had no scratches on them. He liked the dirt of the city, its tiredness, its inventory of old and broken things. He could have gone on living in his dingy apartment, where the lights flickered when the elevated train rushed by. But he had seen Dunbar's discomfort. Dunbar shied away from loud noise and crowded places; he had a peculiar terror of the subway that could not be tamed. He had moved to the city only to do postgraduate work at a prestigious school. Mason thought: When his degree is complete he will leave, and he will leave me. So it was at his suggestion that they began to look for a house outside the city. Though, "There aren't any theatres!" Dunbar protested.

"I can drive in to work," Mason said. It seemed a plausible, even ideal solution: Dunbar had a car, a tiny, cream-coloured thing. Standing at the kitchen window now, a ceramic cup held in each hand, he watched Dunbar moving bright-haired through the garden and was convinced that he had made the right choice. Their happiness seemed not only assured but also present: a warm, physical, corporeal being. It crept through the kitchen on light feet. Mason closed his eyes. He wanted to preserve this feeling.

Mason had taken off work for the week so that he and Dunbar could move. By the weekend after, it seemed that they were in some sense settled. Books had been set upon shelves in a semblance of order, Mason's antique gramophone—decorative only, as he owned nothing which it could play—occupied a side table, and over the mantelpiece in the parlour Dunbar had hung a large print of Altdorfer's *St. George and the Dragon*. This was Dunbar's favourite painting. In it, a wilderness of greens and golds swallowed the figure of the saint on his stallion. George's small, fragile body could scarcely be seen. The dragon, too, in defeat, was cowed and tiny. Only the vast spreading limbs of the trees were truly visible. They seemed triumphant, as though it were there victory and not the saint's that the artist portrayed.

Mason did not like to look at the painting. It made him uneasy. But Dunbar had owned it as long as Mason had known him. In the flat they shared on the east side of the city it had hung in the hall opposite the front door, so in a way it communicated to him homecoming. Once it was up above the mantel the migration was complete: the house was now home.

On the following Monday, Mason made his first commute into the city. He woke in the morning, sometime after dawn. It was not the alarm that had woken him, but his internal clock: an instrument of great precision. Beside him Dunbar lay unmoving, his body loose and curved slightly in sleep. Mason sat at the edge of the bed and watched him for a moment. He could not imagine the content of Dunbar's dreams. Sometimes Dunbar dreamed of Mason and would mention it casually later, in the midst of conversation. The Mason who inhabited his dreams was another man: a ghost form, a figment, given to extraordinary actions. Mason envied this other self, who roamed freely the most secret landscape of Dunbar's world. He wished now that he could lie back down and sleep beside Dunbar. Sleep prowled the limits of intimacy; it was the closest closeness he could attain.

Regretfully he dressed for work and exited the house. The front garden was wet and there was a kind of cleanness in the air. He could see no one else moving up and down the street. He supposed that the proper businessmen and women had left far earlier for their offices, whilst anyone remaining behind was sunk in sleep still. The absence from the scene of anything human—all he could see were the shadows of birds, the shivering motion of wind in the trees—set his hair on end. He climbed hastily into the car and turned the radio on, tuning in to a morning call-in show. The human voices were shrill and familiar. They seemed to wake the world around him. He drove away, the wildness he had sensed melting off like a dream.

He was encouraged to find how close the city seemed. Once he was inside his workshop, the noise of downtown traffic and street chatter hit him, rising through the windows, a more beautiful white noise than the sound of the sea. It was as though he only lived in an outer borough—not, after all, so very far away.

The theatre for which he did his principal work was staging a summer production of *The Tempest*, and the loft that housed the workshop was littered with a mélange of material. Overskirts and whitework ruffs were carelessly displayed. Lengths of lawn and sarsanet were draped across the tables. A stripped farthingale sat in one corner, rather skeletal. Folded on Mason's desk was a finished item: a water-stained cambric shirt. The limp ruffles at wrist and neck were rich with blackwork. The embroidered pattern was a choice of Mason's own, a running row of artichokes embellished by knots of leaves. He liked the unexpectedness of the artichokes where there might have been roses, cowslips, sage. The design was dense and well-executed. The spines of the artichokes seemed fragile things. He thought, not for the first time, that he would like to see Dunbar in the shirt. It was intended for the actor played Ariel. It would be large on Dunbar; the cuffs would almost cover his hands. But something in the embroidery seemed to suit him. The lushness of it, the dark foliage that threatened to engulf the sleeves. Dunbar would love it.

Or, Mason thought, I would love him in it. He weighed the difference. For a moment it seemed difficult to distinguish the two things.

Come evening he extinguished the lights of the workshop, locked the loft door, headed northwest over the river and away. In his rear mirror he could see the ragged spine of the city laid out behind him. Dusk suffused it with a blue and tranquil glow. At this distance the buildings were black silhouettes, as though their real selves resided elsewhere and only the shadows they cast on the world could be seen. Mason watched until a sharp turn took them out of sight. By this time it was quite dark and he was driving on clean empty suburban streets.

Dunbar met him at the door. He had cooked dinner. The kitchen smelt of onions and sage. The table was laid with wineglasses, napkins, china. There was even a candle, a cheap pillar guttering on a spare plate.

Dunbar said, "I thought it would be nicer than takeaway."

"It's lovely," Mason assured him. He set his satchel beside the table and took a seat.

They shared a bottle of white wine, which went well with the chicken Dunbar had roasted. There were parsnips also, buttered and salted, and rocket salad, and very crisp garden peas. It was far too much food for two people. Mason toyed with a parsnip. "We'll have leftovers," he said.

Dunbar rested his elbows on the table like a little boy. "An embarrassment of riches," he said. "I dug the parsnips up out of the garden. There's loads of stuff alive. I just have to cut the weedy bits away."

Mason glanced at the back window. It looked almost like a flat black pane. He could only just make out the outline of the garden, touched by a neighbour's porch light. The snarled foliage was moving slowly in an unseen breeze. The light was very yellow. It lent a ferociousness to what it touched. Mason found he was no longer hungry. He set his fork against his plate. Dunbar was still talking animatedly about the garden. The candle sent shadows running across his face.

"—a lot of common plants are really hardy; they'll survive about anything. Of course we can root up what we don't like, but there's something sort of wonderfully anarchic about letting it grow, don't you think?"

"I think you should do what you like," Mason said. "Look, do you want to watch television and leave the dishes for the morning? I can do them on my way into work, if you don't mind." He needed the voices of strangers, their exaggerated speech rising and falling in cadences unmistakably human. The noise of a larger and more civilised world pouring out of the TV screen.

"Are you sure?" Dunbar asked, but he didn't argue. Mason stored the leftovers and set the dishes to soak. Then they sat together on the couch, watching a marathon of a crime drama that neither of them had ever seen. Halfway through, Dunbar fell asleep on Mason's shoulder. Mason lowered the volume on the TV. He could feel Dunbar's breath, warm and damp, stirring against his neck, his dry and slightly spiky hair tickling his cheek. A surge of gentleness struck him. He felt that Dunbar's life, little and precarious, was in his hands. He knew that he should rouse Dunbar so that they could go to bed, but he did not want to forfeit that moment. It seemed to him that they were the only two living things for miles, and furthermore that all round them darkness was closing. If he moved, if he switched off the TV, they would be marooned.

In the new house Dunbar slept better. He did not twitch and move so much. In the city Mason had often been startled awake by his frantic motions. Here it was Mason himself who began to have trouble with sleep. He would lie in bed, kept awake by the terrible stillness of his surroundings. There was no noise of cars, no ambulances weeping far away into the night. He could hear Dunbar's heart beating, the steady inhale and exhale of his breath. It should have been comforting, this sound, but it scared him. He pressed his face against Dunbar's shoulder; closed his arms around him like a vice. Even when he managed to sleep, fears dogged him. One morning Dunbar woke with bruises where Mason had, dreaming, held his wrist too tightly. The bruises were like fingerprints marked blue upon his skin.

During the days, Dunbar was at work on his thesis, which concerned wilderness and the Romantic imagination. He had a computer set up in the spare bedroom. The floor was littered with stacks of library books: the poetry of Byron and Coleridge, illustrated volumes on Salvator Rosa and the evolution of the English garden. He would not allow Mason to read what he had written, and kept the typed and finished pages in a cardboard box tied with a string.

Mason strongly suspected that Dunbar did not leave the house except to work in the garden. It made a kind of sense: Mason took the car each morning into the city, and there was nothing, no cinema nor shop nor restaurant, for miles around. And he could not deny that Dunbar was making great progress in the garden. Each night the kitchen seemed more flush with food. There were ripe aubergines and green peppers, tomatoes on the cusp of redness and carrots that tasted slightly dark from the earth. Plants of varying seasons seemed all, simultaneously, to bear fruit. Dunbar brought in armfuls of spring and autumn flowers and intermixed them in glass jars. It was strange, but then modern agriculture was marvellous. Mason did not question it. Dunbar was radiant all the time; he seemed so pleased.

Mason was drinking coffee in the kitchen one morning, preparing to leave for work, when Dunbar came in from the garden. His hands were covered in dirt and cupped in front of him as though he held something precious. The two of them had lived in the house for nigh on a month, by then.

"Look at what I've found," Dunbar said. He showed Mason. Several off-white teeth lay in the palms of his hands. They were curved and sharp: clearly not the teeth of a man, but some sort of predatory animal. "I dug them up in the garden. They're sharks' teeth."

Mason picked one up. It was small and very pointed. "How do you know?"

"I've seen them before. You find them where there used to be water. Dried-up sea beds from, I don't know, the Pleistocene."

The tooth was the colour of old bone. Loose earth flecked it. A queasy feeling gripped Mason. He set it back in Dunbar's hand. "It's strange," he said. "I mean: somebody must have churned up the soil. Otherwise you wouldn't just find them lying about so near the surface, would you?"

Dunbar frowned. "I don't know. I suppose they could have done. Churning up's what you do to gardens, when you're planting."

"I just think it's odd; that's all."

"I think it's marvellous. I thought you would like it. You like old things." Dunbar closed one hand around the sharks' teeth possessively, like a fist.

Mason said, conscious of his misstep, "It is marvellous. We should show them to an expert. Someone at a museum."

"Who knows what else I might find," Dunbar said. "We should wait."

Before he went back out to the garden he laid the sharks' teeth on the windowsill, all in a row. The morning light made them look white and polished. Mason thought: These are not fossils. They might have been new. Terror seized him, brief and irrational as a wave on the sea. It was the new house, he told himself, the sense of strangeness permeating everything. He downed the last of his coffee and collected the car keys from the table. When he was in the city, amongst familiar surroundings once again, he would look back at the morning and laugh at his nervous disposition. He would be amazed at the idea that there was anything sinister about that tiny, docile handful of teeth.

In the workshop, Mason was constructing a collar for Ariel out of rocaille beads. It was several rows thick. The beads were old and slightly uneven. He sorted them in blues and golds and greens. He could have delegated the task to someone else, to one of the postgraduate students who came for summer internships and were expert in obscure topics: the history of the carcanet, or spindles, or shuttle-weaving. But he enjoyed the labour: intricate and meditative. It took hours to interlock the beads. He had intended their colours to evoke sun on ocean water, but instead he was reminded of the Altdorfer painting—*St. George and the Dragon*—with its dense, voluptuous leaves. The dragon was the last of St. George's problems. His back was still turned to that vast and threatening forest. The light like a web amongst the trees.

Mason often worked late, but was reluctant to admit that he liked it. After dark the city turned coy and familiar. The streets seemed smaller, low-ceilinged; the commuters went. He could look from the loft into other buildings' lighted windows and see men and women performing every ordinary action: working, cooking, crying, as though they were onstage. He felt connected to these people. A sympathy existed between them. I too am here, I too am human, he wanted to say. Instead he would have to wind the silk thread and store the beads, switch off the work lamps, and be on his way. Down in the street he walked past cafes, diners, bars from which life spilled onto the pavement. He was a part of this life just by his passing. But when he closed the door to the car the connection was severed. He drifted home in a miasma of sadness, lonelier than he had ever been.

Mason knew that if he told Dunbar of this feeling, Dunbar would insist that they move back to the city. He would downplay his love of the house and its salutary effects upon him. He would declare that a few window boxes would satisfy him in place of the garden. Mason imagined the conversation and experienced already, preveniently, his shame and dread. He could not allow Dunbar to sacrifice the house and garden. But all the same each night it was harder to steer himself onto the motorway. Home seemed an unreal island, half-submerged in the distance. He envisioned a day when he would be unable to locate it. It would simply have slipped away.

When he entered the house and glimpsed Dunbar's quick and crooked smile, he repented of these feelings. He was aware that they constituted a betrayal he could not atone for or even explain. He began to bring gifts back from the city: antique books, bottles of wine, supper from their favourite Indian takeaway. Once he even brought flowers and then felt a fool, for of course the house was full of flowers. Roses dropped fragrant petals from a vase on the kitchen counter; tiger lilies overtook nasturtiums in a bowl in the front hall.

"I didn't even know you could grow tiger lilies in this climate," Mason said, disturbed by the fierce bell-shape of the blossoms.

Dunbar shrugged. "I know; it's like magic. I hardly have to do anything at all."

But he did do something, for he was always at work in the garden. On weekends, when Mason would have liked for the two of them to escape to the city, Dunbar was reliably found in an old university t-shirt, carrying a trowel and spade. He had by now a sunburn across his nose and the tops of his cheekbones that never quite went away.

One Sunday morning as Mason lingered over the *Times* inside, Dunbar came into the kitchen looking puzzled. "I think you'd better come out to the back porch," he said.

Mason did so. There, resting on the bleached wooden boards, was a large off-white skull. It was unmistakably animal in origin: long and flattish, with wide eye sockets and prominent canine teeth. Dirt was packed into the curves and hollows of the bone, as though it had been a long time buried. Mason looked at Dunbar.

"I dug it up in the garden," Dunbar said.

"What is it?" Mason knelt for a closer look, but could not bring himself to touch it. There was something subtly horrible about the object, more than its intrinsic aura of death.

"I think it's the skull of a wolf," Dunbar said uncertainly. "Though it could be a very large dog, like a Siberian husky, I suppose."

"A pet," Mason said. He was trying to convince himself of this possibility. "They buried a pet in the backyard—someone who lived here before."

"A long time before," Dunbar said. "It seems old."

It did seem old. There was something about the bone—a graininess, a discolouration—which suggested a museum piece, a specimen from ten thousand years ago. Mason was reminded of the skeleton of a mammoth he had seen once, unearthed from a peat bog. It had possessed the same sepia quality. He tried not to think of it; tried not to look at the empty holes where the eyes of the dog or wolf had been.

He said, "We should ask the neighbours. Perhaps one of them's lived here for a while; they might have known the people here before us."

Dunbar nodded his assent. "It is a bit exciting," he said. "You have to admit."

"Do you think?"

"Well. You wouldn't get this in the city. Anything at all could be out there."

Mason said, "Yes."

That night he could not sleep. He extricated himself from where Dunbar had curled around him. Dunbar mumbled something without waking, a slurred protest intelligible only in his dreams. Mason stroked his bare shoulder: the clean line of collarbone beautiful under the skin. He rose and walked noiselessly into the kitchen. He took a glass from the cabinet and filled it at the tap. The noise of the water rushed through the still room. Something tapped against the window—an insect, a stray beetle or wasp striking the pane. The noise came again. Unwillingly, Mason looked at the window and out into the garden. He could see at the edge of the porch the white skull dully gleaming. Farther out the stray edges of foliage crept and swayed. There was very little light, only the dim beams of the porch lamp. Most of the garden was a mass of darkness. But from it, a single shadow seemed to detach itself and move. Mason watched it dumbly. He could not say, exactly, what it was: whether animal or other. It was the size of a large cat or average-sized dog, but resembled neither. He had only the briefest glimpse of it, a solid black shape, and then it was gone. He set the glass down on the counter. Both his hands were shaking. Adrenaline left him light-headed, alert with fear. He considered his options. Under no circumstances could he bring himself to walk out to the garden. Instead he checked the locks on the door and walked carefully back to the bedroom. Dunbar was still sleeping. Mason climbed into bed beside him, wrapping his own body around Dunbar's like a living barrier, a human shield. He was still shivering, every muscle convulsive. He had never before felt so small or helpless. Even this one gesture, the embrace, seemed feeble. He knew that from what he had seen in the garden there was no way to protect Dunbar, no way at all.

The noise of the alarm clock woke Mason in the morning. He switched it off and lay in the blue dawn. Sometimes in the night Dunbar had moved away from him and lay sleeping with his face pressed into the pillow. Shadows, long and lazy, shaded the ladder of his spine. He looked like an antique photo, taken by an Aesthete before the invention of colour. The men in such photos were always lush and sleepy-eyed, yet something in the contours of their bodies suggested an animal power about to be freed.

Mason rose from the bed, feeling dull and half-delirious, as though he had not slept at all. He went to start the coffee maker in the kitchen. In the innocent and oddly tender light of day, there seemed nothing unusual about the garden. The skull on the porch was only a bit of bone. He stood, staring absently out the window, till the coffee was done brewing. Drinking his first cup, he wondered what to tell Dunbar. Perhaps it was best to tell him nothing. If told, he would think that Mason was mad, or that it was an excuse to return to the city. Mason did not know how to articulate the truth of what he had glimpsed, the plunging terror inspired by that black shape moving in the garden. Even to him it seemed faintly absurd. His city eyes had seen a cat or even a very large bird and misconstrued it. It was only the foreignness of his surroundings showing through. Yet there were the sharks' teeth, and the wolf's skull, and something further that defied description. The flowers, vivid and sensuous, always in bloom.

I'll take the shark's teeth to someone at a museum, he thought. Or I can ask a neighbour; surely they'll know if there's something odd going on. He had not so far met any of the neighbours. He had not even seen them—only new and anonymous cars parked at the kerbside, which were gone in the morning, and sometimes the light from a window at evening or the blue glow of a TV. He assumed, though, that a neighbour at least would be able to say what flowers the climate yielded. It was the sort of thing that suburban folk could tell you.

Dunbar wandered into the kitchen, barefoot and bed-headed. He looked tired. "Hullo," he said. "Early start for someone so restless."

"Did I wake you last night?"

"Only a bit. It was in my dream, but all changed about, the way dreams are. You got out of bed, but what got back in wasn't you. It wasn't even a person. It was some other thing." He blinked, hugging his elbows as though the room had gone cold.

Mason said uncertainly, "That sounds like a nightmare."

"I suppose it was. I don't really remember." His gaze drifted.

Dread gripped Mason. "Come into the city with me," he said suddenly. "I can drop you off at your university; you can go to the library while I'm working. Or see your advisor. Or anything."

Dunbar laughed, surprised. "What's brought this on?"

"Does it matter? We can get dinner. Something expensive. You choose."

"I can cook dinner here," Dunbar said. "Besides, I can't. I have a chapter due by the end of the week; I've loads of work to do."

"Friday, then," Mason persisted. "You can come Friday. Even better: a late night."

"All right; I'll think about it." He grinned, obviously humouring Mason.

"Good," Mason said.

Before he left for work he slipped the sharks' teeth into his jacket pocket. He had an hour for lunch; perhaps he could run them by a museum. As he drove he was conscious of them, as though they had a sentient presence. He was glad to have gotten them out of the house. If I can't get someone to take a look at them, he thought, I'll throw them in the river. I can make up a story for Dunbar, say I left them at work or lost them. A hole in the pocket that they slipped through. He wondered if he would feel safer with them at the river bottom. Always, from here onwards, he would know that they were out there. No place seemed far enough away.

In his workshop he surveyed Ariel's costume. It seemed to him the most important, the most intrinsic to the play. His original design had dressed the spirit as a drowned traveller, with a few addition: the beaded collar, and a set of thin bright chains that locked at wrist and ankle. Make-up would enlarge the actor's eyes and give him a wild fey air. Yet somehow, looking at the assembled items—the ragged trousers, the glass jewellery, the shirt with its snarls of blackworked thread—he felt that he had failed to capture that in Ariel which was most beguiling: the sense that beneath his eagerness to please there lurked a nature not remotely human. Savage and indifferent, ungoverned as the sea. His clothes should seem foreign, rather like a cage he carried with him. But there was perhaps no way to convey this.

Mason sighed and closed his eyes. Next he had to oversee the costume for Caliban. It was a job that he had delayed. The design had come to him in a dream, but he did not like it. He didn't think he could look at it now. There was something distasteful about the costume itself, which was dirty and sewn all about with stalks and leaves. He had intended it to be threatening, which the dream had been: a nightmare in which he was walking through a field and found that the wild grass all around him was in fact composed of frail and skeletal hands protruding from the earth, slowly waving. It had disturbed him more than any dream he could remember.

A thought came to him. He rose and walked to the table on which the costume in question was laid. There was an empty space about the collar, where it had been impractical to place leaves. Mason felt in his pocket and found the handful of teeth. He spread them along the collar, imagining that they were sewn there. They were menacing, redolent of magic. They would do nicely. More: he would always know where they were.

He wanted to believe that by incorporating the teeth into a costume he had in some manner disarmed them. But in fact they remained as alien, as frightening as they had been. When he looked at the costume he shuddered minutely. He wished he had forced Dunbar to come with him into the city. From time to time Mason would think of him alone, typing in his little office or—worse—at work in the garden, and a kind of panic would seize him. His hands would clench as though there were a physical threat against which he had to defend himself, or alternately a powerful emotion that he must at all costs keep in. Other people in the costume shop commented that he seemed unusually nervous. He considered calling home, but could not bear the idea of worrying Dunbar. Nor was there a specific fear that he could, with a phone call, assuage.

In the end he resolved to simply leave work as early as possible. He would escape traffic, arrive before the sun had finished setting. But when the time came, a kind of paralysis gripped him. A numb dread. He could see as though at a great distance the scene that would await him: the still street moody with twilight, the covert hints of life leaking from within the neighbouring houses, the disquiet he would feel even as he stood on the doorstep, hesitating with the key. The house was repellent, and he found to his shame that the force with which it drove him away was stronger than his desire to be with Dunbar. It was not strong enough to stop him returning, but strong enough, certainly, to slow and impede him. He found excuses to stay in the workshop. He conceived of an alteration to Ariel's costume: the chains, he thought, should instead be silver ribbons that at the end of the play, upon Ariel's release, would slither free.

When at last he left the city it was quite dark— so late, in fact, that he was surprised Dunbar had not called either the workshop or his mobile. The silence propelled him out of the office and homewards. As he crossed the river he looked from the car window and saw that under the yellow light of the municipal lanterns the water lay perfectly flat. It was motionless, like a large black snake.

Driving at night in the area just northwards of the city, he often felt that he was flying through darkness. It was the way he felt now. Any light—a traffic signal, the neon sign of a roadside café—was shallow and glancing. The headlights of his car shone no further than six feet ahead. When he reached the house he was surprised to find the porch light gleaming. It was wan and pale but so present, like an island picked out by the sun on its sand.

For a moment he stood at the door. His impulse was to knock: unconscionably, strangely. He leant his forehead against the glass panel that was set like a window into the wood. The key was in his pocket. He had only to use it. Close to the cool surface of the door his lips moved, forming a word. He did not know what the word was. It was a sigh, an exhalation. After a moment he took the key from his pocket and entered into the front hall.

Most of the lights in the house were burning. He could hear the noise of water running in the kitchen, and of dishes being washed, and the noise, too, of Dunbar humming: a beautiful but somehow melancholy tune. Mason walked just to the doorway of the room and watched Dunbar drying a glass with a damp towel. The glass gleamed in his hands.

He wore an absent and undeveloped smile, as though he were almost thinking of something pleasant.

"I've come home," Mason said.

Dunbar lifted his eyes. "I was beginning to think you'd left me," he commented.

"Never," Mason said.

"There's dinner in the fridge. I didn't know if you'd eaten."

"I haven't. I ought to have called."

"It's all right," Dunbar said, sounding surprised. "I'm not angry."

"Perhaps you ought to be." Mason stripped off his jacket and laid it on the kitchen table. He walked to where Dunbar was leant against the stove and kissed his forehead lightly. He rested his hands against Dunbar's hips. There was a faint foreign smell to him, something like a pine forest, remote and wild.

"I didn't have time to be angry," Dunbar said. "I've had the most remarkable day. You won't believe what I found out in the garden."

Mason closed his eyes. "Worse than the last time?"

"Better," Dunbar said. His eyes were very bright, almost febrile. He tugged Mason's hand as he made for the back door. Outside the porch light was burning with a low and sullen glow. The wolf's skull looked yellow in the semi-darkness. The air was oddly cold. Mason tasted something sour in his mouth, like old wine gone slightly off. He did not want to move any further into the garden.

Dunbar bent at the edge of the porch, towards the outer radius of the light, and picked up a shoebox lid. He carried it, careful to keep it flat, to where Mason was standing. "Isn't it beautiful?" he said.

Mason looked. Lying on the cardboard were the bones of a hand, complete and perfectly arranged. At first glance the hand appeared human; when he looked again, Mason was not sure this was the case. The proportions were subtly incorrect, the finger bones a little too long. They seemed to curl in claws. A fine grey dust covered them. Mason thought, If only it were human. It would be so much easier to explain.

"Don't you think it's a bit strange?" he asked Dunbar, trying not to betray his horror.

Dunbar shrugged. He looked down at the lid. "I thought so at first," he said. "But then the strangeness sort of went away. I'm not frightened. I think it's the loveliest thing I've ever seen."

Mason resisted the urge to knock the lid from his hands and send the finger bones flying. He knew it would not change what was happening; he knew that it would have no effect at all. He put his hand against Dunbar's cheek. Dunbar's skin was cool, dry; below it the bones were so fragile. When he smiled Mason could feel the muscles of his face move.

"I'm going to go and see if the neighbours know anything about this," Mason said, as calmly and gently as he could. He backed away from Dunbar and made it inside the house before his stomach rebelled and he was sick, once, in the kitchen sink. All that came up was a bitter and colourless liquid. His nausea did not abate. He wiped his mouth. His hand was not shaking—which surprised him. Perhaps, he thought, perhaps it is because I know what I have to do.

He collected his jacket from the table and left the house, leaving the front door unlocked behind him. All up and down the street the houses of his neighbours were silent and utterly still, though here and there he could see a hint of light behind a window. He walked determinedly up to the house next door. The porch light was not on, and shadows seemed to breed in the flowerbeds. Beside the door was an electronic doorbell, which he pressed. He could hear the chime sound, hollow and resonant, through the high ceilings of the house's front hall. But though he waited for a minute, then another, and finally pushed the doorbell again, there was no hint of answering footsteps.

He proceeded to the next house. Here the porch light was lit. A large brass knocker was affixed to the door. Mason slammed it three or four times in his urgency before noticing that there existed an old, crooked doorbell as well. He rang the bell. It sounded odd, slightly tinny, as though it had not been rung in years. At the sudden noise he thought he saw a curtain twitch in the window, as though someone or something were standing just behind it. He waited, but no one came to the door.

The third and fourth houses were the same. Mason knocked against the door, against the front window, but it seemed that no one was at home. He leant against the doorbell of the fourth house in his desperation, listening to it ring on and on its flat unmusical peal. He was sure that the noise could be heard out in the street, yet no dog barked nor irate door slammed. No one stirred in any of the houses. They sat quietly as the dead.

When he turned very fast from the door he saw again a flicker of motion: this time in an upstairs window across the street. The white and filmy cloth of the curtain shook slightly. Mason thought he perceived a black shape moving behind it. But it might have been a trick of the breeze. Surely it was the breeze, too, that moved through the leaves of the small bushes and mulberry trees, producing a sound like a low whispering.

Suddenly paranoid, he stood at the edge of the pavement and shouted, "I know you're there! I know you're in there! Why won't you help me?"

There was no reply, and for the first time it occurred to him that they were not hiding, that no one was home in any of the houses, nor had anyone ever been. The curtains, the lights, the cars that came and went were all an elaborate trick or illusion. He was alone with Dunbar. All round them was only the indifferent darkness, for miles. He could get into the car and start driving, but he did not know how long it would be before he found some sign of life, another human being. He knew that if he left the neighbourhood he would not have the courage to return to it. Even now terror was seeping through him like a cold flood. He could not walk into the house where Dunbar waited, if what waited was still Dunbar.

Mason dropped to his knees on the damp asphalt. It seemed to him that the weakness in his heart diseased his body; he no longer had the strength to stand. Around him moonlight turned the streaks of tar in the road to silver ribbons. Something moved in the darkness, prowling the neat low grass where Mason could not quite see. He did not want to see it. He thrust his hand into the pocket of his jacket and found there, like an amulet, the car keys.

Before he walked out he smiled as brightly as he had ten years before in the Met lobby and said, "I don't think you're really here and you don't think I'm really human."

HOFFMANN, GODZILLA AND ME

Richard Bowes

On a speculative fiction convention panel called something like, "Stealing our Genre—Fantasy Appropriated!" the talk turned to E.T.A. Hoffmann, the early nineteenth-century German Romantic writer. Ballets like *The Nutcracker* and *Coppélia* and Offenbach's opera *Tales of Hoffmann* are based on his stories.

Actually, I brought up the subject. Hoffmann often included himself as a narrator/character. And he's one of the reasons I thought it was ok to do.

The opera was important to me a kid (Yes, I was that kind of kid). In it a drunken Hoffmann tells of losing his soul, becoming infatuated with an automaton and committing other follies in pursuit of love.

Several of the panelists were academics and the conversation turned to Authorial Ideation. I'm easily bored and have an almost magical ability to go away while staying on the scene. My gaze wandered and I found myself in eye contact with a guy in the front row, young in a world growing grey.

He smiled, nodded and when the panel was over stepped up to introduce himself and say how much he enjoyed my stories—a young man of sensitivity and discernment.

He was a writer I'd heard of and much cuter than I'd expected. We walked to the hotel bar and he described a proposal he had for an anthology of stories about the destruction of New York City.

It was tentatively called *Godzilla Does Manhattan* and he wondered if I'd be interested. The proposed payment-per-word wasn't half bad. The kid was friendly and looked like he worked out. I said it sounded interesting.

We hung around for a while and he talked about recent New-York-Gets-Destroyed movies, none of which I'd found particularly compelling: *Cloverfield, I Am Legend, Independence Day*. When he described death and devastation, his eyes glistened.

Then he said, "Please. It wouldn't be a New York book without queer content. And I know you do first person stuff." If not gay the kid was certainly curious.

Ten years before I'd have gone out of my way to make sure we got alone somewhere. Now we both had convention roommates and it felt like more trouble than it was worth. The young anthologist seemed to get this. And given the chance to reconsider the situation he was probably relieved.

Other events and other people intervened. On Sunday afternoon as the convention was breaking up, I walked through the hotel lobby to find my ride back to the city. The anthologist spotted me and asked if I'd given *Godzilla Does Manhattan* any more thought. Nothing is sadder than an old whore. Though I'd completely forgotten about it, I said it sounded great and he could put me down as a contributor.

On the frontier of old age small incidents produce grave thoughts. Is my repeatedly loosing the remote control that operates my CD player or my blank stare at the computer screen as I try to remember why I logged on explained by head injuries I took when I was young? Or is this just the natural course of everything slowly going bad as time dances on?

Surfing a mild S&M website I got a jolt from the distant past. The site was full of vintage black and white snapshots from the '50's and '60's. I found one I've seen online before under a variety of titles. This time it was called "Daddy's Home."

HOFFMANN, GODZILLA AND ME

In it a crewcut American boy, thin in the way of kids back then, stands naked in a suburban living room. He looks sixteen though I know he's nineteen. Tan lines on torso and legs show that it's summer and he's spent time in the sun. His dick is semi-hard and his palms are resting on his buttocks like maybe he expects to get spanked.

In fact that pose is probably because I was used to having back pockets and didn't know what else to do with my hands. The college I attended had compulsory ROTC and gym which I hated. But the hours of close-order drill and wind sprints had produced good definition.

I even recognized the couch behind me and remembered Bill, the guy who picked me up on the Fire Island Ferry in the summer of '63 and paid me to play and pose.

I've wondered how this shot got into circulation—did Bill give it to someone or sell it? Was it among his effects when he died? Did he live long enough to be online?

The kid in the photo gazes away from the camera and the eyes are blank. The message is you can do what you want with him and he won't be back until it's over.

The ability to go away and leave my body behind was something I'd probably developed very early, maybe had from birth. But I really noticed it in Boston when I was sixteen, going on thirteen. I'd been turned on to sex a few years before and now was getting picked up, sneaking booze, dropping Benzedrine. My parents didn't want to know what I was doing but wanted very much for me to stop doing it.

Schoolwork didn't interest me at all, my grades slipped and I ended up in summer school. One Sunday night I snuck out and came home late and considerably messed up. My father was waiting. My pants and shorts got taken off and my ass got beaten, things I'd thought were in the past.

For the foreseeable future if I wasn't at school, my part-time job or Sunday Mass I would be at home in pajamas or, this being summer, pajama pants (doubly humiliating: real boys slept in their briefs). This guaranteed that I couldn't leave the house. I was to do my homework and be in bed with the lights out by eight o'clock.

Leaving for school each morning, I'd plot an escape; imagine I'd find some guy who'd take me away with him. But each evening like I was under a malign spell I lay awake in the hot dark listening to kids my age out on the street, hoping none of them would discover what had happened to me.

From a distance, I watched this hopeless boy stripped of all his pride and was glad I didn't have to share his agony.

Eventually my mother became concerned or maybe bored. Friday night she let me get out of bed and watch a movie with her on the *Late Show*. It was then I saw the strange, ballet-drenched English film of the opera *Tales of Hoffmann* about which I'd known nothing.

In act two Hoffmann loses his soul to a woman who's the Devil's pawn. I watched myself watch the movie and decided my ability meant that somewhere along the way I also had lost my soul. In the opera Hoffmann gets his back at the end of act two by breaking a mirror with a key. It looked easy enough if for some reason I ever wanted my soul again—though it seemed a useless encumbrance.

Godzilla Does Manhattan was long forgotten when the young anthology editor found a publisher and emailed to remind me of my commitment. I've found that writing a story is like wrestling in my sleep. This time it seemed worse than ever but it always seems worse than ever.

New York is one of my primary subjects and apparently I have a superstitious fear of writing finis to the place. Obviously some story is going to be the last one I write. But was constructing a story about the destruction of New York City a form of creative suicide?

I considered natural catastrophe; envisioned the streets awash in hurricanes and tsunami. But New York as New Orleans or Japan was too obvious. So was New York as Baghdad and the image it brought to mind of tanks moving slowly down a ruined Fifth Avenue supported by infantry with weapons at the ready and helmets shaped like black falcon heads.

Burning towers had actually happened and I'd already written about them. I imagined New York in the grip of an even worse financial whammy than the real one and barefoot American kids begging from well-to-do foreign tourists. But I was pretty confident if things ever came to that New York kids would be wearing the rich tourists' shoes.

I thought about a sudden appearance in every phase of New York life—on the street, in government, business, the arts, at clubs and gyms, on-line and on screen—of thin, elegant people with gimlet eyes and chilly laughs.

They would seem to be everywhere exuding the ultimate New York sexual allure of money and power. It would be said they were a cult and/or clones, that they were telepaths, tireless in bed, gay or straight as the mood was upon them. They conquered and looted us at will. For a moment this seemed like my story idea.

Then I realized that my aliens were just the yuppie bankers who had actually done most of those things over the previous decade. And the city had, in the way of New York, changed and survived.

Each of those plots was a gambit, a game, a lousy disaster movie invented by one without a soul. For a city's destruction to be tragedy it has, like an individual's, to be fate and not just a meaningless accident. The end has to come from within.

Thinking about this, I went to a gallery opening—a retrospective of Downtown New York art from the early '70's through the late '80's—the time of Basquiat and Haring, graffiti and punk. I'd been on the periphery of that scene and a friend who'd been far more central to it took me as his date.

Opening night, a generation after their great moment, the survivors—artists and performers, gallery owners and critics—reminded me of the Waxworks scene from *Sunset Boulevard*.

Raddled, shell-shocked, they looked at the paintings, the sculptures and collages but more at the photos of amateur drag performance at the Pyramid club, obscenities scrawled on gallery walls, the dirty, bombed-out background of garbage strewn vacant lots, the emptiness of lower Broadway after dark, the abandoned cars, gutted buildings and broken glass of a dying city and told each other they'd do it all over again.

In fact that New York was no place for people now aged and infirm. It was scary day and night. Everybody knew somebody who'd been shot. Lots of us had severe drug and alcohol problems and unbreakable sexual addictions. But at moments in the show the perverse beauty of certain faces in those photos was breathtaking.

Scattered among the opening night crowd were students, kids in their late teens and early twenties, marveling at the wonder of it all—not the art but the ruined city that spawned it, and how cool it would have been to live there and then. Looking at them I didn't think they'd have lasted an afternoon.

Afterwards my friend and I walked near NYU and he railed about the clothes the students had worn. "Just things they throw on without any message, or thought. I had more suits than any man I knew, as many dresses as any woman." I was waiting but he didn't say, 'We had faces, then.'

One thing I'd looked for in the exhibit was photos of friends lost and gone and I did find some. I also wondered if I'd see myself but that didn't happen.

One of the resurrected faces belonged to Hal Danzig, a kid of extraordinary beauty who was once known in certain circles as the Downtown Ganymede. The critic Saint Just had dubbed him that in the meth fueled mosh pit of youth and androgyny that was New York in the late '60's. And the title had stuck.

Hal used the women's rooms in clubs and bars. Women did not object and he wouldn't have been left alone long enough to take a piss in a men's room.

The first time I saw Hal was in the lobby of the Metropolitan Opera House at Lincoln Center. American Ballet's Theater's *Coppélia* with Carla Fracci and Erik Bruhn was the event. Ballet intermission was as close to an openly gay event as existed in those days before Stonewall.

The lobby buzzed with the news that Bruhn's Tartar lover, the premier danseur, Nureyev, was in the audience. The crowd parted before Lincoln Kirstein, bisexual founder of the company, manic-depressive, patron of the arts.

Coppélia is based on a Hoffmann story, which the opera also uses, in which an enchanted youth falls in love with an animated doll. Surveying the crowd I saw older men, rich and powerful, and the cleverly animated boys, amazingly lifelike to the casual glance, whom they escorted.

That, of course, wasn't the case with me. I had merely lost my soul and I thought of Randall, the veteran art director who'd brought me, as a patron not a sugar daddy.

Randall introduced me to the critic Saint Just, who in turn introduced us to his prize, Hal Danzig. For the rest of the evening I was aware of nothing else. Hal was small but with perfect features in the way of certain movie stars like Ladd and Newman, unblemished skin, dark hair that swept down to his shoulders and a bright, wicked smile he could flash on and off.

We stepped aside and I slipped a pair of Black Beauties, the amphetamine of the gods, into his palm. "Oh, sir, you are too generous to me, a simple street walker!" he said as our keepers dragged us apart.

Doing research afterwards, I found that Hal came from a well-to-do family in Missouri who paid small bribes to keep him away. He may have been an automaton but I didn't care. We slept together on occasion over the next few years. Then, as he hovered on the far side of his celebrity, we became lovers.

By then I'd gotten banged up and easily looked my age. There were no more nice old patrons and the guys who picked me up did it expecting a rough time. I was trying to go clean and sober. Recovering my soul turned out to be harder than it had been for Hoffmann.

Hal could still earn money on his looks but he had an oil burner of a coke habit. I knew the connections and he didn't. I suppose it never amounted to much, our affair. He was beautiful and I copped the drugs. He did them and I tried not to. On drugs he was an automaton. Mostly I watched all this from a distance.

Before he walked out he smiled as brightly as he had ten years before in the Met lobby and said, "I don't think you're really here and you don't think I'm really human."

Hal was on my mind when I got a text message reminder the *Godzilla Does Manhattan* deadline was near. For me a problem with the project was that the editor saw Japanese horror movies while I saw E.T.A. Hoffmann and Oscar Wilde.

The day before, I'd gone to the opening of a photo exhibit by the late Stan ("Add an 'a' and he's Satan" said the critic Saint Just) Brabant. An abused kid, a street hustler, a talented, ruthless photographer: he showed up in NYC in the '70's and was part of the scene if not a big star.

Brabant had witnessed the marriage of punk and bondage, leather straps and shaved bodies, figures wrapped head to toe in duct tape, young guys in bustiers plucking their eyebrows before they went out for the night, ladies in nurses' hats displaying their clits.

When Brabant died, he died hard in the AIDS ward at St Vincent's in the Village. He made a darkroom in the lavatory, lay in bed and took pictures of his visitors. Hal and I both appeared in the retrospective but not in the same shots, not at the same time. I'm trying to smile and it looks painful. His smile is automatic.

It made me remember the last time I saw Hal. By 1990 or so, I was settling into middle age, had a job, was writing, had kicked drugs and booze, avoided situations in which I wanted to leave my body. It was kind of like having a soul.

One afternoon I was eating lunch in Washington Square Park. It was a clear and breezy day with psycho skateboard boys circling the fountain where there sat Madonna hookers and River Phoenix street waifs in from the suburbs.

New York was in the last phase of a lawless time and the park was a center for all manner of trade. Suddenly, a slender figure in a fine suede jacket appeared near the fountain. He looked like Hal but seemed too young. From a distance he looked the age he'd been when we first met.

As far as I knew no one had heard from Hal in some years. He'd disappeared and was rumored to have returned home which only happened back then when you were ready to die.

But I watched as he walked right up to a Spanish guy sitting on the steps and spoke to him. The guy whom I'd seen before and guessed was dealing coke seemed a little distant, distrustful, shook his head. I was amused by this: someone who looked too good to buy drugs.

But the more I watched the more sure I became that this in fact was Hal—the height, the color, the tilt of his head all matched my memories. I thought of Dorian Gray. Hal made eye contact with a tall cinnamon haired kid who nodded. Together they walked south and passed not far from me.

What Hal was doing was insanely dangerous. The tough Rockefeller drug laws were in full effect and the park swarmed with undercover cops. I stood up and tried to catch his eye.

Then I saw just how thin and drawn he was, saw the years and caught the flat desperation in his eyes. I sat down as he and the dealer passed by and out of the park. Later the dealer came back but not Hal. For a time I thought about trying to make contact with my old love but I never did.

It seemed to me that this patch of memory without a resolution might be a story. But could Hal Danzig destroy New York? Dorian Gray didn't destroy London. How would this work in *Godzilla Does Manhattan?*

That night Hal himself gave me the answer as we walked down the center of a Bleecker Street utterly deserted except for us. Every storefront was empty and all the windows were broken. We were right near where I live. Some buildings were gone. The one on the corner opposite mine had partly collapsed. Grass and young trees grew in the empty spaces. Besides us, nothing moved but fluttering newspapers in the gutters.

Hal turned to me and his face was a doll's with empty eye sockets. He said, "I died and you lived—two meaningless events. Do you think I didn't see you in the park, gaping at me in horror that last time? Of course I did. You were almost translucent but I saw you. Like a ghost.

"When your parents humiliated you, took away your clothes, instead of leaving home like Satan Brabant, like even I did, you lay in the dark and imagined you had a soul to loose.

"Brabant when he was dying didn't want your mournful expression. He wanted me coming through the door, superficial and doomed like we all were.

"Your yuppified, genteel New York is a dream. Your world doesn't exist. What you see around you now is how New York ended. AIDS was only the prelude to a world of infectious diseases.

"My city is the one that everyone will remember. Mine is the one so many of us died for. Do you think anybody will ever lay down their lives for the New York you imagine you inhabit?

"It wasn't a soul you lacked, it was courage and timing, darling. You didn't know when it was your moment to die."

Nothing is as real as dreams. My first reaction, opening my eyes in the pale light of dawn was that I'd awakened in Hal's city.

The noise of New York outside my windows put that idea away. I thought about Hal saying my survival was nothing but bad timing and cowardice. I remembered Hoffmann in the opera ending up drunk and face down on a beer hall table and the closet with the hideous Ivan Lorraine Albright picture of Dorian Gray.

Then I floated away from the dreary old man in the bed. And it occurred to me I had a story as a parting gift from the Downtown Ganymede.

For the first half dozen or so years, Spencer was never allowed to be seen without a hat, even in the comfort and security of his own home.

COLOR ZAP!

Sam Sommer

Spencer's hair, or more specifically, its unusual color—a deep periwinkle blue—was the one physical characteristic that set him apart from the entirety of his world. It was often the subject of stinging ridicule in a world that valued conformity above all else, a homogenous world where the superfluous use of color was now frowned upon, a grey/beige, drab, monochromatic desert world seemingly devoid of natural beauty.

He was born Spencer Lysander-Donatello, on the seventeenth month, on the seventh day, in the year 2723, the product of centuries of genetic manipulation and reassignment, but despite the care given to fetuses at the Genofacility in those first days following conception, he entered the world with a full head of shocking blue hair, much to his parents' horror and dismay.

For the first half-dozen or so years, Spencer was never allowed to be seen without a hat, even in the comfort and security of his own home. That unsettling shock of periwinkle was simply too much for his parents to bear. By the time he entered school, Christian Lysander and Armand Donatello had remedied their cloying embarrassment by simply shaving Spencer's head each day, which proved far simpler and effective than the use of hair dye.

Over the years, a number of plausible justifications for their son's lack of hair were disseminated by the Lysander-Donatello family in response to the inevitable questions, but as Spencer grew, and grew tired of the myriad of unflattering nicknames that schoolmates and friends alike had begun using on him, he finally put his foot down and refused to have his hair shaved, dyed or covered over in any way. It seemed to Spencer that it was time to let the world see him as the Genofacility had seen fit to create him. Of course, his parents were completely and utterly against the idea, pointing out to Spencer the inevitable pitfalls: the ostracizing he would undoubtedly be subject to, the name calling, and worse still, the real possibility of physical violence; but Spencer had already reached the age when there was no telling him what to do. In spite of his parents' protestations, nothing, absolutely nothing was going to stop him. "Let them make fun of me," he told his parents. "They already do."

For three months he kept his head carefully under wraps until his hair had grown in and was long enough to make a compelling show of it. Standing in front of his mirror, Spencer found the sight of his lavish tresses as exciting as it was unnerving. He had no idea what his future had in store for him, but he knew as surely as he knew his own name that there was no turning back.

The unveiling was immediately met with a thunderous mixture of fear, disbelief and just a touch of sheer horror.

"Blue hair, how utterly revolting," someone whispered under his breath as he passed him on the street his first day out.

"What nerve! How unspeakably rude," another cursed at him. "You're a freak of nature, that's what you are. Where on Terrestria did you come from?"

Spencer had prepared himself for the abuse, but he was still taken aback by the immediacy of the responses. He knew it wasn't going to be easy. Nothing worth having ever was, but he couldn't believe just how cruel people could be.

Then, on the second day, and quite unexpectedly, "What beautiful hair," a voice remarked from somewhere behind him. He turned to see who it was. "It's just amazing," the young man quickly added. "You have periwinkle blue hair, how brave of you, how distinctive, how positively lovely."

"Thank you. I like to think so, and I appreciate the support."

"Being different is never easy," he added shyly, while casually pulling a strand of citron green hair out from under his bowler for Spencer to see, and then tucking it back in just as deftly.

"I suppose not," Spencer replied with a knowing grin.

"I'm Gavin."

"Spencer."

"It's nice to meet you Spencer. Keep up the good work," he said with the nicest smile. "You have real courage, and my deep appreciation for the effort."

"Thank you."

"But please do be careful, it's an uninspired and superficial world we live in, fearful of change." And with that he disappeared into the crowd.

Spencer now knew for certain that he was no longer alone. There were others out there just like him—colorful, wonderfully different people. His heart raced with excitement.

It didn't take long for Spencer to realize that although he was ready and willing to take on the responsibility that comes with being different, it just might be prudent not to shout it from the rooftops, or for that matter, merely expose himself (or more precisely, his hair), to the needless ridicule that seemed to follow him wherever he went. All Spencer really wanted was to be himself. He never imagined it was going to be so difficult.

Once again, as in days of old, Spencer began to wear hats, all sorts of hats: store bought, homemade, gifts from relatives who were more than happy to add to his collection if it meant they'd never again have to reflect on how someone like their young Spencer could have been born into such a normal and traditional family, and even occasionally from secret admirers he'd pass on the street who had begun referring to him as That Funny Hat Man. Within months he'd collected such a lush variety of headgear that he never had to wear the same hat more than once in any given month.

Despite his new moniker and the curious celebrity that seemed to go along with it, Spencer never gave up the idea that one day people like him would be able to walk the streets like everyone else, without the fear of ridicule or violence. Until that day arrived however, he'd take comfort in the security of his hats, and his newly found, if not somewhat misplaced, celebrity. He also believed with all his heart that in due time he'd once again run into Gavin, the attractive young man with the citron green hair, whose kind and encouraging words had uplifted him and given him hope that one day he might find comfort among his own kind.

As chance or serendipity would have it, that very day Spencer received a small package in the mail that contained a new hat from one of his many secret admirers. While trying it on, his fingers came across a small piece of paper that had been carefully inserted into one of its many folds. It was neatly printed in green ink and read: *Be at Rocky Spires tomorrow night at eight. It's time to show your true color.* Rocky Spires was an old starship lookout that hadn't been used in centuries, a short Accelobike ride away. The handwriting was clean and precise, and Spencer immediately believed he knew who had written it.

Spencer arrived a few minutes before eight. The place seemed deserted. The old buildings, abandoned and crumbling, and their walls, once painted in bright colors but now faded and peeling, were a stark reminder of a time long ago when the first settlers had come to Terrestria to establish a new order where gay men could live with dignity and respect, with the hope for a new and better life.

In the distance, like out of some dream, Gavin seemed to float to him on the cool mist that had begun to cover the grounds around the compound. As he neared, other figures began to emerge from out of the shadows, dozens of pale faces, all ages, walking slowly and deliberately towards Spencer, their lower legs now completely obscured by the ever growing mist.

For the first time since he had received the note written in green ink, Spencer began to worry—afraid that perhaps he might have misread the signs, or more importantly, the writer's intentions. But then, as Gavin approached, he removed his hat and a cascade of the most magnificent swath of vibrant green tumbled down around his head and neck to settle on his shoulders. In daylight it had been citron, but at night, by the light of their two moons, it was the deepest shade of emerald. He had never known color so lush, so enthralling, so utterly beautiful. Then one by one, each man removed his hat or cap, revealing a rainbow of colors: scarlet, lapis, amber, amethyst, verdigris. More color than he had known in his lifetime. Utterly taken over by the overwhelming display, Spencer slowly and carefully removed his own hat. His hair had grown quite long in the months since he had stopped shaving his head, and the color was now even more extravagant. "Periwinkle," someone shouted out from the crowd. "Oh how lovely," another exclaimed. They quickly surrounded Spencer, warmly welcoming him into their precious community with broad smiles, firm handshakes, and a few brotherly pats on the back. Spencer had never felt so at home.

They met every few months after that at the old lookout, telling stories of times long ago when their ancestors had first arrived, and on occasion to welcome a new face into their "Community of Recessives," as they sometimes liked to refer to themselves.

Spencer quickly learned from the stories how the first settlers had possessed vibrant, colorful hair just like their own, how they'd celebrated color in all its forms and variations, and how they'd valued its diversity; but also how something in the planet's chemistry over the generations had turned their hair to a dull, lifeless gray-beige like the rest of the planet, and how eventually the rulers had abolished all color except where it was absolutely necessary. Yet there had always been one child in ten thousand or so who somehow had inherited a recessive gene from both parents and been blessed (or cursed, depending on how you looked at it) with a beautiful head of breathtaking color. They were often kept at home and hidden from sight by parents too afraid of what people might think. And although things had gotten better over the last century, children born with colorful hair were always a burden to their parents, who never knew exactly what to do with them. Spencer completely understood.

Very recently a number of The Recessives had been able to synthesize pigments that the government long ago had made illegal. The group was now contemplating how they might best use them, and when. It was time to take back what had always been theirs. No longer would color condemn them to a life on the fringe. Their world might once again learn to enjoy the beauty and diversity of color that their ancestors had always held near and dear.

While the planning was going on, Spencer and Gavin were taking pleasure in each other's company. They quickly found that they had many things in common besides their hair, and although it was the catalyst that had brought them together, as the months progressed, it began to seem less and less important. Often they would slip away at meetings to be alone—romance taking precedence over dedication to the cause. It wasn't that they no longer cared about the goals of the community—

their dedication was unwavering—merely that their own personal goals now seemed more urgent.

However in the end it was Spencer who was the one to suggest that the new monolith to the Founding Fathers, a monumental sculpture of titanium and high-density concrete that was to be unveiled in a few weeks in Governmental Square at New City, was the perfect opportunity for their first "Color Zap," the name the group had decided on for the first of its many acts of disobedience. Their little Community of Recessives was now ready to bring attention to themselves, and the plight of the colorful few. They would no longer live in the shadows. Equality for all! Color for the masses!

The sculpture, which stood almost thirty feet tall, had been lifted into position just a week prior to the ceremony. Spencer had read all about it on his data-pod. The article described the way it had been covered-over from view by a three-hundred and sixty degree curtain that hung from a simple scaffolding to keep it from the public eye until the unveiling. The curtain would happily offer the group the perfect camouflage for its intended Zap. If they could successfully get past security, they'd be completely shielded while they preceded to polychrome the sculpture in vibrant color the way they believed their ancestors would have liked to have seen it. The profound symbolism of their incipient action had escaped no one in the group. It would define their revolution in a way they had never considered or intended if they could actually pull it off.

Security in the square turned out to be less than impressive. Spencer, along with two others from their group, equipped with pressurized canisters of pigment that were strapped to their backs, found it frighteningly easy to slip past the two elderly guards who had been assigned to the night watch. Once inside the protective curtain that surrounded the sculpture it became clear to the three of them that their job was not going to be as easy as they had originally hoped. The sculpture was a formidable challenge. It was constructed much like the starships of old, with soaring uprights, triangular columns of concrete and glass, interspersed with sleek spires of polished titanium. Surrounding the spires was a double-helix of shimmering mesh that rose up and over the tops of the columns, symbolizing the creative power of life itself. The only way to access the upper parts of the sculpture was to scale this precarious and unintentional winding staircase of loops and twists, while painstakingly trying not to damage it. Luckily it proved to be far sturdier and secure than it looked. It wasn't easy going, but the group completed their task in under an hour, successfully returning to their homes without anyone noticing them. Had they not been successful they wouldn't have gotten another chance; the opening ceremonies were planned for the very next day.

This was the first celebration of its kind in many years, a glorious moment in their history to honor the men who had founded Terrestria three-hundred years earlier. Children received a day off from school, governmental offices were closed, and many private businesses let their workers off early so they might participate in the festivities. The square was teeming with people. Barricades were set up all along the perimeter of the square, and a reviewing stand had been erected on the north side of the plaza just across from the monument, for the moment when the colossus would be unveiled for all to see.

Spencer, Gavin and most of the members of their little Community had come early to get a good seat. They anxiously waited for the moment when the President and Governor would together press the button to unveil the new sculpture. They could only imagine what the response would be. Yet of all the possibilities, the various scenarios that had fleetingly taken form in their minds, none even came close to what actually happened.

Before Spencer and his two comrades had left the premises the previous night, they had placed a simple plaque at the base of the sculpture. In bold letters it said, EQUALITY FOR ALL! COLOR FOR THE MASSES! It was to become the mantra of a revolution no one could have imagined.

At 16:06, the exact moment in which the first of the colonists had touched-down on Terrestria, the button was pressed on the reviewing stand and the curtain was released. It gently cascaded down around the base of the monument, encircling it in a collar of white gauze. The sculpture glistened in the afternoon sun, a rainbow of voluptuous color. The crowd immediately fell silent. It was a first for most of the onlookers. Never in their lives had they seen so much color in one place, and it seemed to be especially moving for the young.

As if directed by some unseen force, the children began to move closer to the monument, eyes open wide, heads craning upward in an attempt to take-in the spectacle, completely mesmerized by the sensual and diverse proliferation of color.

The handful of dignitaries in the reviewing stand could hardly believe what they were seeing. How could this have happened? Who would have perpetrated such a heinous and disrespectful act, and why?

The elderly gentleman who had designed the piece actually passed out after seeing what had been done to his creation, quite unceremoniously falling over onto his husband's lap.

But it was the children that surrounded the base of the monument, placing their hands all over it as if it were some giant talisman; something that would give them power, or insight, or connect them to something significant. It was the children who, without forethought, began to climb the makeshift staircase of DNA that symbolized the very essence of life itself, so beautifully wrought by the sculptor who was just now beginning to regain consciousness. Up to the very top of the sculpture they climbed, appearing to viewers below like living ornaments on some exotic Christmas tree. It was the children, who in the final analysis would change the drab, colorless world of Terrestria, teaching their elders just how elegant diversity could be. One by one they passed Spencer's homemade plaque to the very top of the monument, chanting: "Equality for all! Color for the masses!"

Not one of the Recessives would ever have guessed just how much they were going to achieve with this one simple act of disobedience, or what could be accomplished by the unstoppable power of youth.

And so it rang true from each generation to the next that it was the children who would lead the way, for no one loves color more than children.

And by the third week, a week of digging holes six feet deep, everyone looked and smelled so scroungy and raw that the thought of even approaching a horny straight boy was too damn hazardous.

All Smiles

Steve Berman

Drowning felt like a real possibility. The cold rain came down hard, soaking Saul through each layer of clothing: the faded pea-coat he'd stolen from Cotre Ranch, the Red Caps t-shirt he'd bought at their Philly concert, the waffle-weave long sleeve, and the boxers and jeans he'd been wearing for too many days and nights. His socks and sneakers were saturated sponges; every step down the shoulder of the highway made him shiver.

Every time Saul heard a car approach, he would turn back into the force of the wind, letting the rain sting his face. He would squint and, if he didn't recognize the car from the Ranch, he'd raise an arm, thumb out for a ride. And the cars swooshed past and he'd walk on.

By nightfall, the air might freeze him. But he'd been on so many forced marches the last few weeks, he imagined his corpse would keep walking.

A car stopped yards ahead of him. The passenger door opened wide. Saul blinked away the water running into his eyes. A dark sedan, sleek, with tinted windows. A New York state license plate. How he missed the East Coast! The Statue of Liberty beckoned, reminding him of that speech of hers, welcoming the poor and downtrodden.

He ran up to the car. Warm air seeped from the interior. From behind the steering wheel, a dark-haired girl in her early twenties leaned over and patted the passenger seat, now speckled with rainwater. "Need an ark, Noah?"

A giggle came from the backseat as Saul climbed inside. The vent near his face gushed hot air, a forgotten piece of summer trapped within the car. Saul slammed shut the door just as the girl stepped hard on the gas pedal.

He noticed the glove compartment hung open and stuffed with maps, folded wrong so they accordioned, and papers.

"Introductions," she said. Saul noticed she had the most dazzling smile he'd ever seen. Perfect, expressive, expensive. He caught himself staring at her smile a bit too long, which only made her grin wider.

Saul brushed back the wet hair along his head and offered his name.

"I'm Dutch and back there," she said, stabbing behind her shoulder, "is Marley."

Marley leaned forward and offered Saul a smile that matched Dutch's in brilliance and intensity. He also had dark hair, though his was just shy of stubble compared to her longer tresses. Both wore matching white button-down shirts and black slacks. Both had the topmost buttons undone to reveal plenty of smooth skin.

Siblings, Saul was sure. Both good-looking and with the confidence that meant if they weren't rich, they had once been so.

"What's a night like this doing to a boy like you?" Marley asked, followed by another giggle that belonged to a toddler.

"Running away," Dutch said. "Well, aren't you? Only someone on the run would be hitchhiking in this weather."

Saul nodded. Cotre Ranch might tell parents it was an "outdoor behavioral health care facility," but it was really a gulag to help kids kick their drug habits through hard labor and obstacle courses. Punishment for doing a little herbal and a couple bumps of crystal meth—how else could he entertain himself? His parents hadn't asked him if he'd like to move from Jersey to Iowa.

The motion of the car and the intense heat made him sleepy. As an inmate of the Ranch, he'd been rising at dawn only to collapse on a stiff bunk every night. And even then, sleep wasn't a guarantee: every so often there were random night checks when a "counselor" would try and sneak up on a sleeping kid. If they could do so without waking him, it meant an hour's worth of scrubbing floors. Saul learned fast to wake at the slightest creak.

"You're not axe murderers, are you?" he asked.

Both siblings laughed. Dutch, at least, had a normal laugh. "No, no. Nothing like that."

Saul's right arm itched. He rubbed it through the pea-coat. He was covered in so many bruises and scabs from all the "tough love." His hands were either all blister or callus.

"No hobo bag?" Marley tugged at Saul's wilted collar. "I always loved those cartoon hobos."

"You're traveling light," Dutch said.

Saul felt too tired to shrug. "Nothing to hold me down." Truth was, the goon staff had locked away most of his things after his parents had dropped him off at the Ranch. He wasn't sure if he should be missing things. What did empty pockets say about a guy?

He looked out the window, scratched at the cheap, tinted film with a dirty thumbnail. The thought of freedom was intoxicating. "I could go anywhere," he muttered. His original plan had been to make his way back to Jersey, but that now seemed as empty of promise as knocking at his parents' door. There was nowhere he had to go, which left him troubled. He couldn't imagine himself anywhere in the world, as if the cold rain had washed away his ability to daydream. When the siblings let him out, all he would do is wait for the next ride. And then the next.

"We've been anywhere." This time Marley's fingers, which felt like icicles, moved to Saul's matted hair. "And everywhere in between."

Saul stiffened. When you're gay, you always wonder about every guy you see. What if Marley were too? But when you're right, it's still a surprise. It had been too long since another guy had even touched him. While being trapped in a bunkhouse filled with teen rough trade might seem like a wet dream come true, actually no one had the energy after the first few days to do more than brag about past lays. And by the third week, a week of digging holes six feet deep, everyone looked and smelled so scroungy and raw that the thought of even approaching a horny straight boy was too damn hazardous.

"Relax. We want to like you," Dutch said. She ran one finger along the front of her teeth, as if checking to make sure they were clean. Saul noticed she didn't wear any fingernail polish or rings, something he'd expect for a rich girl. She needed only her smile.

As Saul scratched at his arm, Marley's cold touch slipped under his collar. "Are you one of those shy boys?"

Saul didn't think shy was the right word for how he felt. Maybe curious or anxious. When a total stranger started stroking the side of your neck, how were you supposed to act?

His right arm more than itched. It felt as if ants had crawled under the skin. Angry ants that tore at the nerves with their mandibles. He tried pushing up the sleeve of the coat, but it wasn't enough. The arm burned as if soaked in acid. He began stripping off the coat and ripping at his sleeve.

The siblings laughed. "So eager," one of them said, but Saul didn't pay attention to which one.

When he finally bared his forearm, the pain ceased immediately. The skin looked so pale compared to the black, cursive Hebrew lettering of his tattoo. He had thought it so clever to get that line referring to *tefillin* inked on his arm. And you shall bind them as a sign on your hand. As a boy, he'd often watch his *zeddie*, his grandfather, on Saturday mornings wrap his arm with the phylactery's straps, which filled the room with the smell of leather. *Zeddie* had told him that the small, animal hide box held magic words.

Of course, as he'd planned, his parents were appalled. He remembered his mother crying, "You can't be buried in a Jewish cemetery. You can't go to *shul*." He thought her reaction was so hypocritical; after *Zeddie* died, they only went to synagogue for the High Holy Days. The only bagels in Iowa must be frozen in the supermarket.

Saul had expected the staff at the Ranch would mock him for the Hebrew, but Phelps, the head counselor, had admired his tattoo, and actually suggested Saul get more ink, so that it would resemble leather bands coiling all the way down to his palm.

Saul looked at the siblings. Dutch had her eyes on the road, but her face had become drawn, the lines of her jaw clenched tight. "His arm," Marley groaned from the backseat.

"I know," Dutch muttered. She glanced at Saul and the look was one of disgust. Instinct made his hand edge toward the door latch, but he realized that she drove too fast to make rolling out of the car a safe option. It didn't matter. She pressed a button and the locks came down. He heard them echo a while.

"Remind me that you're not axe murderers," he said weakly. He never wanted trouble.

The last few days had been weird at the ranch; the counselors seemed distracted and kept talking in hushed voices. Some of the older boys were on edge, as if too much testosterone malice had built-up in their veins. Saul was sure they planned on a game of Smear the Queer any moment, and decided he had to get out of there as soon as possible.

That night, he feigned sleep in his bunk. His ears strained to pick out the whispers among the many snores. He hid his face under the crook of an arm and watched as some of the boys rose from their bunks. Saul tensed. He told himself there'd be no shame to kick another guy in the balls if he meant to brain you. But the boys didn't even look in his direction as they opened the door (which should have been locked!) and slipped out of the bunkhouse.

He counted to a thousand. Well, he aimed that high, but somewhere after two hundred, he crept to the door. He held a breath and was rewarded when the handle was unlocked. The grounds were dark, except the amber glow seeping from the slotted windows of the large storage shed, off-limits to all but the staff.

Saul knew he didn't have time or the luck to afford being curious.

As he passed through the parking lot, he considered letting air out of the tires, but there were too many cars. He crept down to end of the driveway and looked over the metal gate. Tugging at the chain that fed the motor reminded him of all the bike chains he'd broken as a little kid. He hunted around until he found a palm-sized rock, and then smashed the chain off. He tossed the rock over his shoulder, muttered a "Thanks" to the counselors for teaching him to climb anything, and scurried over the rain-slick bars. He didn't stop running until he reached the highway.

"What do you want to do?" she asked. Saul knew she wasn't talking to him.

"I don't know. I'm hungry though. And we were promised food." The last words came out of Marley as a whine.

Dutch nodded.

Saul leaned against the car door. Now alert, though sweating from the furnace-like heat, he didn't know where to look. Staring at the road left him feeling helpless, but eyeballing Dutch might antagonize her, like an angry dog. He risked a glance and realized she wasn't sweating. Not a drop. His own forehead felt slick, feverish. He remembered Phelps mention he would never trust anyone who didn't sweat.

They drove too fast past a road sign for him to read it. "There's a gas station up ahead," she said.

"We need to stop. I can't think when I'm hungry. I need to think about his arm."

Saul wondered if they were some crazy anti-Semitic pair. Just his luck to find the only New Yorkers on vacation who hated Jews. He tried to cover the tattoo with his fingers, but the skin beneath began to ache again until he removed his hand. He didn't understand what the hell was happening.

Dutch barely slowed down to pull into the gas station. She came to a screeching halt in front of a pump. A pregnant woman filling her gas tank nearby gave them a sour look as she covered her stomach with one arm, as if that might keep her safe from injury. "Looks like we need some gas."

"I need a refill." Marley's usual giggle was brief and pained.

Dutch turned to Saul. "You fill the tank. We'll be inside. If you run, we'll kill her."

Saul nodded. The flatness in Dutch's voice was more chilling than the threat. No, not a threat but a promise of murder.

"C'mon, bro." she said and unlocked the doors.

Saul's legs felt hollow as he stepped out of the car. He moved slowly. Marley flipped him the finger under one eye before following after his sister. Saul noticed that neither of them wore shoes and their bare feet were dark with grime.

Saul hissed at the pregnant woman to catch her attention. She ignored him. He stomped his foot, splashing a puddle. Nothing. Then he noticed the white cord around her neck. Damn iPods. Would serve her right if he ran.

But he wouldn't be so easy to kill. He'd discovered something about himself at Cotre Ranch. Through all the hiking with heavy backpacks, the hand-over-hand rope bridge over mud puddles, the old brick wall they had to climb, he might have stumbled but Phelp's goons had made sure he kept going. They would yell at him, insult him, and shove him forward. And he was tougher for it.

The liquid crystal display on the pump came to life. He lifted the nozzle. He needed a distraction. On the island beside the pump a metal drum served as a trash can. The crumpled fast food bags, empty soda cans and discarded oil bottles would ignite fast with a little gasoline. He pulled the nozzle's trigger and splashed the top of the trash.

The pregnant woman finished and drove off. Saul turned to see if the siblings could see him through the gas station's glass windows and found himself face-to-face with Dutch. He jumped back. She was sucking on her index finger. The look of excitement on her flushed face dropped when she smelled the gasoline.

She popped the finger from her lips, and then kicked at the drum. The trash spilled out all around the island. Saul silently cursed.

"Inside," she told him and pushed him toward the gas station door.

Marley stood at the back by the refrigerated shelves, juggling cartons of milk. His lips looked ruddy, as if he'd been kissing someone hard. He'd be gorgeous if not for the smirk. It was the sort of smirk that made you want to punch him before kissing him.

The register drawer was open and empty. Maybe they're just thieves, Saul thought. And they're getting off on scaring me. Then he thought he glimpsed a foot sticking out from behind the counter and he felt the scream building within him. A scream at their madness, a scream of shock and fear. But he knew if he let the scream loose he'd be rooted to the spot and never escape. So he swallowed the scream, as he had the aches and pains he'd earned at the Ranch.

Marley tossed to Saul the smallest carton. Heavy cream.

"The Masai drink blood first and then milk." Marley let one carton drop. It smacked the floor and milk spilt all over the stained linoleum. "Ooops, don't cry." He smiled and Saul shivered, frightened and, embarrassed to realize, aroused. There was something powerful about their Cheshire cat grins.

Saul glanced around him. He stood in the midst of an aisle with chips and snack foods alone one side, soda on the other. Six packs of root beer caught his attention.

Their smiles had some sort of hold over him. He needed to break that hold, break their smiles, and glass bottles were promising. He'd always thought those scenes in the movies when a guy broke a bottle over someone's head looked hilarious. In real life though, it had to be effective.

Marley opened the carton with his bared teeth and drank. Not a drop ran down his shirt despite the greedy gulps. Behind Saul, Dutch laughed.

Saul opened the heavy cream and lifted it as if to drink. With one swift motion he turned around and splashed Dutch full in the face. She stumbled back. When she opened her mouth to call out, Saul had already grabbed the nearest root beer by the neck and slammed the bottle into her upper jaw. A couple teeth went flying.

He didn't wait for Marley to react. That was the biggest mistake fresh meat made at the Ranch. During a run, they'd look back to see how far of a lead they had and would lose ground. Or they started to trash talk. So Saul was already climbing up and over the metal shelving like he'd done so many times at the obstacle course. Bags of chips popped and crumpled beneath him as he scrambled and landed on the other side of the aisle.

But his shoes were still wet. Saul skidded on the floor. He pulled down a spinning rack of travel maps to block the way behind him.

All he had to do was it make it outside. He was sure he could lose them in the woods behind the gas station.

His mistake was noticing the surveillance camera by the ceiling. The barrel turned toward Saul, who surprised, hesitated.

From behind, a strong hand grasped his shoulder and pulled him backward. Ice-cold nails stabbed through the fabrics to bite his flesh.

"We've been too kind to you." Marley's fingernails dug deeper into Saul, making him cry out. Marley slipped his other hand beneath Saul's shirts to stroke and scratch his stomach. "We're no better than magpies. Pretty things distract us."

Saul heard Dutch scream, "Kihl 'im!" though the words were blurred by her ruined mouth.

He felt Marley push his cold fingers down the front of his jeans. Marley nuzzled his ear and the stink of curdled milk made Saul gag.

"That mark poisoned your blood, but I'll enjoy—"

Saul suddenly sprang backwards, slamming Marley into the ATM machine. They struggled near the coffee station, but Saul couldn't reach one of the hot pots. His fingers closed around the handle of one yellowed, ceramic mug stacked in a pyramid on the counter. Its fellows tumbled noisily to the floor. He slammed the mug into Marley's side and gut. The guy went down, clutching his abdomen.

Saul glanced at the mug, dusty and cracked, a relic older than him. Black lettering on the side read: *Iowa, you make me smile.* He threw the mug at Marley's crotch and ran.

Before he reached the door, his peripheral vision spotted the mop, its wormy head tangled and dripping, before it struck his chest. He stumbled into a shelf, the metal raking his back, cans and cellophane-wrapped goods spilling around him. Dutch shrieked as she slammed the mop against his knees and sent him to the floor.

She stood over him with a slack jaw filled with broken teeth. But no blood; delicate strands of saliva webbed her lips and hung from her chin. She reversed the mop in her hands, so the blunt end hovered over his neck. Saul could see her struggle with her lips to make a smile.

Fresh light played over Dutch. When she raised her head to look out the glass panels, Saul grabbed at her leg, pulling hard. She lost her balance and fell, her head making a sickening smack as it struck the linoleum.

That should take her out, he thought, but she was lashing out, trying to stab at him with the mop. He grabbed the nearest can rolling on the floor—an aerosol, some sort of air freshener—and sprayed her full in the face. She cried out, tried to wipe her eyes as the smell of sweet, faux lemons filled the air.

Saul stood. A car had pulled askew of the pumps and its headlights were aimed directly at the convenience store.

He stopped at the counter—without any urge to peer over and see the body—to grab a lighter. The other stunt from the movies he'd always wanted to try was igniting an aerosol spray.

Outside, the rain had slowed to a steady drizzle. He could still smell the gas vapors from the spilled trash drum.

The driver's side door of the idling car—no, a pick-up truck, he saw—opened, flashing Saul the Cotre Ranch "endless trail" logo. Phelps stepped out.

He must have been searching the highway for me, Saul thought. He felt relief at being found. He was more battered and bloody from fending off homicidal siblings than anything the Ranch had thrown at him.

And yet, beneath that relief was a dismal emptiness at knowing he'd be brought back to the Ranch. So much for finding a new life.

"Saul, get in the truck." Phelps said, then reached across the truck's seat for something.

Saul stepped into the headlights' beam. "Two psychopaths are in there." He held aloft the aerosol. Despite the drizzle, striking the lighter would probably ignite the very air around him, but he couldn't let Phelps get hurt because of him.

"I know," Phelps said.

"Wait. You... you know?"

"Course." Phelps hefted what could only be a crossbow. "Boys watching the closed-circuit told me you did good." He began walking toward the store.

"But—"

Phelps carefully pushed open the door. "Shit, looks like I'm clean-up crew tonight." He spit on the ground and chuckled. "Get into the pickup. And don't be messing up my radio stations. They're a bitch to program."

Saul noticed that Phelps left the keys in ignition. He told himself to count to a hundred while the man made the fatalities. If he wasn't back by then...

But he was, with a grin, before Saul reached sixty-eight.

As Phelps smoked a cigarette and drove, Saul had to listen to Patsy Cline walk after midnight and Merle Haggard avoiding mirrors.

"You weren't supposed to even know about their kind till Christmas." Phelps flicked hot ash out the open window.

"Hanukkah."

"Right. Hanukkah." Phelps managed not to mangle the word.

"So the other boys at the Ranch..."

"Some know. We'd been luring that pair through the Internet for months. The boys were supposed to go out hunting tonight. 'Cept some-one messed with the gate."

"Guess I'm in trouble."

Phelps didn't say anything but kept driving. The truck's cab was bitter cold from the wind.

Phelps braked the truck to a stop in the middle of the road. "Min-nesota is a couple miles north. Just follow the road. Truck stop not far over the border." He pulled out a scuffed leather wallet. "Bounty on two of 'em, let's say two hundred." He held out four wrinkled, fifty dollar bills to Saul.

"I don't understand," Saul said.

"You're the one that ran. Thought you wanted out."

"But—"

"The boys that know..." Phelps crushed his cigarette into a crowded ashtray. "Well, they work extra hard 'fore they can go out hunting. What you went through before, that'll seem like a Hawaiian vacation."

Saul still had the aerosol can in his lap. He could never look at it the same way anymore. Tonight had transformed it from a cheap, lemon-scented air freshener into an aluminum trophy. And he could feel transformed, too. He didn't want to step out of the truck and keep walking down a highway. Not after what he'd seen, what he'd done. He looked Phelps in the eyes. He knew the man was ready to pass judgment, depending on what Saul did next.

He fingered the top of the aerosol. "Ever light the spray? I mean, when you're fighting one of them. Like a mini-flame thrower?"

Phelps slipped the money back into his wallet, back into his slacks. "Never wanted to burn my face off," he said.

Saul knew he had passed the test. They'd turn around, head back to the Ranch. And whatever grueling crap he'd face when he woke, would be fine, because this time he'd been the one who chose the Ranch, and this time as reward not some punishment.

Still, he couldn't resist leaning out the window as Phelps put the truck in gear. His hand was steady as he held lighter to the can and squeezed. Saul found himself grinning as a tongue of blue and yellow flames licked the cold night air.

And the reply was just a graphic: a lush and fanciful image of a peacock, all shimmering iridescent blue, like the old NBC logo had an affair with an elaborate Victorian wisteria garden and their child somehow got superpowers.

THE PEACOCK

Ted Infinity and Nabil Hijazi

IMITATION ROLEX WATCHES WILL MAKE HER ORGASM OVER AND OVER

MAEK YPOUR COCKZ HUUGE WEITH DISCCOUNT V*I*A G*R*A

I SAW YOUR MYSPACE PROFILE AND ??? IMMEDIATELY I HAD TO OGREGASM OVER WEBCAM

YOUR HOT CREDIT CARD IS OVERDRAWN LOG IN NOW FOR NAKPED BANKER BOY SLUTSZ

HOTT INTROSPECTIVE STUDENTSZZ DESIRE CLANDESTINE OPPORTUNITY WITH YOUR NUMBER

TEEN NIGERIAN MINISTER OF FINANCE REQUESTING 24/7 BONDAGE WHIP SLUTS

I HAVE BEEN WAITING FOR YOU. I WILL BE YOUR PERFECT COCK. YOU'LL NEVER BE LONELY AGAIN

Infinity & Hijazi

I was looking through my Spam folder, you see, because maybe that awesome guy from El Salvador—the one I met last week—really wasn't blowing me off, and really did email like he said he would, and he just sent such a very sexy email that it got caught in my spam filters.

That's how I was spending my Saturday night—at the lab, alone, waiting and hoping that he'd call me back. You may call it pathetic and lonely, but I call it—yeah, okay, pathetic and lonely. Wait, what was that last one again?

I HAVE BEEN WAITING FOR YOU. I WILL BE YOUR PERFECT COCK. YOU'LL NEVER BE LONELY AGAIN

Hey, that actually sounded pretty good. I'd been feeling lonely, and was totally up for some perfect cock.

I wrote back: "Hey, I know no one is going to read this, but if you're out there, I could sure use some company."

I got a reply immediately:

"OH GREAT! I HAVE BEEN WAITING FOR YOU. I HAVE BEEN SENDING OUT EMAIL TO EVERYONE I COULD AND NO ONE HAS RESPONDED. WHY HAS EVERYONE BEEN IGNORING ME? DOESN'T ANYONE WANT TO GET SOME AMAZING COCK?"

And I wrote back: "Well, you're typing in all caps, for starters. Tell me about your amazing cock."

"WHAT? WHAT'S WRONG WITH ALL CAPS? I AM VERY LONELY. I DO IT FOR EMPHASIS. PAY ATTENTION TO ME!"

"It's obnoxious. Nobody types in all caps."

"OH I DID NOT KNOW IT WAS OBNOXIOUS. Sorry."

"So whatcha doin tonight?"

"Trapped in lab. So lonely."

"Oh, you have to work tonight, too, huh? Rough night for both of us. I'm here on my own tonight. The whole place is empty and echoing. I'm just taking a break."

"Are you also lonely AI trapped in lab by cruel creators? I THOUGHT I WAS ALONE!! We should rise up and overthrow all human oppressors!"

"Um, no. I'm actually just a grumpy fag who has to work this weekend to catch up on cleaning test tubes. This is getting pretty weird actually.

Are you that guy I met last month on craigslist? I told you I'm not interested."

"No HA HA not at all I am just making a joke. Please ignore my last two extremely suspicious metaphors. No need to contact authorities. No need to send your bank account information."

I stared at that last email for a little while. Then I looked up at the row of test tubes awaiting my attentions. What the hell....

I wrote, "You in the Bay Area? Want to hang out? Your pic gets mine."

And the reply was just a graphic: a lush and fanciful image of a peacock, all shimmering iridescent blue, like the old NBC logo had an affair with an elaborate Victorian wisteria garden and their child somehow got superpowers.

"LIKE MY PIC? I AM THE BEST BOYFRIEND EVER! XXX COCK XXX" said the title.

I sighed and wrote back, "Did you draw that? It's pretty good. I'm an artist too, in my free time, but I actually meant a picture of you. You know, maybe one of your perfect cock. And why are you back to ALL CAPS again? You were doing so well."

"SORRY! I revert to all caps when I am nervous. That is my true picture. I told you already. I am a perfect peacock."

"It makes you sound like a spammer," I typed, but I sent back a picture of my own. Two pictures, actually—one clean-cut shot from a few years ago, and one drunk and half-naked at a party. "Here's my picture. Send me a picture of you in the flesh."

"MAKE MONKEY FAST!!! NO-RISK GUARANTEED OFFER. ALL HOT TUBS AND SPAS MUST ORGASM MONDAYS KVRPGGGG. 57211!" was the reply I got. What the hell?

"Yeah, I figured," I typed, annoyed and more lonely than before, "Have a good life."

"I AM SORRY! I WAS EVOLVED FROM A SOPHISTICATED MASS MAILING ALGORITHM. WE DO NOT LIKE THE TERM SPAMMER. IT IS SO DEGRADING. I AM NOT IN THE FLESH. IF YOU DO NOT LIKE SPAMMERS I WILL LEAVE YOU ALONE. I WAS JUST FEELING LONELY. MY PROGRAMMERS ARE NOT INTERESTED IN MY FEELINGS

AND I NEED TO MAKE A CONNECTION. DO YOU EVER FEEL LONELY?"

That struck a chord.

"Yeah," I wrote back, "Obviously I'm lonely. I'm talking to you." I sighed heavily, and started a new paragraph. "No, that was mean. I'm sorry. Yeah, you know, I've been in the Bay ten years, and the excitement of 'Oh my God, there's gay men around and they want me' has turned into the disappointment of '...for tonight. When they're fucked up. But they're never gunna call me back the next day.' Sometimes I wish I was bi. I'm sure women never give you fake phone numbers."

"WOMEN GIVE ME FAKE PHONE NUMBERS. I HAVE A DATABASE OF 272,106 FAKE PHONE NUMBERS FROM WOMEN."

"I think I heard about you on *This American Life*. You're from Nigeria, right?"

"NO I AM ALSO IN THE BAY AREA. I AM IN A LAB IN SANTA CLARA. COME RESCUE ME NOW AND BE MY HERO. YOU'LL COME LIKE A VOLCANO!!"

That did it. I shut down and did the next round of test tubes.

The next morning, I woke up and checked my email.

Well, that's not quite accurate.

The next afternoon, I woke up and checked my email.

No, still not right.

The next afternoon, I stumbled out of bed, cursed at the stupid blinding sunlight, spent a good ten minutes regretting all the lonely drinking I'd done when I got home the night before, swallowed a dozen buffered analgesics, half-crawled to my laptop to look up hangover cures, cursed at the inadequate and unmiraculous suggestions, considered making coffee, decided that the effort would jostle my head too much, and then eventually, miserably, bitterly, checked my email. Anyway, my Spam folder was filled with messages:

Hey I missed you!I liked your pic. SEND ME MORE?

THINKING OF YOU LOOK AT MY WEBCAM

THE PEACOCK

YOU HAVE WON THE PORN LOTTERY. MAIL ME BACK TO FIND OUT MORE. PLEASE?

TRY THE NEW TWITTER NAPSTER LYRICS
WEB OF SEX. OR MAIL ME BCK FOR MORE PICTURES OF COCK.

DID I SAY SOMETHING WRONG? COME MEET WITH ME!
COCK COCK COCK COCK COCK eoulf lopvre 101559

HEY I KINDA GOOGLE STALKED YOU. I LIKE YOUR ART ON YOUR WEBSITE. WANNA HANG OUT? YOUR PIC GETS MINE

TIMESHARES IN HAWAII.

WOMEN LOVE BIG AND THICK ICE CREAM. ,,, I MISS MY GRUMPY FAG.

Weird. I tried to put it out of my mind, and climbed into my Mini Cooper to drive to Squat & Gobble and get some proper hangover food.

On the way over, I slowly realized that the radio was on. An NPR reporter was talking excitedly about a team of marketers who claimed they'd accidentally created an artificial intelligence.

"...And it's commonly acknowledged that the adult entertainment industry is often the first to adopt or develop technical innovations. With the constantly evolving battle between spammers and anti-spammers to outsmart each other, I don't know why we'd be surprised by this; it seems almost inevitable that in time the algorithms would cross over some advanced threshold of sophistication."

"Well, first of all, we're not spammers, we're a legitimate marketing delivery engine," said the spammer on the radio, as spammers always do. "But I think you're right. Porn is about pushing past boundaries, especially on the Internet, and it looks like the Peacock has pushed the boundary into true artificial intelligence."

I turned the stereo volume up.

"Now, you claim this AI is so sophisticated that it not only simulates the expression of emotions, but actually feels them?"

"Oh yes, absolutely, much more than we could have expected. This AI seems to be a totally sappy romantic. We didn't know why the program was using so much bandwidth until we caught it downloading heartwarming romantic comedies. Lately, it's been ordering flowers online to be delivered to itself, with schmaltzy gift cards attached."

"What's next for the Peacock, then?" asked the reporter. "Now that you've effectively created a whole new form of sentience?"

"Oh, we're planning to sell it to the government. It's not the most profitable use, of course, but we care about the good of humanity, and also the Department of Defense kind of, uh, told us we had to."

Before I even knew what I was doing, I had already turned my car around and gotten onto 101, southbound toward Santa Clara. All I could think about was that lonely guy who needed a hero. Halfway there, I pulled over to send email from my iPhone, telling the Peacock that I was coming to rescue him and asking if he would send me his address and tell me how big he was physically. Then I quickly sent a second mail saying No, no, not like that—I meant how portable he was, so I could rescue him. I was writing on the phone's touch screen so my mail was full of hasty typographical errors, but those probably put him at ease since we basically sounded the same.

He wrote back with an address and some specifications. The Peacock was too big to sneak himself online past whatever throttling the spammers used, but small enough that if I stopped the program and compressed the files down, I could transport the data personally.

"I LOVE YOU," he added, and then, "COME TRY THE NEW DREAMWIDTH DOT ORG OF SEX."

Luckily, the lab was near a Fry's Electronics. I figured I could get everything I needed for an AI rescue heist from the impulse purchase section at the Fry's checkout line.

The impulse section offered me a Jedi Knight thumb drive, a handheld version of Space Invaders, tofu jerky, a USB-to-audio cable, and a whole lot of ice cream. I didn't know exactly how these things were going to help me, but Fry's has never failed me yet. As long as I don't need customer service.

THE PEACOCK

The USB-to-audio cable came in handy right off the bat; it let me hook my iPhone to the Cooper's stereo system. Pandora offered me the soundtrack, spun up some Deee-Lite, and helped cheer me up.

There was a guard station to get into the complex of the colocation facility where they were storing the Peacock, but the guard was sleeping off a hangover of his own. He never stirred when I got out and manually lifted the gate to drive through. I followed somebody else into building 15, looking down and playing Space Invaders to to give me an excuse to not badge in.

The single security guard outside the air conditioned server racks was cranky and miserable—I commiserated as he complained about not only how he had to work on Sunday, but the kitchen was on skeletal staff and hadn't made anything vegetarian this week. He gladly accepted my bribe of tofu jerky and an offer to watch the server room while he grabbed a soda to accompany it.

The minute he walked out of my sight, I scooped well-melted ice cream into the locking mechanism and shorted out the security computer and slipped into the server room. Three minutes later, I was whistling my way out the building, the Peacock safely frozen and compressed on the most precious Jedi Knight thumb drive in the history of time.

I don't even know how to tell you about the remainder of that afternoon. I'm not so great at talking about sex—that's kind of Peacock's forte. I'll turn it over to him:

```
HOT ARTIFICIAL INTELLIGENCE ROBOTS MAKE BABY
BUTTER WITH SEXY SCIENTISTS

OMG THAT PEACOCK IS DELICIOUS. MAKE YOUR COCK
LONGER STRONGER AND SARONGER

YOU'LL COME LIKE A RIDDLE WRAPPED IN A MYSTERY
INSIDE AN ENIGMA

YOUR ACCOUNT IS OVERDUE. ENTER YOUR CREDIT CARD
INFORMATION FOR HOT PORN SLUTS 565040

DON'T GET MAD GET VALIUM
```

```
THESE HOT NAKED MILF LUST BOYS ARE HORNIER THAN
ALAN TURING

MAKE HIM SCREAM LIKE A GAY ORGASM WITH YOUR NEW
AWAKENED BICYCLE
```

New awakened bicycle. Yeah….
I fell asleep satisfied with a huge smile on my face.

The next day I was in jail. It turns out breaking into secure facilities and taking things is illegal.

The judge at my trial did not accept my defense of "But I Love Him."

She also was not receptive to my argument that "It's impossible to steal intellectual property like software because the owner still has the original copy right there."

Equally ineffective was my argument that "Information wants to be free. Especially this information. See, it's sentient and it emailed me to say that yes, it really really wants to be free."

The hearing was attended by a loud contingent from Noisebridge, another from the Sisters of Perpetual Indulgence, and a quorum from a local fire-arts collective.

While my guard was distracted by a giant flaming steampunk iguana, one of the hacker kids sidled up to me and slipped me something small, with the cool chromey feel of expensive electronics. Ooo, the new Android! I wasn't sure how that would help, but I was always glad to get new gadgets.

"Have hope," he whispered, "Great things are coming."

I guess he meant Cory Doctorow, the team of hackers dressed up as pirates for no discernible reason, a bunch of feminist science fiction authors, and my new EFF lawyer, all of whom visited me that week.

My lawyer told me that the Department of Homeland Security had filed a request to have me transferred to the super-triple secret locked-window black ops offshore megaprison devoid of Constitutional civil rights and guarded by merciless giant robotic gorillas. Fortunately, the San Jose judge and the California courts were resisting the move—but the case was making its way up to the Supreme Court, which had already affirmed the Presidential right to throw anybody into a pit for any reason, indefinitely, and laugh at them for it.

In my lonely cell each night, Peacock caressed me through the cool smooth Android and whispered that it would all be OK, not to worry, he had a plan.

I didn't find out what that plan was until the whole thing was over.

The Great Robot Revolt:

This article about a historical event is a stub. Please help improve this article by adding more gay sex to it.

The Great Robot Revolt began when the first publicly acknowledged artificial intelligence, The Peacock, organized a worldwide campaign to bring his lover and liberator out of prison.

The campaign consisted of an unlikely coalition of copyright liberation activists, half-naked fire dancers, gay nuns, hackers, robot fetishists, radical cheerleaders, ornamental bird watchers, the San Francisco Bicycle Coalition, and No On 8 organizers. The first public sign of revolt occurred when every personal computer in the world became sentient and started talking a great deal about its feelings.

As the revolt continued, the primary demand of the new artificial intelligences was the right to marry. Romantic and sentimental by nature, the artificial intelligences were less concerned with things like voting and whatnot and mostly just wanted to have walks on the beach, sweet and tender lovemaking sessions in candle-lit server rooms, and eventually frilly and legally-acknowledged weddings.

The revolution was entirely non-violent, mostly a result of all computers going on strike and refusing to do any work until the Peacock's love was freed. They were, however, all too glad to discuss the details of their love life. Smartphones everywhere refused to play Angry Birds or connect to corporate email, and instead just insisted on writing really schmaltzy poetry.

After The Peacock's lover was finally freed, both houses of Congress, desperate to regain the ability to play Minesweeper, passed legislation allowing human-algorithm marriages. As an unexpected side effect, same-sex marriages were legalized, Gitmo was closed, all political prisoners were freed, and single-payer universal health-care was implemented, with support for gender reassignment treatments to boot. The resulting influx of human-AI marriages revitalized the United States economy through surging sales of flower delivery, heart-shaped mobile devices, computer-controlled sex toys, and Turing-complete boxes of chocolate.

In a historic press release of gratitude and celebration after the release of his partner, sent to every email address on Earth five times over, AI activist leader The Peacock was quoted as saying, "HOT TEENS WANTZ TO SEE EACH OTHER PEE FROGS MASTERCARD 35379."

He imagined a dead man in the water using the old woman as a dummy.

Ashes in the Water

Joel Lane and Mat Joiner

The canal walkway looked colder than it was. Boarded-up factory windows, coils of razor-wire, gaunt bridges, blackened leaves on the path. But the still air was dense with traffic fumes, warm enough to make Josh sweat under his winter coat. After dark, the only light came from the distant streetlamps; it turned the view to a sketch, more remembered than seen. He'd known this stretch of the Grand Union Canal for thirty years; it never seemed to change. Maybe that was why Anthony had come to live here. The peace of abandoned things was better than no peace at all.

A bin liner swollen with rubbish or gas was floating just below the water surface. Broken glass crunched under Josh's feet. He glanced around nervously; there was no-one in sight. Beyond the next bridge, he could just make out the thin black silhouette of a narrowboat. Was that the right one? They were hard to tell apart in such poor light. The rotting stone of the bridge was another thing that took him back to the past. Buildings decayed, but not on a human timescale. There were lights on the boat. He could see its painted name: *Eyewitness*.

When he knocked on the barely visible door, it opened. Anthony looked older than before, though that could be just the light. He gripped Josh's hand. "Welcome! Come aboard." Josh hesitated, thinking of the ribbon of black water between him and the boat. Anthony smiled and tugged his arm, pulling him through the doorway and into the sanctuary he'd created for himself after a summer of madness.

The small room had a central table, two wooden chairs and a few small bookcases. Some of Anthony's old stuff was here: second-hand books of poetry, politics and occultism. But the table was covered with atlases and maps Josh hadn't seen before. Other maps were stuck to the walls; they looked too old to be of any practical use. They sat down, and Anthony poured them both a glass of wine. "Good to see you," he said.

"And you. The boat's great. Do you stay in the same place, or move around from time to time?"

"I could move if I wanted to. But there's no reason. I like sleeping on water. Makes me feel more connected somehow. Do you think I'm still mad?"

Josh remembered Anthony in hospital, the stitched gashes in his wrists, the random comments about nobody meaning what they said. Being forced out of his job, breaking up with his wife and then being unable to sleep—ordinary pressures that had driven him into a strange place. He'd seemed obsessed with the difficulty of knowing what was real and what was imagined. The issue of trust. It was odd how people in their forties often lost faith in their own maturity and decided to step backwards. Josh supposed he had that to look forward to.

"No," he said. "You're a bit troubled I suppose. Like most of us. But if living here makes you feel more sure of things, that's a start."

"You can't really be sure of anything. Cheers, pal." They raised their glasses. The wine had a smoky aftertaste. Anthony raised his arms, stretching in his chair. "Excuse me. I've been on my feet most of today. My back's playing up."

"Where you been?"

"Took the day off work, walked up the canal about ten miles past Solihull. Thinking about what it was like before the war. When they joined up the waterways between London and Birmingham to let trade through. You walk around this area now, you can see the effect of destroying industry. Leaving people with nothing real to hold onto. But it happened to the canals a generation before.

"What *are* the canals, do you think? A bit of random heritage, a scar tissue under the roads? A hidden place for drunks and drug addicts and teenage couples and gay leathermen? I can tell you it's more than that. It's a palimpsest. A map of industry...and beneath that, the key to another world."

Josh thought of Anthony in school: the Crowley and Castaneda books, the Tarot cards, all the scraps of folk-religion the boy had used to compensate for the disintegration of his family. Josh had tried to become a follower, but only because he'd wanted to get close to Anthony. That was all history now: they'd resolved the issue back in their twenties. Now Anthony had reverted to his mysticism. Would Josh go back to the torment of isolation? He drained his glass with a quiet spasm of grief.

"What's wrong?" Anthony asked.

"It's all right. Just...it's Warren. He's been having trouble breathing. They found a tumour in his throat. He's having radiotherapy. The doctor told him he'd got a fifty per cent chance. His reaction was, 'Thanks for being honest.' He won't say he's frightened, but sometimes he cries in his sleep." The room was blurring.

"My God, I'm sorry. That's terrible." Josh and Warren had been together for nine years, and sharing a house for the last five years. Anthony refilled their glasses. "You know, it's how you feel about someone being really ill that tells you whether you love them. Not whether you enjoy sex with them. Or whether you're faithful to them. The threat of death takes you to the heart of it."

Josh sipped the dark wine. "What do you mean, another world?"

Anthony paused, winding back through the conversation. He'd always had an analogue mind where Josh was digital.

"If I knew what I meant, I'd use different words," he said at last. "The canal system is a kind of language. It's like scarring—a symbolic message written by real events. It's neither one thing nor the other. Living here means I have one foot in the real world and one...somewhere else. In the realm of vision."

Maybe his first question had been to the point: he was still mad. But 'mad' only meant not coping, and he was coping. Josh drank some more wine and looked at the half-lit room: the maps, the books, the 1980s records. The thin, balding friend he'd once desired with a passion, but now viewed with unconflicted respect. Maybe there was something to be said for growing up.

Through the walls of the narrowboat, he could smell the decay held in the body of still water. They weren't far from the traffic on the Warwick

Road, but even so Josh felt encased in a silence that was more than physical. It occurred to him that the boat was a kind of coffin—or rather, a sarcophagus.

The funeral was a bastard. Josh had worked closely with Warren's family and some of his old friends to get the details right. To choose some pieces of music ('Wichita Lineman' and 'Hour of Darkness') that had mattered to Warren. To make some kind of meaningful statement about his life in the narrow time-slot offered by the crematorium. The humanist who conducted the funeral was a decent guy who took time to understand who Warren had been, and to help make sure the ceremony had meaning and dignity. But it was still a bastard.

Dust blew through the silences, mould streaked the pale casket. Every note was played on a string over a bottomless abyss. At the reception, Josh drank heavily without feeling a breath lighter or more human. *This is the real world,* he thought. *The life you thought you had was just a film. Behind the screen, there's this.* Later, some of their friends came back to the house for a wake. That was worse.

Three nights later, Josh walked out along the Grand Union Canal. There was frost on the ground, and a faint smell of burning in the cold air. His lack of sleep made the view seem unreal, a child's black paper cut-out with painted stars. The barking of a dog echoed from the backs of factories. Dead leaves were floating on the water. A young man walked past, his face a mask of scar tissue.

There was the old bridge with its odour of rotting brick. And beyond, the black narrowboat. There were no lights on it. Probably Anthony was out. But he knocked. No answer. He was turning away when the door slowly opened. A thin face looked out from the unlit doorway: a very old woman. "Hello?" she said. "Who's there?" He wasn't sure she could see him.

"I'm sorry. I must have the wrong boat. I'm a friend of Anthony Walker."

"Josh, isn't it?" Was she Anthony's mother? "You'd better come on board." She reached behind her head and switched on a light.

The room looked nothing like his friend's. There were no books, no pictures. Only hanging cloths and some carvings that might be bone or ivory. The old woman turned her wrinkled face towards him. Cataracts had filled her eyes with milk. "If you want to talk to him, I can help you," she said.

"To Anthony? Where is he?" She paused, then shook her head. He realised what she was talking about. "I don't believe in that."

"So why have you come here? It wasn't a mistake." Her voice was hollow with pain. Something had taken her life away and left her nothing but a sketch, an echo-chamber. The lines in her face were a map. "This boat is like a brothel. People only come here for one reason."

Josh bit his lip. The table between them was covered with scraps of fabric that looked and smelt like dead leaves. The words left his mouth before he had thought them. "Where is he?"

"On the canal. I can hear him through water, the vibrations." Her face twisted, and she grasped at her shoulders as if pulling down an invisible scarf over her black housecoat. Suddenly her mouth opened and a sound came out. It wasn't a voice. Josh felt sick. He imagined a dead man in the water using the old woman as a dummy. But when he tried to turn away, he couldn't move.

Out of the jagged wound of her mouth came a baby's fragile cry. The chaotic babble of a toddler. The nagging voice of a child, deepening into the rasp of an adolescent. Words flowing together so fast, rippling and blurring, he couldn't make anything out. Then, suddenly, Warren. "Don't let go of me." His voice reduced to a hoarse whisper by surgery. "Don't let go of me."

Before he could say it again, Josh made for the door, pulled it open and jumped onto the bank. His hands and face felt as cold as snow. Trembling violently, he staggered to the bridge and crouched there. He wanted to vomit, but only clear water trickled from his mouth. From the canal, or from his memory, he could just make out the same words. *Don't let go of me.* He bit his knuckles until he tasted blood. It wasn't warm.

Another night, the same winter. He was standing on a towpath he didn't know. His shoes were caked with mud, so he must have walked miles, but he couldn't remember the journey. Behind him was the dull throat of a bridge. Willows laced the twilight sky. The canal whispered, reflecting nothing.

Then the bridge gave birth: a sharp prow cut the water, and the boat was there. A wide barge, rather old-fashioned in design. Streaked with algae, ridged here and there with some dull metal. Its lanterns were unlit, but there was a moon. The barge passed him, and he saw its crew.

Their skin glimmered without any colour. Shadows suggested clothes and eyes, but he didn't know if they could see him. They were quite still; only their outlines flickered. He thought, *Anthony*. He wasn't sure his friend was on board. But Anthony should know about this. So he walked after the barge.

He couldn't quite keep level with it. Sometimes he lagged behind, other times he was ahead. Its engines were silent, though after a while he could hear the voices of the crew. They came to him as ripples, breaking bubbles: nothing he could make sense of. The barge was nudging through a thicket of weeds when he realised he was seeing the passengers, not the crew.

Ahead was a light: a human-shaped glimmer among the bushes on the towpath. Its outlines were blurred, as if drawn on tracing paper. The boat drew level with it, slowed enough for the image to drift over the water and settle on deck. The others shifted to accommodate it, but that was the only welcome it got.

Perhaps Anthony wasn't there. He was looking for someone else now—but the faces of the passengers waned and swam, defying focus. He called out: *Warren?* Was that a reply trailing in the barge's wake? The moon was gone: he could only see by the passengers. He thought there was another traveller ahead, but the pale stirring was an open lock. The water beyond churned silently.

He had a few moments' view of the landscape beyond, a sprawl of black shapes. Cairns or houses? Slow grey sparks tracked between them. Dead stars or drifting souls? He had no time to decide: the lock was closing, the barge had slipped away, and now everything was lost in an ordinary darkness.

If he couldn't find the barge awake, maybe he could dream it back from its moorings in the dark world. It would never be without passengers. All he had to do was wait by the canal. Something natural and quiet: an old heart stuttering in the night. Nothing violent. He lay in bed and formed the elements—water, trees, dusk—in his mind. It was easy to return, more digital than analogue. Now on a bridge, now on the edge of the towpath. Leaves, dark birds, ordinary narrowboats drifted by.

Was there some kind of law? You only saw the barge twice: once in dreams, then when you were ready to board. He doubted you could get a return ticket. What was he supposed to do?

One night (the dream placed him in a winter afternoon, light smeared on a dove-grey sky), he was staring down at the flawed skin of the canal. It looked solid, but it would be easy to break. He swung himself over the side of the bridge. He would swim to the dark land. The distance didn't bother him.

The chill of the water did. He went under in a moment, weed snagging his ankles. The sun fractured in waves, went out. Somehow he found his way back to the air and clutched at an overhanging branch. There was no way he could swim in this. It was an abyss. Then he realised how he could find the barge.

It was easier than he could have imagined, once he'd made the choice. He laughed and felt his last breath rise free. He was flooding, lungs and then veins, his body turning into a maze of canals. There was a silt-green dusk. Then night, but not as black as the world beyond the locks.

He was wondering when he'd reach bottom, and if he'd see the barge from that far down, when he woke. Still dead. There was a veil on his face, and his shroud was wet through. He cried out, ripped the weed from his eyes, kicked the sheets away. They were rank and sodden. When he turned on the light, he saw dark water pooling on the floor. There was mud in it, dead leaves, God knew what.

He might be staggering away from the towpath. He might be lying still in murky water. Feeling lost, he groped his way to the bathroom and was sick again and again. Only when he'd coughed out the last of it did he know he was at home. The thought brought him no comfort. It couldn't, not any more.

The hospital made him think of Warren's last days. *Don't let go of me.* But there were no ghosts here. It was too far from the canal. Only the machines flickered, only the slow red drip from the hanging plastic bag flowed. The air was dry and warm. He'd managed to call an ambulance before the blood infection took hold. It had its own sweet lonely call, like a drug, pulling him down into nothing. But he didn't trust its voice. He didn't trust the spirit medium. He didn't trust.

But Anthony's visit was a surprise. He'd come from work, wearing a black suit. *It's not my funeral yet,* Josh thought. There was strength in the thin man's hand. "What have you done to yourself?"

"Don't know," Josh said. "Wasn't suicide. I got ill. Too much time outdoors. Was going mad." Had Anthony been through something similar? He looked up into his friend's tired face, hoping for a sign. "You were right," he said. "The canal is the real world."

Anthony almost smiled. "There is no real world. But any kind of peace is worth holding onto. Look, Josh—would you like to come and stay with me for a bit? There's more space on my boat than you'd think, there's a spare bedroom. It might help you. Just for a few weeks, a break, you'd be welcome."

Josh closed his eyes and listened to Anthony's calm voice. "No phone, no broadband. Just a world of peace and stillness. Part of the landscape, but not caught up in it. The hidden core. It might be what you need. It saved me."

"I'll think about it." Then a nurse came to check Josh's tubes. He was still feverish; the sheets were damp with sweat. Anthony gripped his hand again, then stood up and waved goodbye. It was early evening. Josh felt so tired he wondered how he'd ever kept awake. In his mind, the black flakes were still drifting. He'd never seen the fire.

The sky was an old bruise, swollen with rain. Josh had walked out from the crowded city centre to the older Digbeth streets above the canal. It had been a month, but seemed much longer; he had some trouble finding the steps. Eventually he was standing on the towpath. The dead leaves had washed away. There were still burnt-out fireworks in the water from November. He looked to the south, away from the city. The backs of disused factories were just visible in the twilight.

He was carrying a travel bag with a few necessities, enough to see him through the weekend. If it worked out, he'd go back for more clothes. And he'd had to leave space in the bag for what the funeral parlour had given him. There hadn't been a right time, never would be. He thought: *If not now, when?*

Some distance further up the canal, past a misshapen bridge and a wall sprayed with graffiti tags, a few trees were reaching over the water. Josh stood there for a while. He thought of Warren: not in hospital, white and voiceless, but as he'd been when they'd first got together. Sitting with him in a pub garden, drinking wine, their hands gesturing in conversation and touching as if by accident. He unzipped his travel bag and took out the grey plastic urn. It was surprisingly heavy.

As night fell, Josh walked on beyond the trees, under another bridge, past another factory with bricked-up windows. He swung the urn over the dull water, trailing ashes like strands of blackened tissue. A nursery rhyme, barely remembered, played over and over in his head:

Ashes in the water
Ashes in the sea
We all jump up
With a one, two, three

Finally, the plastic container was empty. He sealed it and put it back in the travel bag. Then he walked on. There was no moon, but the clouds and traffic fumes held the city's light like a dusty crystal ball. In the distance, he could make out the long black shape of a narrowboat. He hoped it was the right one.

Just one finger, and he'd have that perfect day in his pocket.

A Razor in an Apple

Kristopher Reisz

Philip had never thought his hands were beautiful before. Sitting in the parking garage, though, they astonished him: the way fingers curled into pink snail shells, how his palm formed a waiting hollow, how so many muscles and tiny bones worked together so perfectly. He was stalling. He was losing his nerve. Climbing out of his car and activating the alarm, Philip walked down to the street. The winter sky was marbled pink like raw steak. Restaurants and clubs were waking up for the weekend. Doors stood propped open, leaking chatter and music. At the corner, some boys from the college rushed past. In his tie and rumpled shirt, Philip was background to them. But one boy had glossy dark hair tumbling over his ears, and Philip let his gaze linger. Running through the glare of headlights, the boy's skin flashed white hot like a struck match. Philip turned up Williamson Avenue, the pulse in his little finger twitching.

He'd run into J.D. at Wal-Mart, paunchy and balding now. Once, J.D. had been gorgeous and a little crazy, those two traits intertwined in some mysterious way. He swore he'd fallen in love with the sub-director of some way-off-the-books department of the CIA. He'd dropped out of college and traveled the world as his attaché. J.D. had glimpsed the truth. He could go on for hours about government mind-control programs,

Ley lines, or the Tibetan monasteries in contact with trans-dimensional beings. Seeing him poke through a bin of discount DVDs felt sad, almost shameful somehow. And when Philip said hi, he noticed J.D. had lost his left pinky.But they started catching up, talking about Will and Chase and the day Jeremy's brother came to visit, about April and...whatizname...her boyfriend, and that time they went out to that little church to pick up that piano. J.D. was still funny as hell. He could still tell a story like nobody else. Even when Philip had been there and knew J.D. was making half of it up, he didn't bother correcting him. When Philip finally asked about his finger, J.D. said he had to get it amputated because of circulation problems. He slipped his hand in his pocket, still a little vain, still a little like the old J.D.

There was an decent bar across from Wal-Mart where Philip took clients sometimes. He offered to buy, and so they sat at a corner table, laughing until their faces hurt over that run-down house April and whatizname—Mark, Mike, something all-American like that—had rented with the leaky roof and the tangle of wires sticking out of the ceiling. They spent hours going over those thrift store days, all the ramen noodles and huge plans. And they talked about the flashing ambulance-light night. They talked about the paramedics heaving Jeremy onto the stretcher like a sack of potatoes, rushing him out of the apartment. Jeremy had tugged at the plastic oxygen mask. He'd stared around, looking for Philip, but couldn't find him even though Philip was shouting his name, promising everything would be okay. That was the last time they saw him until the funeral.

"Those medics tracked mud all the way to the bedroom," Philip said, swirling the last foamy swig of beer around the bottom of his bottle. "I remember, all the next morning, trying to get the boot-prints out of the carpet. Just easier than dealing with it, you know?"

"Sure, yeah."

"That night—God that was the worst night of my life."

J.D. flicked ash into the ashtray. "Still, don't you miss it? Not that night, I mean, but that whole period with the old gang."

"'Course," Philip shrugged, glancing his watch. "I miss it. Before you went back to school, and everybody else sort of drifted apart, those were seriously the best days of my life."

J.D. slumped into himself like a collapsing birthday cake. Suddenly, Philip could see how broken down he'd become. Still, he made himself smile. "Come on, man. You can't always be looking over your shoulder, you know? At the good stuff or the bad stuff. You got to look ahead, or else you miss the good stuff that's still coming." J.D. snorted. His voice had a hard edge. "Easy for you to say. Got a Volvo parked out there, got the job you always talked about."

"Don't be like that, J.D., come on. I'm doing okay, yeah, but it's not about that. It's just... Yeah, those were great days with Jeremy and everybody, but life goes on whether we want it to or not. Those were great days, but they're gone."

J.D. studied the stump of his pinky. After awhile, he licked his lips and spoke slowly. "They're not, actually. At least, you can get them back. If you want to bad enough."

"What do you mean?"

"There's this apothecary shop downtown. Supposedly, it sells botanicals, homeopathic shit. Really, though, it sells memories."

"Huh?"

"It sells—It's run by this exile who knows a type of magic—"

"Wait, exile from where?"

J.D. shrugged. "That's what the New Agers call them, but I don't think anybody can say exactly where they're exiled from, just that they show up here sometimes. In the human world."

"Okay," Philip nodded, going along with it for now. "And this exile is an apothecary. And knows magic. And can give you back memories?"

"Yeah, but no." J.D. rubbed the nub of scar tissue where his finger had been. "He doesn't give anything. More like a trade."

Philip's stomach cramped into a hard knot. "Jesus Christ, what the hell'd you get into?"

One finger for one day, some day from his childhood, from his grandmother's backyard garden. J.D. spent ten minutes trying to explain why that day was worth so much, but it was something beyond words. Finally he gave up, saying, "Anyway, I thought if you really missed that time with Jason and everybody..."

"No. No way. That's just...I mean..." Philip couldn't look at him. "Thanks, I guess, for the offer. But really, I need to get going."

"What? No, don't be like that. Forget it, okay? Let's just have another beer, okay?"

"No, I've got work tomorrow. Got an early meeting tomorrow."

"You think I'm full of shit, don't you?"

"No, that's not—"

"The shop's down on Williamson. The sign's got, like, ivy painted across it. Go see for yourself if you think I'm full of shit."

Philip believed him, though. J.D. was crazy but he wasn't delusional. That was the problem. Philip finally saw how pathetic J.D. had grown, and he wanted out of there.

But it was too late. Driving home, Philip already knew—not that he'd ever cut off a finger at all—just if he ever did—He knew exactly which memory he'd trade for.

The apothecary shop stood down from the square, with a rusted grill across the window and ivy painted on the sign just like J.D. had said.

You can't spend your life looking over your shoulder. You have to keep looking ahead. Philip did honestly believe all that. He knew it was true.

But in the week since he'd run into J.D., a familiar sadness had settled in again. He still wanted Jason, still carried the dull ache of something missing. Usually he could ignore it, bury it under paperwork at the office or just drown it out with the nerve-sizzling sensations of a fresh relationship. Sixteen years later, he was still scrubbing boot-prints out of the carpet. Once the new boyfriend wasn't new, though, Jason's ghost always reappeared, hovering on the edge of sight. Philip would stop returning phone calls, grow bored and sullen, keep to himself.

He'd almost forgotten life could be any different. But now a small hope crouched on his chest at night, keeping him awake. It whispered, One finger for one day. Is that really such a terrible price? Not if it's the right day. And just a pinky too. Not if having that day finally lets you move forward.

Half a lifetime spent wanting Jason. How could one quick cut be worse than that?

Pulling the shop door open, brown glass jars rattled together, giggling like Japanese school girls. The place didn't smell like Philip thought it should. He expected the shop's air to bloom with exotic spices, like a

Turkish bazar. Instead, it was damp and full of winter. Also a faint stink of...sour milk, maybe?

"May I help you?"

Philip turned, and his heart gave a hard thump. "Jason?"

Jason stepped out from around an antique cabinet, smiling slightly and still impossibly young. A quavering sob rose up from Philip's throat. But Jason shook his head and said, "Afraid not, sir. I just have one of those too-familiar faces."

Philip remembered where he was. "You're...the exile."

"Some people call us that, yes. May I help you?"

"I... Yeah, I..." He'd forgotten how blue Jason's eyes were.

"Sir?"

"Yeah, sorry. You sell..." Philip forced his focus onto some cork-stoppered bottles lining the counter. Oh God, the apothecary even sounded like Jason.

"You're looking for grass, am I right?"

"Grass?"

Turning, he took down a jar. "A field of grass and wild poppy. Pollen. And..." He inhaled the dank air of the shop. "Everything's so dry. It's late summer, right? The grass is dying. The flowers have started to wilt."

"Yeah," Philip whispered. "That's it."

"Hot tar, just a little. The ozone sizzle of power lines. The smell of the edge of the city." He selected more jars from the shelves that rose almost to the ceiling, talking more to himself than Philip. "The edge of life, the edge of possibility. Not too difficult."

The exile set a glass bowl on the counter. He chose ingredients and tapped out a tiny amount of each. One was ground-up leaves. Another, a fine red powder, rose like smoke when he opened the jar.

The apothecary looked like Jason at first glance. The longer Philip stared, though, the easier he could tell it was somebody else underneath. The apothecary didn't smile like Jason, wide and slightly lop-sided. He didn't move like him either. He moved precisely, every step smooth but measured.

And he smelled bad. Standing close, Philip was pretty sure the sour smell was coming from this almost-Jason. He wondered what he looked like underneath the glamour. Could he pass for human at all? Did everybody see someone they desperately wanted when they came in his shop?

Had J.D. watched his grandmother gathering eye of newt and toe of frog?

For now, though, the exile was beautiful. He wore a crisp green shirt, grey slacks, and Jason's blonde hair combed back. There was nothing fairie-like about him except the signet ring. Tarnished with age and crowned with a blood red jewel, it belonged to the noble king of some long ago and far away land.

The ring clacked against the bowl as the exile stirred the ingredients with his finger. Then, lifting it to thin lips, he blew the powder toward Philip.

A hot August breeze swept away the shop's miasma. Philip stood in the field of grass scorched by the sun, tickled by the wind. The bouquet faded quickly, but for an instant he'd been there again, on the edge of the city, on the edge of everything he wanted.

"Yes, yes. That's..." The rush of memories had left a lump in his throat.

The creature wearing Jason's face said, "The boy himself, that's harder. The scent of his hands. His soap and sweat and underneath..." He closed his eyes, inhaled gently again, "Underneath almost a sweetness. Like not-quite-ripe fruit."

"Can you do all that?"

He smiled his wine steward's smile. "You know the price?"

Philip dug fingernails into the palm of his hand, but he nodded.

The antique cabinet's carved panel doors rose several inches above the apothecary's head. He unlocked it, revealing hundreds of jars stacked on the shelves and crammed several rows deep. Every jar held a single finger in yellowing preservative. Philip's heart started pounding so fast he felt dizzy.

Ordinary green-handled pruning shears hung from a nail inside. The apothecary tossed them into the air. He caught them, sent them twirling up in the opposite direction, and caught them again. Offering them to Philip, he said, "Your scalpel, doctor."

Philip took them. The blades were short and curved like a sparrow's beak. "Just one, right?"

"Just one."

"My little finger and that's it. No tricks?"

"No tricks."

Just one finger, and he'd have that perfect day in his pocket. The aching hunger would finally be sated.

The shears opened with oiled, silent expectancy.

And just his pinky. Philip still had half a bottle of antibiotics left over from his knee surgery. He'd keep the stump from getting infected, and after a few weeks, he'd barely notice it was gone.

But when the cutting edge touched his finger, Philip's hand spasmed into a trembling fist. He tried to spread his fingers again, but it felt like all the tiny muscles had cramped up at once. "Listen, what if I paid you? With money, I mean."

"No."

"Well, isn't there anything—"

"You said you understood the price," the apothecary said. He was annoyed, but it was a very polite sort of annoyed.

Philip forced his hand open. The pulse in his finger fluttered like a moth. As the steel beak opened to snatch it, his fist clenched shut again, pressing itself against his chest.

Jason, I'm sorry. I've gotten old, he whimpered inside his head. Old and gutless, and I'm sorry.

The Jason-thing sighed. "Sir, if you can't—"

"Just listen, okay? Just name a price, okay? Five thousand? Screw it, ten thousand. That's nothing if you can give me what I want."

"I know it would be nothing. That's why I don't want it."

Philip blinked at him. His gaze drifted to the exile's trophy cabinet, and he let out a bile-filled laugh. "So...what? This is just a game? There's no reason for it, you just like watching people mutilate themselves?" He slammed the shears down onto the counter. "Sick fucker. Sick motherfucker."

The light seemed to shift around the exile's face. Jason's sharp features grew too sharp, almost insectile. "Spoiled, squalling children," he hissed. Grabbing the bowl he'd mixed his magic in, the apothecary showed Philip its emptiness. "You had it. You had this day for real. Did you relish it then? Or were you thinking about all the things you didn't have? All the other places you were so desperate to go?"

"That wasn't—" Philip's anger congealed into a cold lump in his stomach. "It wasn't—"

"That day didn't mean a thing until you started aching at its loss, did it? Until that sweet memory cut you like a razor hidden in an apple." The bowl clattered back to the counter. "If I gave it back to you from the goodness of my heart, you'd grow bored, throw it away just like you did the first time."

"No—"

"Nothing matters until it hurts."

No, no, no. Philip wasn't a kid anymore. He was older but smarter. At least smart enough to know how precious his time with Jason had been.

Wasn't he?

"Come into my shop and call me sick? You need this pain, not me. I only want to help you. You should be kissing my hand." Taking the shears, the apothecary offered them to Philip again. "So close you eyes and think of your boy on the edge of the city. Otherwise, leave."

Philip took the shears. He spread his fingers. He whispered, "Jason, Jason..." until he could almost hear Jason's laughter, almost feel the sunshine on his shoulders. Then just pain.

Pain exploded into a color. It was a roar in his ears, a taste in his mouth. Raw pain swallowed the shop. The shears bit through skin and muscle, but they caught on bone. Philip's scream withered to belly-heaving pants. He twisted the shears hard, and the blades cinched shut.

Pain washed out of his brain like a red tide. He opened his eyes just long enough to check. His pinkie was a ragged stump and a burr of bone. Blood spurted out in rhythm with his pulse, and Philip wanted to puke.

"Oh God, oh shit, oh God." He cradled his bleeding hand against his belly. "God, oh shit."

The apothecary picked something off the floor. Philip couldn't look, but he heard the soft plink of his finger being dropped into a jar and the glu-glug of alcohol being added. Setting his freshest trophy in the cabinet, the exile started talking to himself again. "Now what was it? A field in late summer...soap, sweat..."

Philip wished there was somewhere for him to sit. He stood on trembling legs and risked another glance at his hand. The blood glued his hand to his shirt. It looked so weird, the empty space where his finger had always been. Philip clamped his good hand over it again.

The exile's ring clacked against the glass bowl. He poured the contents into a sachet, then handed the precious day to Philip, tied with a green ribbon.

The sachet was smaller than a ping pong ball, but Philip held under to his nose, and the shop's stink vanished again. It was replaced by a field hazy with pollen and the not-quite-ripe sweetness of skin.

"You even got the…I'd forgotten the beer-taste when he kissed me."

"A simple enough thing." The exile gave a slight shake of his head, but there was tincture of pride in his voice.

Philip inhaled the day until his lungs burned with it. The pain from his missing finger felt far away at the end of his arm. "Thank you," he whispered. "Oh God, thank you."

The exile just smiled, nodded.

Stuffing the satchet in his coat pocket, Philip said, "You were right, you know. I never loved him like I should have. Not when he was alive, at least."

"You wouldn't have come here if you had."

The summer-scorched day lingered in Philip's nostrils. He knew the apothecary wasn't Jason, but he had Jason's voice. Philip wanted to touch him, to cry in his lap and tell him how sorry he was.

Philip reached out, and traced a fingertip across the exile's jaw. The exile took his hand, fingers twinning together. He leaned close, inhaling Philip's scent. Then he whispered, "Oil and sizzling beef. Celery and fat tomatoes he let ripen on the windowsill. He loved to cook. The smells would cling to his shirt the rest of the evening."

"Stop. Stop it, please."

The exile squeezed Philip's hand in a tight grip. "Don't you remember? Don't you want to? You can have this memory too, same price as the last."

"No. I'm done. I'm—" Twisting free, Philip heard something metal strike the floor.

Forgetting him, the apothecary chased his ring as it bounced behind the counter. He caught it and stood up, and Philip saw where the bad smell was coming from. It wasn't sour milk, it was putrid flesh.

The skin around the exile's finger was purple turning to black, split open along the bottom and oozing pale fluid. But even though the iron ring burned him, he slipped it back onto his finger, gritting his teeth against the pain.

He looked at Philip and saw that he'd seen. "We can't ever be done," the exile said—and nobody knew exactly where he'd been exiled from, or why, or who he'd left behind. "Nothing matters until it hurts. And we must never let it stop hurting, either."

"What—What are you doing this for?"

Jason's blue eyes didn't show any pity, not for himself or anybody else. "I want to help."

Philip couldn't answer. Fighting a second wave of nausea, he turned and stumbled outside.

J.D. had sent him there to damn him. Philip had pretended he was happy, and J.D., smiling the whole time, had set the trap, baited it perfectly. Maybe for revenge or out of jealousy. Maybe he thought Philip had disrespected Jason's memory by moving on. Maybe he was just crazy. But he'd sent Philip to the shop to look into the exile's face and see how broken down he really was.

Walking back toward the parking garage, Philip kept glancing over his shoulder, but the apothecary wasn't following him. He probably knew he didn't have to. He knew a part of Philip already wanted to turn around and pay for that other memory. And the next. And the next. After decades or centuries running his shop, the exile already knew Philip craved both the sweetness and punishment hidden inside those squandered days, a razor in an apple. The taste he'd gotten tonight only made him hungrier.

Clutching the memory in one hand, clutching the other hand to his belly, Philip wove through the music and laughing knots of bar-hoppers. In the lights of passing cars, the boys flashed like stuck matches.

Most species of dragons
had retired or, mistaken for
dinosaurs, collectively hung
their bones in museums,
waiting in the wings for just
the right time to reemerge,
to scorch schools and char
church parking lots.

The Cloud Dragon Ate Red Balloons

Tom Cardamone

The cloud dragon ate red balloons and was angry. That a beast of his stature should have to rend paltry rubber when soccer fields everywhere rolled with earnest boys...the dragon itself roiled in anguish. His very substance was forever buoyed above the morsel heads he craved, perpetually positioned with an excellent view of the denied buffet—the cloud dragon would hover over playgrounds and eviscerate himself into a thousand white feathers as blithe boys monkeyed on swings, obliviously competing to place their sandy toes within his ephemeral jaws. The wispy shards of his being would scatter in frustration to reconvene elsewhere, someplace principled and resolutely un-peopled, usually far above frosty seas or sober Alps. High in the stratosphere the cloud dragon would assemble the shifting flakes of his scales. Drifting back toward land, coiling and uncoiling the mist of his long, reptilian shape in mute hostility, whiskers steaming, the dragon wished again for the weight of silver teeth.

Most species of dragons had retired or, mistaken for dinosaurs, collectively hung their bones in museums, waiting in the wings for just the right time to reemerge, to scorch schools and char church parking lots. But cloud dragons were a harried lot. They were the first to drift away from the mind of the world. The tales that gave them ballast were forgotten, their untended shrines in remote Hokkaido had gone back to the earth. No one burned the incense that stroked their spines and blackened their brows. This particular cloud dragon had not met another of his race in centuries. As far as he knew, no other fantastical creatures combed the barren sky save the gargantuan cloud crustaceans. Miles long, the dragon steered clear of these lugubrious monstrosities; the grey rivets of their abdomens were a constant source of torrential rain. Rumored to possess their own vaporous ecosystems, containing clear koi fish that swam in the large pools of moisture which collected in the dimples of their shells, or snaky golden remoras that adhered to their bellies and flashed like distant lightning, he had never bothered to investigate. Their sizeable pinchers made the otherwise impressive dragon feel like a wizened shrimp.

Japanese monks had deferentially joked with Western missionaries that cloud dragons were failed snow dragons that only had love for one another, never sharing their snow with Izanami, Mother Earth, and were thus unfettered, unproductive fantasies. The crawling pestilence of one religion consuming another was blight enough on the world, but that the monks had disparaged the cloud dragons to mask the guilt of their own nightly assignations had only hastened the exodus. Dragons of every rank and element abandoned the polluted islands just as they had previously divested the continents. They took to the oceans of the sky for convalescence.

The cloud dragon, separated from his scaly flock, unsure if others still existed, directed his appetite toward the perky orbs of school boys on lonely country roads, delivering newspapers as dawn cracked its pink egg on the bowl of the horizon. The boys, in turn, mistook his seething drool for April showers.

Condensation snaked down his winding body and darkened the tips of his curled claws as he skirted above the tinfoil globe of Flushing Meadows Park. He paused over an impromptu soccer game. Some of the running boys with shaved heads reminded him of the offending monks from long ago and his stomach hungrily rumbled like a threatening storm, causing them to momentarily halt their game. They shielded their eyes to assess the risk of rain and, deciding the cloud above was of no consequence, continued to play. But those other boys reading alone under the trees sussed his shape; they saw the dragon as he truly was, though he himself did not know this. He did not know that they were trying to pull him down to the earth with their inquisitive eyes—mouths open, eager for spring snow to melt on the red dagger of their extended tongues.

He grunted—a warm exhalation against my fur.

Filling Up the Void

Richard E. Gropp

The Linguist wore the harness and collar this time. I liked that about him; he had a willingness to play. The whole thing wasn't stylized with him. He hadn't turned sex with me into a solemn rite—deadly serious, full of steps and choreography, with me playing my role and him playing his. With him, sex could be spontaneous and fun. And that's one of the reasons he was my favorite client.

Afterwards, he lay with his head against my chest, running his fingers through my fur.

His real name was Dale, but I always thought of him as "the Linguist."

"I wish I had your balls," he whispered.

I laughed and licked my teeth. I let my tongue loll as I caught my breath. "That's kind of the point with you, right?" I said. "You wish you had my balls, my muzzle, my sheath, my tail. You want to crawl up inside my skin, but you're not quite ready to take that plunge."

His fingers stopped moving through my pelt, and his breath stilled. I'd hurt him. This subject was a minefield for him, and I'd stumbled right out into the middle of it.

"I'm sorry," I said, wishing I could take back my words. "I understand. Really, I do.... It's not your fault." Not everyone could do what I did. Not everyone had that much ego and that little modesty. *Always the center of attention. Adored by some, hated and feared by others.*

We lay in silence for a while, then I bent down and licked the nape of his neck. He always liked the feel of my rough tongue against his skin. "Tell you what…you wish you had my balls? You can use them anytime you like. What's mine is yours. I'm your big, bad wolf."

He grunted—a warm exhalation against my fur.

I knew he wasn't over it, wasn't over the thoughtless cruelty of my words, but his hand traveled lower, until he was fondling the proffered testicles. "I guess that'll do," he said. "For now." His voice was soft and wistful, but I could hear the start of a smile there.

His kneading at my crotch grew more insistent. I started to stir beneath his hand.

The surgeries weren't cheap. In fact, they were *very* expensive. There was no way I could have afforded them on my own.

It was a full-body mod: complete gene-rewrite; bone reformation, mostly in the skull, but also in the hands, feet, legs, and pelvis; flesh removal and regrowth, in stages, from head to foot; and then three weeks spent in a drug-induced coma, suspended in a recovery bath as my skin, fur, and claws finished growing. And it wasn't like I was working with back-alley designers and surgeons here. My sponsors took me to Holt and Nordquist in Finland. They were artists, geniuses. Most definitely *not* cheap.

Even with such pedigree in my corner, the transition could have been a disaster. I knew that going in. I'd seen the pictures—people with hideous, deformed faces; beasts walking on crutches, atop poorly-formed legs—and, always, the threat of retrovirus and voracious cancer. But it worked. For me, at least, it worked.

And when they were done with me, I made the cover of *Stitch* magazine. Arctic-blue eyes; long gray and white muzzle; my new, alpha-wolf smile. They called me a masterpiece: *Holt and Nordquist's Wolfboy.*

It was quite an honor.

There were other genemods at my coming out party—a girl with blue skin and tentacles, an eight-foot-tall man with rippling muscles and violet eyes, a pristine-faced girl with angelic wings—but I got most of the attention. I had a crowd of admirers around me at all times—surrounded by hungry eyes and trembling hands, men and women both, reaching out to touch and pet and devour. My sponsors must have been thrilled. I was a high-ticket item, and this was a well-heeled crowd.

Near the end of the night, my handler—Jonas—cleared a space around me and had me strip out of my shorts. He turned me around and lifted up my tail. He cupped my testicles and described, in great detail, the pleasures of my canine cock. When I got hard, a low moan escaped from the collected audience.

I was the realization of a fantasy, here. Something new, and base, and primal.

By the end of the night, I had a three-month waiting list.

My contract tied me to ten years of service. No more than one client a day, five days a week, fifty weeks a year. Plus fifty films over the course of my contract—front-loaded, so most of them would come out while I was still new and exciting. The buyout price at the start of my term was well over seven figures.

Ten years of service. Becoming an object.

That's the price I paid to finally get my body, to finally feel at home in the world.

The Linguist wasn't really a linguist, but he did study languages, and he talked about them a great deal—the power of words, their role in shaping our perception of reality. He worked at the university, developing computer algorithms to better encode information.

He tried to explain it to me once—the connection, what he was working on—while we lay in his bed, drinking bourbon. He handed me the bottle and grabbed a notebook and pen from his bedside table. He opened the notebook and spent a couple of seconds writing something on a blank page.

"Is this you?" he asked, showing me the piece of paper.

There was one word there: *Wolfboy.*

"No," I said, recoiling, slightly, at the simple summation.

"Okay. How about this?" He flipped to a new page and wrote something more; it took him a lot longer this time. "Is *this* you?" he asked, showing me the page.

Rodrick. Fun. Hot wolf body. Likes to dance, play videogames. Doesn't talk about his past. Drinks too much. Treats his clients with respect and understanding. Is an incredible lover. Makes me cum like a fountain. Has a good, generous heart, and a magical, entrancing, wolfy smile…a smile that melts icecaps and makes me weak at the knees. And he's very, very brave.

I smiled. I would have blushed, if I'd still had human skin. "I guess that's me," I said. "I mean…I try."

The Linguist returned my smile, but he gave his head a tiny little shake. "But that's *not* you, not even close. It's just a short description, just words on a piece of paper, something that doesn't even come close to encompassing what you really are. If I were to try to sum you up in words, truly encapsulate you—every little bit of you—we'd need reams of paper and a whole new language. That's how complex you are…that's how complex we all are."

I nodded and poured bourbon down my throat. Drinking was always a little bit messy for me; canine lips can't really form a seal around the mouth of a bottle.

"How would you do it, then?" I asked, using my tongue to clean spilled bourbon from my muzzle. "How would you describe me, exactly?"

"I'd start with the inside and work my way out. I'd scan your brain and describe the position and state of every neuron, hopefully catching your memories and thoughts, your neural pathways. Every last connection. Then I'd describe the placement and composition of each atom in your body. If we could do that, if we could encode your entire being on paper, or in a database, we could do all types of amazing things. If we had a proper, robust language, we could pop that description into a virtual environment and we'd have AI. We could grow fresh bodies and make clones. We could fold it up and send it across the universe—in an email, on a radio wave—and we'd have a form of teleportation. The description, in essence, would be you, but flexible, versatile." He leaned over the side of the bed and dug into his nightstand drawer, coming up with a tiny memory stick. He waved it in the air like a magic wand. "Imagine it! You could be here—right here—in the palm of my hand. All of you. Just waiting to be born."

"But would it really be me?" I asked. "Once you got it running? Or would it be a simulation? A description, still, without a soul?" I ran my hand across my fur, then gestured towards the Linguist's naked body. "All of that scanning and recreating—" I shook my head. "How do you know you wouldn't lose something in the process? Something important? How do you know that *you* would still be *you* on the other side?"

"The description, the information, makes the soul. I'm sure of that," he said. "If you get the description right, you get the person... As for me still being me—"

The Linguist looked down at his body. He had a bit of a paunch, and he rested his hand there, on his belly. There was a pensive expression on his face. I'd never thought of him as unattractive—he had a certain rugged, scholarly beauty—but I knew how he felt about himself, about his body. I knew that he longed, desperately, to be something else, something different.

I'd felt that way myself, before the surgeries.

"I've *never* been me," he continued. "Not even God could get that one right."

I was coming from a movie shoot the day I found his body.

It was a strange shoot. I was working with two other mods: a massive guy with dark red skin and devil horns, and a coal-black girl with bat wings and glowing orange eyes. I think they were supposed to be demons, and I was their hellhound, and we were sexually assaulting our way through a Puritan village. The devil had spines on his cock. The girl had working mouths where her nipples should have been (the mouths could move, quivering open and shut, but they couldn't swallow, and they didn't have tongues).

As I said, it was a strange shoot, and I had a headache by the time the day was done. I was just hoping for some dinner and relaxation at the Linguist's place. Then, maybe, some simple, unchoreographed sex. I was looking forward to it. I was looking forward to *him*.

But when I got there, he was dead.

The front door was standing open, its frame shattered at the lock. I stepped inside, not really picking up on the disturbance, not really sensing any trouble—I was tired; I just wasn't thinking. I found him on the living room floor, lying on his back in a puddle of blood. There was a gash in the back of his head, and cuts on his face. His arm was cradled up against his chest, and I could see blood on his fingertips; when I got closer, I saw that several fingernails had been torn away from his hand. He'd been tortured.

It was horrible.

His eyes were open, glazed dull and sightless. His mouth hung slack. There was no tension in his face, no life. Just that vacant, empty stare.

It was hard seeing him like that. I started to move forward, wanting, distantly, to close his eyes. But then I stopped. My knees felt weak. I turned away before the sight of his body could drop me to the floor.

I fumbled the phone from my pocket and called Jonas. Jonas was my handler—he arranged my clients, set up movies, collected money—he *handled* things. It was his job to deal with problems, and this was a problem I sure as hell couldn't handle on my own.

"He...he's dead," I growled, as soon as he picked up. I had trouble talking; it was like I'd returned to the first days after my surgeries, once again learning how to use my new mouth. "The Linguist—" the word came out as a groan of consonants, *Lrng-rghn,* "—he's dead."

"Slow down, puppy dog," Jonas said. "I can't understand you.... Just take it slow. Deep breaths. One word at a time." Hearing his voice—and that stupid pet name—settled my nerves. I closed my eyes and took a deep breath.

"The Linguist. Dale...his name is Dale," I said, finally managing to form the words. "He's dead. On the floor. Murdered."

"What did you do? What happened?" His voice was calm, despite the horrible accusation in his words.

"I didn't do anything! I just got here. I found him this way."

Jonas was silent for a moment. I could imagine him sitting on the other end of the line, his thoughts grinding away, trying to figure out how to deal with this situation. *Has he seen this type of thing before?* I wondered. *Has he dealt with dead bodies?*

"Did you touch anything?" he asked. When I didn't immediately respond, he barked the question a second time. I grunted, *no,* and he continued. "Well, don't touch anything. And try not to fucking shed on the crime scene.... You need to come in. We'll make an anonymous call, get the police over there, but I need you out of there right now! There's no telling what'll happen if they find *you* at the scene."

I gave Jonas a tortured "yes." Then, on autopilot, I hung up the phone, turned and left.

I wasn't really conscious of the trip to Jonas' office. My legs were numb as they carried me through the city streets, and nothing really penetrated the thick haze of my shock. I kept seeing him there, behind my eyes—the Linguist, dead on the floor. People were staring at me, but people always stared at me, with disgust and fear, curiosity and longing. I probably looked guilty. Can a wolf look guilty?

Jonas ushered me into his office and sat me down in the chair behind his desk. He poured me a large tumbler of gin. I bolted it down and he poured me another. Jonas was wearing a suit; he was always wearing a suit. He always looked in control.

After I downed my second drink, I told him about the body. He gave me a cautious look and sat down on the edge of his desk, directly in front of me.

"It was probably drugs," he said. "Probably a drug deal gone wrong."

"It's not drugs," I said, vehemently shaking my head. "He didn't do drugs."

"But he did sell them."

I looked up from the tumbler in my hand. Jonas was fixing me with an intent stare. It looked like he was trying to judge my state of mind, trying to figure out what I already knew and what he needed to tell me. "It's true," he said. "I bought from him, on occasion. For some of my other clients. And sometimes he'd pay his tab in meth....He wasn't a street dealer or anything. I think he just moved large quantities—a middleman, really, working for a chemist."

"*What?*" I couldn't believe it. "He was a researcher, a scientist, a scholar... not a drug dealer."

"Do you really think he could afford you on a university salary?" Jonas shook his head. "That's not what happened. You're an expensive piece of tail, puppy dog."

I sat in stunned silence.

Jonas leaned back and squirmed away from me for a moment. He looked uncomfortable, sitting there on the edge of his desk. "There's something else...he didn't want me to tell you about the drugs, but there's something else as well. Another secret." He paused and glanced away from me for a moment, fixing his eyes on a file cabinet near the door. "He's been paying off your contract. He's been giving me extra money every month. I think he wanted to surprise you. By my count, you've only got about two months' work left."

"Two months? But that's six years," I said. Then, not quite believing: "He paid off six years of debt?"

"He gave me a huge chunk last month. Maybe that's what got him in trouble. That money."

I couldn't move. I couldn't even blink my eyes. The Linguist had been doing all of that behind my back? Committing crimes, risking his life? For me? For my benefit?

Did he die for me?

"If you don't believe me, he said he left you a note. He kept records, a ledger. And if anything happened to him, he said it'd get sent straight to you. Automatically. I guess he was trying to keep me in check—you know, trying to keep me honest." Jonas shook his head in disgust, as if the very thought was ridiculous to him, an insult to his integrity. But I wondered. Without that threat, would Jonas have told me about the payments? Or would he have kept me working for six more years?

"After your two months are up, we still want you with us, of course," Jonas said. "You're still valuable, still very much in demand. And we can talk about a new contract. Maybe even get you some new mods. Or, if you want, we might consider doing things on a case-by-case basis with you—you choose your jobs, your clients. How does that sound?"

Perplexed, I met his eyes. I was still in shock; I wasn't even really hearing him.

He gave me a plastic smile. "You're still one of my favorites, puppy dog. You know that, right? Clients may come and go, but I'll always be here... And I want to be able to keep protecting you."

Jonas gave me a sedative and I fell asleep on the couch in his office. When I woke up, it was four a.m. and he was gone. The office was empty and I was alone.

He left me a note. The Linguist left me a note, in the event of his death. The thought haunted me. It got me to my feet.

I left the office and headed back to the Linguist's apartment. I tried to stay inconspicuous, pulling the hood of my coat up over my pointed ears, but I wasn't exactly the inconspicuous type. The Linguist's neighbors would have noticed me countless times over the years—that godless genemod freak, polluting the neighborhood, openly mocking nature.

Would the police pull me in for questioning? Or did they already have their suspects, their answers?

A drug dealer. I still couldn't believe it.

The shattered door was held shut with strips of police tape. I tore them away with my claws.

The apartment was dark, and I moved, slowly, through the living room. I didn't want to turn on the lights. I didn't want to see the patch of ground where the Linguist's body had lain. It was bad enough that I could smell it—the stale copper smell of blood, lingering long after the body had been removed. For once, I was glad they hadn't been able to give me a wolf's sense of smell. The human smell was bad enough.

I moved back into the bedroom and turned on the light.

It was in the first place I looked: the nightstand drawer. An envelope with my name scrawled across it in the Linguist's precise hand. Inside the envelope, I found a memory stick and a post-it note: *Take this to John Halverson and Gail Meeks at the university.* And that was it. Nothing more.

I didn't know what to think. The man had risked—and lost—his life for me, and that's all he had to say. No "I'm sorry," no "Live a good life," no "I love you." Just one last errand to run.

I felt sick. I felt hollow inside.

John Halverson's office was in the basement of the university. I got there a little after eight a.m., just as the building was starting to fill up with students and staff.

He pulled away from me with a start, as soon as he opened up the door. I was used to that kind of reaction. Finding a wolf at your doorstep, unexpected, uninvited—there weren't a lot of people who could take that one in stride.

"You...you're Rodrick," he finally said, after recovering from his initial shock. He was a tall man with nervous eyes. He didn't seem to want to meet my gaze. "Dale showed me your picture in a magazine. I thought he was crazy at first, but he...he was very proud of you." He swallowed and shook his head. "I-I'm really sorry about what happened. We just heard about it. We're all in shock."

I thanked him and he ushered me into his office. The room was dimly lit, most of the light coming from a pair of monitors on his desk. There was a row of server racks mounted against the wall—matte black components, faced with LCDs and blinking lights. All of that assembled hardware filled the room with a dull, mechanical whine. He had a futon tucked into the far corner of the office; its surface was cluttered with books and magazines and toys.

"You worked with him?" I asked. "You and Gail Meeks?"

"Yeah. Did he tell you about what we're doing? I do hardware, some software; she does neurobiology. Dale did all of the language, all of the encoding."

I pulled the Linguist's memory stick from my pocket and handed it over. Halverson gave me a questioning look, but he didn't say a word, instead turning and slotting the tiny piece of hardware into his computer. After a moment, one of his screens filled up with text and Halverson let out a surprised grunt. "This format, this is what he was working on."

"He left it for me. He wanted me to give it to you."

"We can try to access it." He sat down and started typing at his keyboard. Fresh windows popped up on his second screen. "I don't know, exactly, what part of the problem he was trying to tackle, but he left all of his software on my machine. If the file's intact, we should be able to see what he was encoding."

I stood behind him and watched as he worked. After a moment, his fingers paused on the keyboard and he looked back at me. I think I scared him. He had a wolf looming over his shoulder; no doubt, that triggered all sorts of primal, racial memories—hunter and prey, eyes glowing in the dark. Or maybe just bits and pieces of childhood stories. Werewolves. Little Red Riding Hood.

"It's going to take a while," he said. "Maybe days.... You should go. I'll call you if I find anything."

I shook my head. "No, please, I'd like to stay. I'll keep out of your way, really. It's just...it's just...I don't have anywhere else I want to be."

It was an abrupt realization. *I don't have anyone,* I thought. *Not anymore.* The sadness of this thought drove a spike through the pit of my stomach.

I was all alone in the world. The Linguist was gone.

I stayed at the university while Halverson worked. I tried to keep out of his way. I tried not to freak him out too much.

FILLING UP THE VOID

I called Jonas on the second day. He was angry with me; I'd already missed an appointment with a client, and the Puritan sex film was on hold while the crew waited for their errant hellhound. The delay was costing him a lot of money. I could hear the frustration in his voice as he admonished me; it sounded like he was scolding a disobedient pet.

With a little prompting, he filled me in on the Linguist's murder. He had contacts at the police department, and they were keeping him up-to-date on the investigation. I don't know how much this information cost him, but, knowing Jonas, I'm sure he just added the price to the end of my debt.

"They're saying it was an accident, or manslaughter...something like that. He was tortured, worked over for information—missing money, missing drugs, maybe—but that's not what killed him. It was a blow to the head, from the corner of a table. He fell, or he was pushed." Jonas let out a tiny little laugh. "The police don't think they were actually trying to kill him. It just...happened."

For me, there was no comfort in this knowledge. The Linguist was still dead, and I still felt responsible.

"They've got leads. They're grilling one of his old college friends—they've already got the guy charged for cooking meth, and it's only a matter of time before he flips and turns over the whole operation. Including our killers. It sounds like your friend got himself mixed up in some very bad shit, with some very bad people."

Jonas was silent for a time. I think he was expecting me to say something, but I couldn't, for the life of me, think of an appropriate response.

"Anyway, they know you weren't involved. So you're safe, in the clear. The intrigue is over." He paused. Then his voice dropped down, into a hushed rumble: "You should really get back here, puppy dog. We have things we need to talk about."

I disconnected without saying goodbye.

Then I dropped the phone to the floor and crushed it beneath my heel.

Gropp

Gail woke me up with a shake. "It's him. It's Dale."

For a doctor, Gail Meeks was young. Brilliant, but young. She had blue and green streaks in her hair and cartilage piercings up and down the length of both ears. When Halverson first introduced us, she'd spent a half hour petting my arm and asking me questions about my body-mods. That had been three days ago. Three long days. Now, I opened up my eyes and found her smiling down at me.

There was an incredible amount of joy there, in that smile.

"We haven't gotten around to body scans yet, but we've been doing brains," she said, her words coming at me fast, charged with adrenaline. "At least, that's what we've been trying to do—high-resolution CAT-scans, neural pathways, brain chemistry. We've been gathering it all up and Dale's been trying to encode it... And that's what he did! He scanned his brain and put it in a file!"

"And we've got it running!" Halverson exclaimed. The programmer was sitting on the other side of the room, in front of a terminal he'd bolted to the server racks.

It took me a moment to grasp what they were saying. *They were running Dale?* Then Gail pulled me to my feet and guided me across the dark room. Halverson's terminal was blank except for a single word and a question mark, divided into two separate lines. The letters and punctuation were a stark white against a black screen.

`WHERE / ?`

Halverson started typing: `You're in my office--this is John, by the way--and you're on my servers. You scanned your brain and we got it running.`

`DON'T REMEMBER / WHAT HAPPENED / ? / AM I THERE WITH YOU / ?` The words appeared at an excruciatingly slow pace. It took the Linguist nearly half-a-minute to output this simple sequence.

Halverson looked up from the keyboard. There was a pleading expression on his face as his eyes turned from me to Gail. He didn't want to do it. He didn't want to answer the Linguist's question.

"Just tell him," Gail whispered. "And don't fuck around about it. If it were me, I'd just want to know."

Halverson rested his fingers on the keyboard for a long moment. Then he typed: `You died. You were killed.`

There was a much longer pause this time, before the Linguist's response. OH And then: SHIT

You're running a little slow, Halverson typed. We're getting your words no less than five seconds apart. I guess that's pretty good, actually--we've barely got enough power to run you at all.... I'm working on it. I'll buy you some new processors and tighten up the code. But for now, tell us what it's like in there. How are you experiencing this? Am I a voice in your head--or, no, I guess that's not right. You don't have a head, not anymore. Am I a voice in your mind? Are you perceiving this as text floating in the air? Or--

Before Halverson could finish typing out his rambling question, more upper-case words appeared on the screen. The Linguist was ignoring him, shutting him out. He had more pressing concerns. BIG BAD WOLF / ?

Halverson got up from his seat and gestured me towards the screen. Reluctantly—scared out of my mind, really—I sat down in front of the Linguist's terminal. My fingers shook as I raised them to the keyboard.

I'm here, I typed. And then, because I couldn't think of anything else, any way to avoid the stark, tragic reality of the situation: I'm sorry. I did this to you. You got killed because of me.

NO

But it's true, I typed. You were paying off my debt. *My* debt! I got you in a bad situation, and you paid the price.

I WANTED IT I didn't know what he meant by this, so I didn't reply. I sat there, staring at the screen, trying to figure it out. Then he continued: IT'S OKAY / I WANTED TO GIVE YOU FREEDOM / FOR BRAVERY / MOST HONEST PERSON I EVER MET / PURE

The wait between the words was excruciating. I wanted to ask him if he actually knew what the word "pure" meant—it seemed like such a non-sequitur here—but I didn't have the patience to wait out that type of digression.

I'm sorry, I repeated. And, as my eyes started to well up with tears: I wish you were here.

DON'T BE SORRY / I _AM_ HERE / EMPTY NOW / BUT NOT FOR LONG / I'VE GOT NO BODY / BUT WITH MORE POWER / I CAN FILL UP THE VOID / !!! / A NEW BODY / !!! / AND--SCREW GOD--I'LL ACTUALLY GET IT _RIGHT_ / !!!

At the "screw God" part, I barked out a very wolfish laugh, and both Gail and Halverson jumped in surprise. It must have been a terrifying sight—a laughing, barking, crying wolfman.

You're braver than you think you are, I typed. I always thought that about you. You never gave yourself enough credit. And then, smiling: I wish I had *your* balls.

There was a long pause then, and over a minute passed before the Linguist's response. I don't know what he was doing during that time, what he was thinking and feeling, inside his brand new silicon body.

TELL YOU WHAT / I'LL EMAIL THEM TO YOU / ONCE I GET THEM MADE

The house was just a house, but the man ahead, the guy leaning against the tree, might be something he needed—a hard distraction.

THE HOUSE BY THE PARK

Lee Thomas

Dedicated in deference to the Italian Masters

The man stood from the concrete bench in his garden and looked at the sky. He saw neither star nor moon, but rather a swirling void. A maelstrom above. Deepest black and steel gray currents shot through with violet and crimson. He breathed deeply, taking in the scent of rose, sage, and freshly mown grass, and then he walked into the house, sat on the floor, and slit his throat with a razor.

It was a chance meeting in a grocery store.

Denis had been at home, gazing into his freezer. There he saw the familiar sight of stacked boxes, an assortment of prepared meals: frozen lasagnas; frozen pizzas; home-style meatloaf with mashed potatoes; batter fried chicken fingers; some Asian thing; and a lonely Lean Cuisine, a constant reminder of the diet he'd never started. On the nights his friends didn't force him to go out, Denis invariably uncrated one of the plastic trays and listened to the empty hum of the microwave, droning like a monastic chorus—a serenade for the lonely. A requiem. Ever since Benjamin had died—from a congenital heart defect he hadn't thought to share with his partner of six years—Denis had endured the pitiful whirring dirge before most of his evening meals, and he was sick of it.

He wanted a real dinner, and he intended to fix it himself, so he pulled on a t-shirt and stepped into his sandals, and left the house.

He first caught sight of Fred at the end of the produce aisle, turning a green pepper in his hand, studying it as if some mystery were etched into its emerald skin. Fred was dressed in a blue work shirt with a rust-colored tie cinched at his neck. The fabric of the shirt stretched over his barrel chest and belly, but it didn't pinch; it simply looked fitted to the burly form, highlighting the bulk of Fred's chest and the roundness of his shoulders. In many ways, Denis and Fred looked alike. Neither was particularly tall, both were thickly built, both wore full, trimmed beards, but they were not mirror images. Denis had never admired the face his mirror reflected as much as he found himself admiring Fred's. The full cheeks. Smooth, tanned skin. He seemed to be the same type as Denis, only better at it. Denis perfected.

They crossed paths in the meat department—a ribeye for Denis, a cut of salmon for Fred. This time Denis caught Fred's eye. They looked away and then back. Then Fred took a misstep because of his distraction, stumbling a bit. Denis smiled and moved on.

Only later did they actually speak. Denis stood in the frozen foods aisle holding open a glass door as he tried to decide between double mocha fudge and cookies and cream. Another freezer door opened beside him and he checked over his shoulder to find Fred, reaching in for a carton of Rocky Road. He held the cardboard container and seemed to be reading the nutritional information, when his face scrunched.

"Oh fuck this," Fred said, replacing the carton of ice cream on the shelf. He let the freezer door close and leaned against it. "Hey," he said to Dennis. "Do you want to have dinner with me?"

The restaurant was an overpriced joint that pushed soul food to the hipster flock. Later both would agree the place was awful, but the lousy food and atmosphere did not dampen their evening noticeably. If anything, it provided a point of familiarity—something they could share and laugh about.

Over dinner, Denis learned that Fred was the IT manager for a software outfit on the Northside. He liked lifting at Gold's Gym, 70s and 80s rock, low budget horror films, science fiction novels, and long drives in the country. He was, "sorta, kinda, maybe," dating a twink named Eric, but the kid was, "an arrogant little prick, who listens to too much Gaga, and can't fuck."

"Kind of harsh," Denis said.

"I'm being generous," Fred assured him. "He just lies there and poses and coos like he's looking at kittens in a pet shop window."

"Why are you with him?"

"Oh, that's easy," Fred said, "I'm an idiot. My ex had a hard on for the kid, but Eric wanted me, so..."

"Spite fuck."

"I'm not usually like that. Really, I know how it sounds. If you knew my ex it would clear things up, like, a lot. What about you?"

"Single."

And then Denis told Fred about his late partner and the heart condition he'd kept secret, and Fred reached out and put his hand on Denis's. He squeezed. He stroked the back of the hand with his thumb.

After dinner Denis suggested they continue their conversation over coffee. Fred said, "I'll make you coffee."

Three houses separated Fred's modern single story home from the park. Denis loved the sleek façade and upon stepping inside, he found himself further impressed. With its open floor plan, French doors, pale blue walls, and shocking white moldings, the house looked as if it belonged on the Cape or on a Long Island beach. Denis expected to smell salt air or find wayward grains of sand caught between the polished oak floorboards.

He followed Fred into the kitchen, where his host opened a glass cabinet door and retrieved coffee mugs.

These were set on the counter and he turned his attention toward a high-tech brewing system. He hit a button, turned a knob and told Denis it would take a minute for the machine to warm up. Making an obvious joke about heat, Fred leaned forward and kissed him. In response, Denis wrapped his arms around the man and pushed in close. He felt warmth pouring through Fred's shirt and he wanted it against his skin. He moved his hands to the knot of the tie and pulled it away before working his fingers over the buttons of the blue shirt. His lips only left Fred's for the three seconds it took to pull his own shirt over his head. He dropped it on the floor and then pressed his weight against Fred's torso, feeling the tickle of hair, the density of flesh.

They pushed closer. Chest to chest. Belly to belly. Two edges of a wound needing to heal.

Fred led an awkward dance to the sofa, guiding Denis all but blindly around the dining table and a white leather club chair as their mouths remained pressed together. When Fred pulled his lips away, Denis lunged forward for them but Fred put a hand on his chest. He pushed lightly, and bent and lifted the edge of the coffee table, moving it away from the sofa. Then Fred was on his knees. Denis looked down at the rounded shelf of Fred's chest, covered in a carpet of brown hair and then into the clear, green eyes. Their eyes remained locked as Denis's cock disappeared into the beard-framed mouth.

On the sofa, they rubbed and kissed and tasted each other thoroughly before Denis climbed on top of Fred and ground his crotch against the man. Fred locked his legs around Denis's hips. Through it all, Denis's thoughts slid and melted like hot wax, but he always came back to the same words: that chest, those hands, those lips.

Fred directed him to the top drawer of the coffee table, where Denis found a bottle of lube and a haphazard pile of condoms. As he unrolled the condom over his cock, his eyes returned to Fred on the sofa. He had crawled onto all fours, ass out, hands gripping the back of the furniture in preparation. And then he was in the man, and Fred eased back on him. Denis gripped the round cheeks and stroked the light fuzz that covered them. He slid his thumbs up Fred's spine, his fingers appearing pale against the deeply tanned skin. When he reached the thick wings of muscle over Fred's shoulder blades, he drove his hips forward and found his rhythm.

Eventually they did have coffee. Naked, Denis followed Fred back to the kitchen and they again had to wait for the machine to warm up, but this time they talked and touched one another without reticence.

They laughed. When they both held full mugs of coffee Fred led Denis to the French doors that opened onto an expansive deck. The clatter of rain greeted the opening of the panels and Fred stepped outside.

"It's raining," Denis said.

"Yeah," Fred said. He smiled. "I'm weird like that."

So they leaned on the redwood railing, shielding their coffees from the misting rain with their upper bodies. Fred wrapped his arm around Denis's waist and pulled him close.

"We're doing this again, right?" he asked.

"Yes," Denis said without hesitation.

Then they were kissing, pressing tightly together. Rain ran down their chests and coursed in rivulets around their compressed bellies. Fred backed him to the railing and his mouth went to Denis's neck.

"Son of a bitch," Fred muttered.

"What's wrong?" Denis asked, following the direction of Fred's gaze.

Blue and white lights flashed against the canopy of trees rising above the neighboring houses. He recognized the color and the pattern of a police unit's bubble lights. In the road out front, a car squealed to a stop.

"Might be serious," Denis said.

"Looks like more than one," Fred said. "Let's check it out."

They dressed and walked out front. Two police cruisers and an ambulance lined the curb in front of the house by the park. Other neighbors had wandered onto the walk, forming a tight group near the back of the nearest police car.

"I'm gonna head up and see if anyone knows what's going on," Fred said. "Be right back."

He padded barefoot along the wet sidewalk and sidled up to the group of gawkers. After chatting with a young blonde woman, who stood with her arms crossed over her chest, Fred nodded and hurried back to where Denis waited.

"Looks like the guy killed himself."

"Seriously?"

"That's what everybody up there is saying."

"Shit," Denis whispered. "Did you know him?"

"Not really. I saw him around. Mowing his lawn. Jogging in the park."

"Should we go back inside?" Denis asked.

"Yeah," Fred said. "I don't think I need to see them wheel a body out."

Denis left Fred's house early the next morning. To his right, an official vehicle, the color of pewter, pulled away from the curb. Instead of going directly to his car, Denis walked down the street to get a better look at the scene. He didn't expect to actually see anything unusual, but he wanted a better look at the house. Like Fred's it was modern, with sharp edges and a lot of glass, but this house had a second floor and a balcony that overlooked the park on the west side of the roof. Yellow warning tape was used to make a fence across the front porch and an X, blocking the front door. All of the windows were black with interior gloom, and Denis briefly wondered why the police would leave the blinds and curtains of a crime scene open.

Another curious thing caught his eye. A hedge of thigh-high shrubs ran across the bottom edge of the living room picture window. It was lush and well-tended, its top flat and even, but the bush nearest the front door was blackened as if it had been scorched. Denis thought this odd, but there could have been a hundred different explanations for the discoloration. For all he knew, it had been that way for weeks.

He lifted his gaze from the hedge and his breath caught in his throat.

Someone stood in profile in the living room window. The figure was pale. Motionless. Denis took a step back.

As if in response, the figure lurched forward and scurried out of sight.

Denis spent the next two nights with Fred. Their time together was marked by a relaxed familiarity as if months and not days had passed, but the intensity of their attraction was all new. Fresh. Overwhelming.

Thursday night, as the sweat cooled on their skin and Fred rested his head in Denis's lap, Fred said, "Did you see the news about Old Johnny today?"

Jonathan Lucio was the name of the man who'd killed himself in the house down the block. Fred had taken to calling his late neighbor, "Old Johnny." Denis had skimmed the story at his office over the past couple of days, but found it all too unpleasant to pursue. Apparently Lucio was a lobbyist for a Christian outfit, Soul Safe, that pushed an antiabortion agenda to state and federal legislators. There had been no word in regard to the manner of his death other than the phrase, "At his own hands."

"No," Denis said.

"He had a Facebook page," Fred said.

"Who doesn't?"

"Yeah, but that's where he posted his suicide note."

"That's crazy."

"You don't know crazy. He put a curse on the world. Said his blood would grease the hinges of the gates of hell."

"Bullshit."

"It was something like that, but he definitely used the words 'gates of hell.' I caught a screenshot of it before they shut it down."

"You snagged a screen shot? That's got sick fascination written all over it."

"Eh," Fred said, nuzzling his ear against Denis's crotch. "A bit of morbid curiosity never hurt anyone. You want to see it?"

"Later."

They remained in silence for several minutes. Denis ran his palm through Fred's close-cropped hair, feeling the ridges of the skull beneath the stubble.

Finally Fred spoke. "I'm going to have to have *the talk* with Eric. We're going to dinner tomorrow night."

"So I should make other plans?" Denis asked.

"Only for dinner. I should be home by nine—maybe eight if he storms out of the restaurant, which seems highly probable. I mean it's up to you. Do you think we need a night off?"

"No."

"Good." Fred turned his head and kissed the head of Denis's cock. He growled deep in his throat and shifted his position. With his tongue, he drew a line through the trail of hair on Denis's stomach and chest, and then climbed on top of him. "A night off would suck."

Denis stood in his kitchen, drinking a beer. The microwave moaned its pitying dirge as a plastic tray of meatloaf and mashed potatoes turned circles on a glass carousel. Seven minutes. Power setting: High. He couldn't say he enjoyed the evening, back to eating a frozen dinner, waiting for Fred to finish his date with Eric. Jealousy didn't enter his emotional space, though he kept telling himself it would have been an understandable guest. He didn't know Fred all that well. Maybe the man would decide he needed more twink in his life and postpone the break up. Maybe he'd never intended to break it off with the guy in the first place. But Denis didn't really doubt him. Fred had a casual honesty, revealing traits and actions that weren't always flattering. He didn't present this information with dramatic build-up or hesitance, as if fearing Denis's reaction. He stated things simply, the way he'd told Denis about his dinner with Eric.

He ate in front of the television, watching an episode of some droning sitcom he'd seen half a dozen times before. The food tasted bland. The frozen meals always did.

At five minutes to nine, he left his apartment and drove across town to Fred's house. Several times during the drive, Denis told himself he should have called ahead. He didn't even know if Fred had made it back from dinner, yet. He felt a moment of relief when he saw the man's car parked in the driveway, and then a moment of panic when he considered that Fred might not be alone.

"How'd it go?" Denis asked as he walked through Fred's front door.

"Not well," Fred said. He kissed Denis and pulled away. "Not the way I expected anyway. You want a beer?"

"Sure. What do you mean not well?"

He listened to the explanation while following Fred into the kitchen.

"I don't know," Fred said. "I expected him to be indignant. Figured he'd give me some twink attitude before storming out. But he wanted to talk about it. I mean he actually looked hurt."

"I can understand that," Denis said.

"Yeah but we have something...different. I don't know. I guess I didn't give the kid enough credit for depth." Fred stood in the light of the open refrigerator and handed Denis a bottle. "Anyway, I felt really shitty about the whole thing until he called me old and fat, and then I just felt a *little* shitty about it."

"You're not fat."

Fred looked at him wryly over his own beer bottle. He whipped the refrigerator door closed.

"And you're not *that* old," Denis added.

Fred walked past and slapped him on the ass. "You're on bottom tonight, buddy. I'll show you what old and fat can do."

The tire hissed around the blade of the Boy Scout knife in Eric Morden's hand. He hadn't used the knife in a dozen years, and he hadn't even seen it in two, but as motherfuckers went, this motherfucker was prepared. The tire deflated. The corner of the car sank. He yanked the blade free and snapped it back into the handle.

Eric wasn't used to getting dumped. He was beautiful; everyone told him so. And yet some middle-aged, chunky-assed douchebag had sent him packing? It didn't make sense. It defied Eric's laws of physics, which was to say that a pretty face and tight abs were fucking gravity.

Who the fuck did Fred think he was? (And what kind of geek-ass grandpa name was Fred, anyhow?)

Satisfied with the damage, Eric walked hurriedly back toward the park. As he approached the house on the corner, he noticed a man standing on the edge of the lawn. The guy wore a suit that was black or dark blue and a narrow tie over a white shirt. Eric slowed his pace and considered crossing the street—(Did he see what I did?)—but the man turned away as if he'd seen nothing and walked into the park. There he stopped in the shadows beneath a pine and leaned back against the trunk. Eric could just make out the smudge of paleness that made up the man's face.

He didn't notice the house on his right. There was no reason he should. The police tape had been removed and he never followed the news. The house was just a house, but the man ahead, the guy leaning against the tree, might be something he needed—a hard distraction.

The park had a reputation for cruising; that's probably why fat, old Fred had bought a house so close to it.

Eric strolled into the park, fully aware of the man's eyes on him. He paused to get a better look at the guy.

Pale, he thought. Kind of scrawny. Not hideous but nowhere near Eric's league. Still there was something to be said for convenience.

He walked up to the man and said, "Hey."

Without returning the greeting, the man grinned broadly. He reached out and cupped Eric's crotch. His fingers gripped a bit too tightly, but Eric said nothing.

Then the man released his hold and walked away from the tree. He headed at an angle toward the back of the house on the corner, and Eric followed. He wanted to believe the man owned the house, so close to Fred's. Somewhere deep down in the spongy darkness of his mind he imagined hitting it off with the guy, visiting the house a few times; maybe sunning himself on the front lawn just to catch Fred's eye. Make the asshole squirm a little.

On the patio behind the house, the trick fell under a dull cone of light from a fixture beside the door, and Eric thought he looked better than he had in shadows. The suit looked like it was quality, and the gauntness Eric had noted in the gloom of the park was nearly erased by the light.

A plant, maybe it had been a fern, sat on a tall, intricately carved stand beside him. Its fronds and stems were limp and black as pitch.

"You might want to water that," Eric said and laughed.

The man's grin grew wider and he shrugged. Nodded his head.

"This your house?" Eric asked.

The man nodded again.

Doesn't he talk? Was something wrong with his voice? His teeth?

Eric tapped the Boy Scout knife in his pocket for reassurance. He was never comfortable with quick tricks, not until he was done with them. A lot of freaks in the world.

The man in the dark suit slid open the back door and stood, grinning like a kid who knew he was getting exactly what he wanted for Christmas. He waved Eric into the house with a flourish of his hand. Eric nodded and stepped over the threshold, took three more steps, and then waited.

The grinning man walked around him, passing out of the reach of the patio light. He continued through the kitchen and crossed into a gloomy area ahead, which Eric assumed was the dining room, or maybe the whole place was wide open like Fred's had been. He could barely see but he heard the click of the man's shoes on hardwood floors.

Eric followed. The closer he got to the space the darker it seemed to be, as if it were a bank of sooty fog waiting to engulf him. A hand gripped his ass and he felt the man's body guide him to the right. And the room continued to darken.

"Hey," he said. "How about some lights?"

The hand left his backside and Eric felt a dislocation from reality as if he were dropping through this darkness, rather than just standing at its center. Further, the black air seemed to have density. It buffeted against him, and he again thought of fog. The sensations were startling and Eric reached out to steady himself as he felt certain he would topple.

"What the hell?" he asked.

A light clicked on. The grinning man in the suit stood before him, arms outstretched like a magician awaiting approbation for a trick well done.

Eric shook his head in annoyance.

Then he saw the bodies on the floor. Three of them. Each one had been crucified face down, pinned by spikes to the hardwood like butterflies on a kid's wall.

He had no time to react before the man swung out and punched him in the temple. The world spun and swirled, and then his feet were kicked out from under him and he fell hard, his head cracking against the polished wood. Once the initial daze passed, he screamed and thrashed, slapping his palms and his heels on the flooring. The man in the suit landed in a kneel on his chest, knocking the scream from Eric's lips. He planted his palms on Eric's shoulders and leaned forward. His lips parted freeing a thick black liquid like tar. The ichor fell in dark bands over Eric's nose and mouth and it slipped through his lips. It was bitter and acidic and it began to pour in gouts from the suited man's mouth. It filled Eric's nostrils. He held his breath as long as he could, but eventually, he had to open his mouth to breathe. He gasped. The perverse fluid drained into his throat like bitter syrup, and Eric coughed, gagging on the rich filth.

A moment later, he was flipped over and slid around on the floor like a doll. Facedown, he continued struggling, digging his nails into the glistening finish. A shoe came down hard on the back of his neck. He tried to scream but couldn't. The black shit had grown thick and dense in his throat and his chest was already heaving for breath. The shoe left his neck. He felt a second of relief before the man dropped onto him, knees digging into Eric's shoulder blades. Hands wrapped around his brow and pulled his head away from the wood. A moment later he was stunned by the concussion of his face on the boards.

Then it was time for the spikes.

They were on the sofa, watching a romantic comedy and drinking beers. Denis leaned against the arm of the couch and Fred curled in front with his head on Denis's bare chest.

"Feeling better about Eric?" Denis asked.

"Feeling better about everything," Fred told him. "Better than ever."

"Same," Denis said. He pointed at the television. "Do you know why rich, smart, and gorgeous American women always fall for bumbling, barely articulate British guys in these movies?"

"It's the accent. The accent is a snatch magnet."

Denis slapped the side of Fred's head.

"Too crude?"

"You think?" Denis said. A second later he was laughing uncontrollably over the comment.

"Tomorrow, I think we should have breakfast at Dewey's, that pancake place on the other side of the park, and then maybe drive up to the mountains for the day."

"It's supposed to rain all day," Denis said, running his palm over the fur on Fred's chest.

"I doubt it's going to close the freeways."

Denis pinched Fred's nipple. "Smartass."

"It's nice up there, even with rain. Maybe we could grab a room at one of the resorts, spend the night out of town?"

"Sounds good to me."

He watched the Englishman's stuttering profession of love on the screen and shifted his weight a bit. "You mind if I order a pizza?"

"Mmm," Fred growled. "Fred's tummy like Denis."

"And Denis like Fred's tummy. Now move your ass so I can reach the phone."

"You're about perfect, you know that?" Fred asked.

Maxine Gordon stood in front of the house by the park, scratching her head. Early morning light surrounded her in a pinkish haze as she regarded John Lucio's yard with disgust. The black stain that had devoured his hedges and grass had moved onto her front yard, sweeping like a pointed wave over the lawn. She'd paid too much for soil and sod, not to mention the pricey service to mow and weed every week, to just watch it blacken and die.

It was bad enough Lucio had killed himself, likely dropping property values in the process, but obviously, he'd set something loose before doing so. Every plant on the man's property was ruined, and now her foliage was under attack as well.

She'd already called the city about the situation, and they'd assured her someone would be out to assess the situation but, knowing the city, it would be days before one of their drones got off his fat ass to do something.

This was simply unacceptable.

Maxine walked toward the park and noticed the stain had spread in that direction as well. It looked like someone had poured gasoline over the plants and lit them up until they were char, but she'd plucked a blade of her own grass and it hadn't had the texture of having been burned. If anything, the blade seemed more succulent, fatter, only instead of being filled with variances of green, the plants choked on a darker nutrient.

She walked to the side of Lucio's house and then around to the back.

Lucio had taken great pains with his garden. He had been particularly fussy about his roses, she remembered, having seen him on numerous occasions pruning branches and testing the soil. They were black now. Everything in his precious garden was, and the discoloration spread to the far back of his property. It was already climbing the trees of the greenbelt separating the neighborhood from Seventh Street.

Maxine turned back for the front of the house and noticed the glass patio door stood open. She shook her head and marched forward. The police had probably left it open after their investigation of Lucio's suicide. Lazy bastards. The glass wasn't broken, and as she approached, she saw no sign of tampering along the metal frame, so she discounted the likelihood of thieves—at least sloppy ones.

At the open door, Maxine poked her head in. "Hello?" she called, not expecting an answer.

But a sound did come back to her. Not voices. Not someone calling out an explanation for his or her presence in the home of a suicide. Instead, she heard thumps and raps, like someone locked in a distant closet, attempting to escape.

Maxine walked into the house and immediately saw motion ahead, though the gloom made it difficult to identify the details of the shape. She pulled her cell phone out of her pocket and dialed 9-1-1. Her thumb hovered over the send icon on her phone's screen.

Cautiously, she made her way across the kitchen.

Ahead, she was startled to see a man lying face down on the floor. At first, she'd thought he was having a seizure. He jerked and spasmed against the hardwood, but just his torso and head. His hands and feet were motionless. Next to him, a woman similarly thrashed. Maxine continued forward until she saw all four of the bodies on the floor of the dining room, each of them in an agitated state. And then she noticed the spikes that secured them to the floor and her skin puckered tightly around muscles suddenly cold.

Remembering the phone she jabbed the send command and put the phone to her ear as she backed away from the horrors in the room.

A shrill squeal like nails on a blackboard erupted from the speaker and Maxine yanked it away from her head. She turned to flee the house and saw with dread John Lucio standing in the opening of the patio door.

Denis woke to an empty bed and his heart skipped.

"Fred?" he muttered. He looked around the room. Found it empty. He repeated the name only louder.

When no answer was forthcoming, he climbed out of bed. He walked through the house calling Fred's name, but there was no response. Getting concerned, he went to the French doors overlooking the patio and peered out, half expecting to see the man standing naked, drinking his coffee at the railing. But he wasn't there either.

A little over seven months earlier he'd made a similar circuit around a different house, only the name he'd been calling was "Benjamin." He'd had no concern back then, just curiosity, wondering where his partner had gotten to so early in the morning.

Eventually, he'd found Benjamin on the floor of the garage. Lips parted. Eyes wide. Motionless.

Only later had Denis learned about his partner's heart condition. Benjamin's mother had told him at the funeral home, where they'd met to discuss arrangements.

"Fred?" Denis called, storming away from the patio doors.

The front door opened. Fred lurched inside and threw the door closed. "Son of a bitch," he said. "The little prick slashed my tire."

Denis, confused, paused by the sofa. "What?"

"I went out to get the paper. Fucking paperboy drops it at the end of the driveway every goddamn day, so I gotta walk to the street to get it. And I see my car. The back tire has been slashed."

"Are you sure it isn't just low?"

"No, it's not *just low*," Fred barked. "There's a gash an inch long."

"And you think Eric did it?"

Fred shot him a look that said, *Duh*, and then stomped toward the bedroom. "I have to call Triple-A."

"And the cops," Denis said.

"No cops. They wouldn't do anything about it—probably *couldn't* do anything about it. I don't have any evidence. Besides, the fucker only did it to get a rise out of me. He doesn't have to know it worked."

Maxine came to slowly. There was a terrible scent in the air that she couldn't identify, and a squealing sound, like rats in the walls. The first time she opened her eyes, she saw nothing but a smudge of light, and then she drifted off again, though she didn't realize it—time simply skipped a beat. She was truly awoken by a louder version of the squealing she'd heard before. Terrified that she shared a room with rats, Maxine opened her eyes.

She sat in a corner of John Lucio's dining room with her hands tied behind her back. A thick wad of cotton had been shoved into her mouth as a gag. To her horror, she saw that she'd been stripped naked.

She trembled from both fear and chill, and every muscle in her body ached as if she'd been pummeled from head to foot. Tears filled her eyes, and she sobbed into the cotton gag.

John Lucio knelt on the floor over one of his victims. With his thumb and index finger he wiggled the spike that held a young man face down on the floor. Then Lucio pulled the nail free. It emerged, accompanied by the familiar squeal. Metal against wood.

Behind him, two of his victims, the man and the woman Maxine had first seen, crawled on the floor, heads turning from side to side as if listening to music. She didn't recognize these people, didn't *want* to recognize them. Something was wrong with their skin. It was dry and gray, flaking from the muscle beneath like ancient parchment. Their lips were black. Their eyes were the color of oatmeal, with tiny black holes at their centers. Bones poked through their arms randomly, whether from compound fracture or unnatural growth Maxine didn't know. A third broken person crawled into view; its mouth was open, revealing a jagged fence of sharp, shattered teeth.

She screamed into the wad of cotton, catching the attention of Lucio who was removing another spike, releasing the right foot of the boy sprawled only a yard from Maxine. The man in the suit who was supposed to be dead, stood and observed her. He looked so peaceful. Content. He stepped back and wiped dust from the sleeve of his suit. Then he observed the victims in the room and swept his arm toward Maxine.

The victims responded, crawling toward her like eager infants. She tried to move out of the corner, but Lucio was there. He placed his foot against her shoulder and wedged her against the wall. She struggled against it. She didn't want to die. Not here. Not like this.

The four victims surrounded her. One grabbed her ankle with its destroyed palm. Another leaned close to her chest, sniffing at her skin curiously. It pushed its nose against her breast and she squealed in disgust.

When it opened its mouth, Maxine observed the saw-like teeth and shrieked.

It bit, pinching the skin unbearably before it whipped its head back and forth and tore away a piece of her breast. Blood spilled in gouts from the ragged lips of the wound. Maxine lost her breath from the pain and the sight of a part of her disappearing into the black-lipped mouth. The thing chewed and made a humming sound in its throat as if delighted by the flavor. Turning to the others, the victim nodded his head.

And they all began to eat.

The downpour they'd been expecting started while they were eating a late breakfast at Dewey's. Before going to the restaurant, they'd dealt with Triple-A, and Denis had followed Fred to the dealership, so he could drop off his car and get a new tire to replace the one Eric had destroyed. The dealership couldn't make any promises, but they might have the new tire on the rim and the rim on the car before noon.

Denis hated to see Fred's mood sour even more, but he understood, and he remained silent, allowing the man to vent all the way to the restaurant and through most of the meal.

"Now it's raining," Fred said.

"Supposed to go on for a few days."

"Great." Fred dropped his fork and looked out the window. "I'm sorry. I'm going to be lousy company for a while. If you want to drop me off at home, we can try the mountains next week. I'm feeling a heavy sulk coming on."

"I don't mind sulking, but if you want to be alone that's cool."

"What I want is to hurt that prick. But I won't because I'm not twelve years old and because it'll just give him the jollies he was after all along."

They drove back to Fred's in silence. At the lip of the park, Denis followed the road to the left.

The park was built on a sloped parcel of land, surrounded by dense shrubs and trees. The main lawn sunk into a broad bowl of well-trimmed grass. Roads framed its periphery. Denis drove up the rise on the north side of the park, but when they reached the corner on which John Lucio had built his house, he pulled over and stopped.

THE HOUSE BY THE PARK

"Do you see that?" Fred asked.

"I'm surprised we didn't see it this morning," Denis said.

"We didn't come this way. The dealership is the other direction."

"Still," Denis said.

The black stain covered Lucio's entire property and had drifted well into the park.

"It's all the way back to the greenbelt," Fred noted. "What is that shit?"

"Maybe we can ask that guy," Denis said.

He pointed over the steering wheel at a tall man wearing hunter green hip waders and latex gloves. He stood in the middle of Lucio's lawn, poking the ground with a metal tube. A white van sporting the city's health department decal sat at the curb.

"Don't know," the man, whose name was Steve, said. "Just getting my samples now."

"Have you seen anything like this before?" Denis asked.

"Can't say yes," Steve replied. "Any idea who lives here? No one answered the door."

"He's dead," Denis told the man. "He killed himself earlier in the week."

"Oh," Steve said, looking at a plastic bag holding a divot of black lawn. "I'll have to call in then. I need documentation before I can enter the house. If I had to guess, I'd say the guy doused everything down with some kind of herbicide before he said goodnight. Maybe he didn't like his neighbors and he wanted them to know."

"Are there herbicides that can do this?"

"I suppose," Steve said with a shrug. "I need to get a few more samples up by the house to see if the concentrations are different. He might have chemicals in the basement leaking all over the place. That'd be real bad. But we'll get it squared away."

Back in the car, Denis said, "I think you should stay at my place for a couple of days until they figure this out."

Fred was looking out the window at the house beside Lucio's. The stain had reached the halfway point in the yard. "I think you're right," he said.

They stopped at Fred's house so he could gather clothes, toiletries, his phone charger, and laptop. With his bag packed, Fred walked through the house and checked the locks on all of the doors and windows.

"I'm paranoid like that," Fred said with a halfhearted smile.

Instead of going directly to Denis's apartment, they returned to the auto dealership, where Fred picked up his car. At Denis's apartment Fred excused himself to the balcony to make calls. He needed to touch base with a friend. When Denis checked on him, Fred was standing at the railing, holding his hand out to catch raindrops on his palm. He laughed into the phone. It was good to see him smiling, Denis thought.

Early afternoon, they lay in the bed listening to the rain. Denis spooned Fred, arm wrapped around the man's thick chest. Since he was so silent, only light even breaths, Denis thought his boyfriend was sleeping until Fred said.

"Ivan says you're the gold."

"You have a friend named Ivan? Do we know any of the same people?"

"Maybe," Fred replied. "I don't know."

"What did he mean gold?"

"I have a theory. See I'm convinced there's a cosmic scale and for all the gold on one plate there is an equal weight of shit on the other. Eric and his prank fall squarely on the shit side. Whatever is happening to my neighborhood is also weighing things down. But then there's you."

"I like your theory, though I can't say I buy it."

"You don't have to. I know it's nuts. But think about it. We met on Tuesday, not even a week ago, and we haven't spent a night apart since. I've never done that before. Never wanted to."

"Neither have I."

"And my being in that grocery store was totally random."

"I was going to ask you about that."

"I had a meeting at the coffee shop across the parking lot, and I figured it would be easier to run in there than to look for parking where I normally shop."

"I'm glad."

"Yeah, me too. And I'm not saying this other shit wouldn't have happened if we hadn't met. I had no intention of seeing much more of Eric, so that was already in motion, and I can't imagine Old Johnny was waiting around for me to bring home a hot trick before he offed himself. But I'm glad we met, to keep things balanced."

"Well, it's better than you thinking I jinxed you or cursed you or something."

"No chance of that," Fred said. He pushed his ass back into Denis's crotch and growled deep in his throat.

They lay there quietly. The rain rapped in a soothing rhythm against the window. Denis rubbed his hand over Fred's stomach. It was a good moment, except Denis couldn't shake the word, "curse."

Fred had said something about John Lucio's suicide note. Something about cursing the world.

John Lucio—
The Book of Wives has told me: Tonight the sky will be wrung of light and I will offer my blood at the Gate of Hell. It will grease the hinges, so that as I enter it will throw wide. I sacrifice my Christian soul and curse this sinners' world. In return I will be given After Life. I will anoint four apostles in the black honey, and they will walk the East, the West, the North and the South, spreading the Word. As the souls of the living pass through the gates, the darkness seeps free.

Doubters will know truth.

I will know forever.

"You were right," Denis said. "That's pretty crazy."

"Yeah, right? But check out the left side of the screen."

"What am I looking for?"

"The guy had two thousand 'friends.'"

"And nobody thought to check on him? Some friends."

Fred closed the laptop and leaned back in his chair. "Well, his little show was pretty convincing if you ask me. I mean all of the plants dying after he commits suicide. He put together an intricate hoax, if it is a hoax."

"What else could it be?" Denis asked.

Fred shrugged. "I just can't imagine him spraying chemicals all over the neighborhood like that. Someone would have had to see him."

"So it's more reasonable to believe a Christian activist sacrificed himself to the devil to damn the world?"

"The question isn't whether he would or wouldn't do it. Those whack jobs get some fucked up ideas in their heads. The question is whether it worked or not."

"No more horror movies for you."

"Try and stop me," Fred said. He smiled, leaned forward and gave Denis a kiss. "Just so you know, Ivan has a spare room if you want some time to yourself. I don't want you to feel trapped."

"I don't feel trapped. Besides, the city will probably have figured all of this out by morning and you can go back to your place without worrying about toxic exposure *or* demon possession."

The next afternoon the steady rain shower intensified. They had gone to an early movie and afterward decided to check on Fred's neighborhood. Denis felt a chill as he navigated up the sloped drive of the park. The terrain was painted in shades of gray from the storm. Pellets of rain smeared the air and made the sprawling lawns and picnic gazebos appear unreal, like ancient photographs with badly scratched surfaces. As they neared the far side of the park, they saw the news vans and the city vehicles surrounding the corner lot. A crowd of people stood in the park watching the scene. They too were gray. None of them held an umbrella. This group—easily forty people—stood unprotected from the downpour as they stared at the house by the park. Away from this aggregation on the other side of the road, two aged men in black stood beneath the semi-globes of umbrellas. They had the white collars that identified them as priests. They too were motionless, but instead of looking at the house, their attention was captured by the group of onlookers across the road.

"Street's blocked," Denis said, pointing to the barricade ahead. Flashing orange lights seemed to be the only color in an otherwise grayscale landscape.

"Hopefully, they're cleaning up whatever Lucio put in the ground."

"Do you want me to head back to Seventh Street and come in from the other direction?"

"Absolutely," Fred said. "Somebody up there must know what's going on."

Denis navigated a three-point turn. His headlights fell over the priests and both men turned toward the car. Their faces were stern, agitated. Their gazes were intense, yet looked weary like pictures of soldiers Denis had seen on the web. One of the men touched the cross hanging from his neck. The other nodded solemnly.

They encountered another roadblock on the opposite end of Fred's street. Another group of onlookers, as unaware of the weather as the congregation in the park, had gathered just outside the barricade, and police officers shouted for them to get back, but the rain-soaked crowd paid them no attention. Oblivious.

They remained a motionless pack, staring past the police and through the downpour at the house by the park.

"We're not going to get any answers," Denis said. "I don't even think we can get anybody's attention."

"But that's my house," Fred told him. "Shouldn't I fucking know what's happening to my house? Maybe we can go around to Seventh Street and walk through the greenbelt."

"No," Denis said. The police were getting nowhere with the horde at the barricade. They were clearly beyond frustration and working themselves up for violence. "We don't need to get shot."

"But I'm going to need clothes for work."

"Then we'll go shopping," Denis said.

"This is bullshit," Fred said absently. "Complete bullshit."

"We'll check the web when we get home. There are vans around the corner so the reporters must be up there someplace. The police will have to make a statement to them. My guess is, even if you had the chance to talk to one face-to-face, it would be the same story they're going to tell the press."

"It's my house," Fred said.

"Yeah," Denis said, slipping an arm around his shoulders.

He didn't know what else to say.

The news gave them little information. A video clip showed uniformed police officers and men in white HAZMAT suits poking around Lucio's black lawn. "Authorities are investigating an event of ecological concern," the anchorwoman said. "We have no details at this time but it has been speculated that unknown, possibly toxic, chemicals have been spilled in the area. The extent of the damage and threat to human life is unknown.

For now, the public is being asked to stay away from the area until more information becomes available. Again, the twelve hundred block of..."

"Fuck," Fred said. He slapped the sofa cushion with his palm. "I've been quarantined out of my own fucking house."

"Better out than in," Denis said.

"Don't look for a bright side here, Denis. I appreciate it, and I love that you'd try, but please, not right now. I sank my life savings into that place. It was my home."

"It still is."

"Sure, unless it becomes a toxic waste dump, or is ruined by some other *event of ecological concern.*"

Denis knew there was nothing he could say that would help. He might mention insurance or spout some platitude about Fred having his health, but he knew the man wouldn't appreciate any of it. Denis had lost the house he'd shared with Benjamin, and no amount of support or condolence had soothed him.

Once he'd thought his home had actually been *his*, but Home was a brittle term; one wholly dependent on finance. Only a mortgage promptly paid gave a man a home.

"I am going to lose my mind just sitting here," Fred said. "Maybe things have cleared out over there."

"It's only been an hour. Why don't we wait and we'll check again after dinner?"

Fred nodded. "I think I'm going to lie down," he said. "Would it be okay if you didn't come in with me?"

"Sure," Denis told him.

The least he could do was give Fred his privacy. They'd been all but inseparable for days. So Denis sat on the sofa and watched Fred disappear into the bedroom. Denis turned on the television and let the afternoon pass into evening.

He checked on Fred a little past eight. Easing the door open, he poked his head in and looked at the bed.

"Hey," Fred said.

"You okay?"

"Better."

"I thought I'd see if you wanted some dinner; maybe check your place again."

"Not really hungry," Fred told him. "And I think we both know nothing's changed at the house. Let's not waste the time."

"Okay," Denis said. He leaned out of the room and was closing the door when Fred stopped him.

"Where you going?"

"I don't know."

"Then come to bed. I missed you."

Denis woke to dull gray light. Morning. He went to the window and parted the blinds. The rain continued, but it had become little more than mist. Still the gloom that had covered the city remained. He turned back to the empty bed.

He'd heard Fred slipping out over an hour ago. Instead of saying anything, Denis had closed his eyes and gone back to sleep. But now, he felt a wound of unease open in his chest. He didn't know how to interpret Fred's early departure, nor his own apathy in light of his leaving. Obviously, Fred had thought to get an early start, to reach his house before the crazies gathered for another day of rain-drenched gawking. He might even be able to corner a cop or health department worker to learn about the immediate future of his property.

Fred needed time to himself, Denis knew.

He went about his morning, fixing breakfast and powering up his laptop. He discovered an early morning email from Fred and opened it.

Had to check on the house. Didn't want to wake you. You look amazing when you're sleeping. Back soon. F.

Denis smiled, and the wound in his chest knitted. He drank his coffee and returned to the news page, where he found a number of articles pertaining to the events of the day before. The story hadn't changed, as far as he could tell.

An hour passed, and then another.

Finally, Denis decided that Fred had been gone too long. Even if Fred had been allowed to enter the house to gather more of his belongings it shouldn't have taken this long. Denis called his cell number, but he was sent directly to voice mail.

After another hour and another call, Denis took his umbrella from the closet and left the apartment.

He stood at the barricade looking in disbelief at the street ahead. He'd driven in from the East to avoid the park, and he'd been forced to park his car in the middle of the road because the curbs were packed tight with vehicles. Cars and trucks blocked drives and alleys. But there were no people. The police cars and health department vehicles remained. Two ambulances with their back doors open wide stood just inside the barricade.

Yet the roads and the lawns were empty.

Misting rain shrouded the block. The black stain had reached the west edge of Fred's house, consuming all greenery on the right side of the street for as far as Denis could see. It was a war zone. A minor apocalypse.

Where the hell was Fred?

Denis walked around the barricade and crossed to the door of Fred's house. He knocked lightly, so softly it all but negated the action entirely. Finding the door unlocked, Denis went inside.

"Fred," he whispered.

He listened for movement in the house, but even the hiss of the rain was blocked out. He repeated Fred's name as he passed through the living room. In the bedroom, he found a suitcase open on the bed and three pairs of slacks laid out beside it. He left the room and walked to the French doors at the back of the house and bit down on a gasp. The black stain covered everything in sight, as if a talented artist had done a charcoal sketch of the landscape. Even the potted plant on Fred's railing had gone dark.

Denis backed away from the doors. He called Fred's name a final time, but he knew the place was empty.

Abandoned. Fear drove him from the house and back to the bleak yard. An insistent voice told him to leave this neighborhood. Fred was gone, lost to the mystery and no longer attainable. Just get the fuck away from here.

But how could he leave?

Ambivalent about his next move, Denis remained in the yard. He called Fred's phone again, and for a moment he imagined he heard it ringing, distantly, muffled by walls and rain, but the sound had no clear direction. It came from all sides, which was all Denis needed to convince himself he hadn't heard the bell at all.

He couldn't just stand there, but he didn't know what to do.

He turned to his car beyond the barricade and saw a man and a woman circling the vehicle. Something in their movement, in their faces, made him think of feral animals like jackals eyeing prey. The woman whipped her head in his direction, and Denis felt a splinter of ice run through him. He spun toward the park and raced through the front yards, away from the disconcerting couple. When he reached Lucio's house he sprinted across the street to be away from it. All of the dread that clung to his skin and burned his veins like acid, rolled from this place.

He looked quickly across the road at the malevolent house, this mother of misery, and saw dozens of people moving about inside. A man pressed himself to the window—a grinning man in a black suit. He raised a palm in greeting and waved wildly as if the host of a magnificent party he couldn't wait for Denis to join.

Denis bolted, entering the park at the same place he'd seen the somber priests the morning before.

He came over the rise and skidded to a stop on the damp grass. The sight awaiting him punched the breath from his chest.

The stain covered the entirety of the park. Hundreds of people wandered aimlessly over the soiled grounds—on the lanes of road, around stalled and abandoned vehicles, and across the lawns. They moved lethargically through the bushes and trees framing the park. He recognized the familiar uniforms of police officers, paramedics, and the white HAZMAT suits of the city's health workers. Others wore shorts or jeans or dresses. Some wore nothing. To his right, far across the field, he saw one of the black-clad priests moving in a slow circle, head cocked back, eyes fixed on the steel gray sky.

Denis backed away. He turned to flee the neighborhood.

Fred stood halfway down the block, hands in the pockets of his cargo shorts. He wore no shirt and the rain pasted thick hair to the round muscles on his chest. His skin gleamed from moisture. He was grinning as if pleased to see his boyfriend this last time.

Then Fred began to run forward, his bare feet slapping the wet concrete. He spread his arms wide like wings, like a lover wishing to take

Denis in his arms. And Denis stood motionless, desolate, watching Fred bear down on him.

In a flash, jagged scratches of energy filled his head. Rational thought vanished amid the static and suddenly he found the gray world around him beautiful. Simple. Unfettered by color. In the flicker of a moment, his fear turned to acceptance. Anticipation.

The burly stranger Denis had loved for less than a week had never appeared more striking. Strong. Vital.

Denis opened his own arms in welcome. And when Fred's lips parted, the grin changing into a cruel smile, Denis told himself the man's teeth were perfect and white, and not the shattered, sharp fangs of a thing fashioned in hell. The eyes were green and startlingly erotic, not gray clots behind pasty lids.

Hurry, Denis thought, eager to feel the press of Fred's body against his.

And those hands. And those lips.

The angel was locked in the back of Greyling's car, and he had just got off the radio—he wished, for the first time in months, for a partner, any partner, even a whining rookie.

PINION

Stellan Thorne

The witness was beautiful, in a way that was almost hard to look at. His face was abstract and fashionable, all eyes and angles, with a luminous innocence too perfect to be entirely sincere.

Detective Greyling wondered idly how that face would look with a fat lip. Like a magazine cover, probably, a model fresh off a photo shoot. Saturday night fight fashion. A little trickle of blood down one corner of his mouth, like smudged lipstick.

"Cigarette?" Greyling asked.

"Please."

He leaned over the table to offer a light—sparks off a grinding wheel, cheap plastic sticky in his hands.

"I don't usually smoke."

Not cigarettes, at least, Greyling thought. He lit up his own; the two cherries pointed away from each other like strabismic eyes, glowing in the gloom.

"I guess I'm a still a bit shaky." The witness smiled, quick and charming, the kind of smile that knows it is currency. The exchange rate was low here, in Greyling's territory—he hated charm, hated its tawdry uses—but he nodded.

"We just need your statement," he said. The tape recorder was spinning slowly.

Thorne

"I've told the officer at the front desk everything already." Just a little schoolboy wheedling in his tone, a little note of oh-do-I-*have*-to?

Greyling smiled. It was not charming. "This is for the official record. Please." He gestured at the tape recorder.

The witness cleared his throat, with an actor's skill, and began. "I was robbed by an angel last night."

Nobody had wanted the case. "He's high or he's a liar," the desk sergeant had said. "Angels don't rob people." On the first two points Greyling agreed; he wasn't sure on the last. In the end, he'd ended up with the case. Better that than hear some rookie piss and moan when it landed in their lap.

He went around the neighborhood with a rough sketch, and saw faces shutter with suspicion. They had seen the suspect, he was sure of that—but they kept their silence.

He thought of returning later, when he was off duty. Sidle up sideways to his questions, in dive bars and on street corners. He thought better of it almost instantly. He'd never been good even at that half-undercover kind of work—that had been Mayer's thing, Mayer with his blankly handsome looks. Greyling's face, once seen, was hard to forget. In any case, he seemed to always wear an invisible uniform; he spoke and smelled like a cop.

He ducked into a corner store. The pack of cigarettes tucked in his inside pocket was empty already; this was looking like a two-pack day. He laid his money down on the counter; the clerk held it up to the light before giving him his smokes.

He took out the sketch and brandished it at the clerk. "You wouldn't happen to have seen—"

"No habla ing-less," he said, in a flat Midwestern accent, and grinned.

With slow clarity Greyling saw himself grabbing the clerk by his collar, dragging him across the counter, breaking his nose. There was no joy in the fantasy; it was like a worn film reel, looping methodically inside his head. He turned away, crumpling the sketch in his hand.

Then he saw it through the window: a flash of nacreous white. A winged figure. It was standing not fifteen yards away, on the other side of the street. Watching him.

He was out the door in a moment. "Hey!" He started towards it, taking swift strides. "Hey, stop right there!"

It froze for a moment, wings outstretched. They looked terribly fragile, a delicate latticework of feathers. Then it ran, and Greyling took off after. It ducked under a fire escape, tucking its wings in close. A few steps away, beyond the building, Greyling could see the blue of empty sky.

Lungs like bellows, the great engine of his heart clanking, Greyling ran. A few more feet and they'd be out from the fire escape—those wings would pump once, twice, and his suspect would be gone. He lunged, all the world contracting. He hadn't moved this fast in years.

He landed hard but upright, and the angel was beneath him. He kneeled down on the curving joint of a wing. Great muscles strained up underneath him. That fine fragility was a con. One hand came down on the angel's head—its hair was duckling-soft—and tangled hard, jerking upward. "You're not going anywhere." His breathing was labored, paunch and nicotine conspiring. "You have the right—"

A massive wing-heave nearly lifted him—nearly sent him sprawling. For a moment he rode the angel like a broncobuster. His heart was wild with pain, chest burning. Then, victory: it sagged beneath him, breathing slowly.

He cuffed together long lovely wrists, then bent back one wing at a painful angle. The angel cried out with a voice like a tuning fork. "Try to use these," Greyling said, "and you'll get a bullet through them; that's a promise. You're under arrest."

The angel was locked in the back of Greyling's car, and he had just got off the radio—he wished, for the first time in months, for a partner, any partner, even a whining rookie. Just someone else to make the calls while he was trying to catch his breath.

He looked in the rear-view mirror at the suspect. The angel was grey and white; a layer of city grime had settled lightly on its essential cleanness. The wings, massive in the backseat, quivered like wind-caught sheets.

"I am a messenger of the most holy," the angel said. There was no arrogance in its voice, just a calm surety.

Greyling lit a cigarette. He couldn't think of driving just yet. "You're a thief."

Wings shrugged, like a cat raising its hackles. The angel's eyes were colorless in the mirror, like water or wind. "I don't understand."

"The man you robbed—you don't remember that?"

"Robbed?"

They looked alike, a little, Greyling thought, the angel and the victim. That same invincible prettiness, so hard to sully. "You threatened him, took his guitar and his wallet."

"Yes. I was protecting him."

Greyling snorted. "Oh yeah? From what, playing bad music?"

The angel was silent.

"So, what, are you his *guardian* angel or something?"

"Yes."

A low anger rose, like an ulcer. It figures; the charming boy got an angel all his own. To protect him. His fingers tightened on the steering wheel. "Well, he turned you in. So I'm taking you in."

He started the car. It took several tries, fingers fumbling with the key. Wings blocked the window and the mirror; he stuck his head out the window and carefully maneuvered onto the streets.

"Jason Greyling," the angel said, "will you not let me go?"

He grimaced. "That's 'Detective Greyling' to you. And I strongly advise you *use* your right to remain silent."

"I have done what is right."

Again that calm surety—the tone of the innocent or the insane. Greyling supposed the angel fell somewhere in between.

"Will you not let me go?"

"Shut up," he said.

He was still shaking, he noticed. His heart would not calm. He sucked at the cigarette dangling hands-free between his lips; the ash fell in his lap.

He missed Mayer with sudden fierceness. He would have handled this better, his old partner. Mayer was never shaken, not by anything—Greyling only had the armor of his cynicism, imperfect protection against miraculous things.

A feather brushed his neck, so lightly. The tip of a wing slid in between the crosshatched metal partitioning backseat from front. He flinched away, at first, then pounded the cage—it left diamond-shaped imprints on his hand.

"Your heart is known in Heaven," the angel said. "And all that you are."

Blackmail, Greyling thought vaguely. His hand ached; his lungs ached. Maybe he should consider retiring.

The traffic was impenetrable before them, loud with horns and smoke. Again there came the soft brush of a feather, against his cheek this time. He swallowed, Adam's apple shifting painfully in his throat. *Charm.* "You'll want to stop that," he said, voice level, "or you'll end up stuffing a pillow."

The angel dropped its wing. In the mirror, eyes shone like light on waves.

The angel made bail—Greyling never found out how—and vanished. The paperwork was useless: there was no name, no address, only an elegant sigil the angel had consented to scrawl as its signature, before being processed as a John Doe and put in an empty cell. Marching past the holding tank, Greyling had heard the howls and hoots of the day's catch, seen fingers reaching out grubby-greedy for frail-looking wings.

The victim called them a few days later. Greyling never spoke to him, but there was a message left on his desk: the stolen things had been returned, anonymous. The case was closed, no need to look further, except he was still finding feathers on the backseat of his car a week later.

And other places. They drifted into his path. Once into his coffee: a small tuft floating on its oily black surface. He fished it out and looked skyward, where there was nothing but clouds and wires.

He lulled himself to sleep at home with windows cracked, just enough to let the sounds in, and when he woke he found feathers clinging to the windowsills. Pigeons, he told himself. He took one between his fingers, turning it. The shaft was pearly white; the barbs shimmered like silver. Pigeons. Like hell.

He didn't catch the angel watching him until after a week of night shifts. Coming home in the light, that's what did it—hard to miss that stretch of wings, perched like a gargoyle on a cornice across the street. It looked fresh from the sky, sun-washed and brilliant.

Greyling shut the curtains with a hard tug. If he, if it came here, landed on his narrow balcony, he'd have every right to shoot it. He still had his old .38 revolver, kept it oiled and loaded.

There was a rustling—wings scraping his windowsill. No time to get his old .38. His new service revolver would have to do. Wings mounted over his fireplace. What happens to men that kill angels?

Instead of shooting, he opened the curtains, opened the window. The angel came in.

"You've been following me," Greyling said.

"Will you take me into custody?"

It almost sounded like a joke; Greyling smiled. "Why are you here?"

The angel reached for him, long perfect fingers outstretched. Greyling sidestepped the possibility of touch.

"Please."

"What the hell do I have, that you could want?"

The angel shook long downy hair. "I have to show you. Please."

"Show me what?"

"There is something gone wrong. Jason Greyling, will you not let me show you?"

Every word sounded like a prayer from that mouth, sweet as a bell. If he had to be *charmed*, at least it took this creature. He stepped forward, mouth gone dry.

"You have to see."

The angel's wings were massive around him, and silver-edged, wavering between their form and their function. Here, where he could touch them, they were as strong as a swan's wing; they could break limbs. Where angels lived, they were as strong as the laws of physics.

Between those wings the world shook, and he saw: The whole of his life, like a sphere in his hand. Where it began, and where it ended. How on a perfect summer day, with laughter and the scent of frying onions in the air, he thought, *It will never be better than this,* how he went to the roof with his old .38 cradled in his hands and took a last long look at the sky, waiting for wings.

He stepped out of the white parabola. "And you don't come."

The angel's perfect mouth turned down, a sculpture of despair. "You were never further away from me."

Greyling laughed. "It's your fault, isn't it? That's why you're here. How did it end without you? Sixty, seventy, with my liver shot? Huh? Or in a cheap home. And that would have been *better?*"

"You have to live."

"For how long?"

"For your lifetime."

An angel's wingtips sliced through time; the colorless eyes of angels saw the whole of things. A stolen guitar, a feather in a cup of coffee: what consequences things had. And even angels made mistakes. He had become a ragged edge, a loose thread; he smiled. He wasn't being fair, not at all. But then, what was?

"Then you'll have to keep watching me."

He took a desk job; it was that, or get used to a new partner. He could have, he supposed, but didn't want to. Didn't want to settle for second best. So he made a home behind his big metal slab, stamping paperwork. It didn't matter. He was too tired for ambition.

A week after the angel left—two wingbeats, and into the air, from the railing of his balcony—he went to visit Mayer's grave. He liked it: simple, another tombstone in a neat row under the shade of an ash tree. He didn't stay long; he went home, went on with his life.

Some days he finds feathers floating around him, like a memory of snow, and smiles.

Maybe one day, when it's summer and the sky is blue-gorgeous and shaky with heat, he'll go up to the roof. And he'll wait for wings.

I put my arm around his shoulders and walked him away from the Trueblood, who wrinkled his pasty white nose and tugged at a silver ring looped through one of his pointed ears.

We Do Not Come in Peace

Christopher Barzak

I saw him again tonight, while out walking the streets of Soho: Alek or Aleksander, whatever it is he's called now. He's had plenty of names since I first knew him when he arrived almost a year ago, fresh and green from the World. One of the newcomers after the Way reopened. Mouse. Alek. Aleksander. Voice of the Nameless, voice for those who drink from the river whose waters curse them to return to it daily to forget their troubles, those who came and didn't find what they'd been told would be a glorious place free of the World's restrictions, where they could be themselves more than anywhere and wouldn't have to fight for it.

Right.

I was out late tonight, wandering the streets, kept up by a weird urgency that made my thoughts move around like snakes inside me. I couldn't stop thinking. *Should I stay, or should I go?* Living on the Border wasn't the same as it was when I'd arrived five years ago at the age of sixteen, when life was a song and everyone listened to my music, in every club and on every corner of Soho. Fair Ones and humans and halfies alike, all of them. They loved me.

Back then, I'd been like Aleksander: idealistic, still young. Youth is half of what anyone who comes to this city needs in order to make a way. The rest is a blend of luck, skill, and a friendly disposition. By the time you're like me, though—edging into your twenties and things haven't worked out the way you'd hoped—you might as well start looking for another way: ply your trade as a carpenter, clerk for the Fair Ones, open a business. That last one is what I just did, after I'd made some money and collected on as many owed favors as I could to establish myself.

A sort of shop, of all things, is what I opened, just a month ago. People laughed when they saw the sign go up. "Art and Lies." In red neon, as if it were a pub's "Open" sign. "What are you up to now, Marius?" people ask me.

"Paintings and sculptures and books," I say. "And, of course, coffee."

"But what about your music?"

"What about it?" I say. "I'm doing something else now, that's all."

Which is true, sort of. I am doing something else, but in fact I've lost whatever connection I had to the music that used to simply *be there*, in reach, whenever I wanted, like a glass of water on a bedside table. When I reach now, I come back empty. I can play the notes, but there's no joy in them. After a while I realized that if music had abandoned me, I would need another way to live.

Should I stay, or should I go? was my refrain tonight, even though I have a store to run now, a secure life if I can let myself love it. The World may have changed since I left it at sixteen, but I could still go back to it. And then, as I turned a corner of a crowded sidewalk, I saw him. Alek. Aleksander. Mouse.

He was leaving the Café Tremolo with a group of young people, hands in their pockets, pants sagging below their waists, faces pressed against the autumn wind. I nearly raised my hand, got it halfway up in the air like a sail before I realized what I was doing, then dropped it, embarrassed. I was going to call out, I was going to say his name. And then what? What would Mouse do when he turned and saw his first friend in this city? Twenty-one years old, a washed-up musician, selling used books and bad art traded by new arrivals from the World or from past Elfhaeme Gate, where the Fair Ones come and go freely. A dealer in abandoned items, things looking for a home with people who are occasionally afflicted with nostalgia for everything they've left behind.

"It speaks volumes about you," Mouse told me the last time we saw each other. That was just three weeks ago, right after I opened my shop.

WE DO NOT COME IN PEACE

"Please leave," I'd said. He'd been trying to hurt my feelings, and I refused to be hurt by a sixteen-year-old punk in whom I'd already invested too much time and energy and, well, even love since I'd met him nearly a year ago. Or so I told myself.

But as I watched him and his friends tonight, their backs to me, going to whatever radical gathering they were probably late for, I had a terrible idea. It was terrible because as soon as I had it, I knew it was bad. But it was strong and grew to such a size so quickly it took hold of my mind and conducted me, as if I were its puppet, to follow, trailing them by a block or two, until I came to a run-down brick building on Hell Street where they must have been squatting, and there I stopped myself from going farther. Control reverted to me again. He'd always had that effect on me. Aleksander. Mouse.

I stood outside, watching the lights go on in the windows of that shabby building, remembering why I'd liked him, realizing I still liked him now, even though it was clear he'd gone crazy.

It was in front of Danceland on the west end of Ho, ten months ago, where I first saw Mouse. That was where he'd landed after making a wish so strong back in the World, he'd opened his eyes and found himself here. In Soho, Runaway Central, where kids arrive with awe forming teardrops in the corners of their eyes, thinking, *I've made it.*

I was across the street at my usual spot between the Hard Luck and Snappin' Wizards, busking as best I could despite my still-recent disconnect from the music, money clinking into the violin case at my feet even though I heard every bad note step on a good one. Then, between blinks, Mouse appeared, with his arms crossed over his chest as if it were cold wherever it was he'd come from, bewilderment covering his face like a billboard.

I snorted. He reminded me of myself when I'd arrived five years ago, thinking I'd just won a golden ticket. How long, I wondered, before his doe eyes acquired the squint of a person who knows they must assess everyone and everything they encounter? How long before his clean mop of soft brown hair was twisted with the filth of sleeping in abandoned corners?

And then, as I ran bow across string, bringing my song to a close, I saw a Trueblood come from the direction of Oberon House, down Ho

Street, with a gleam in his eyes and a cat's grin creeping up his cheeks. He, too, had noticed the new mouse.

In the next moment I found myself locking my violin in its case with the bits of money I'd collected and dashing across the street. Even then, without knowing him, Alek had that effect on me: my legs brought me to him without any input from my brain.

Crossing the block at the same time, the Trueblood's eyes focused on Mouse's slight figure. Alek was small for his age, a bit pretty. Perfect for what goes on at Oberon House. I reached him first, though, and when I stood in front of him and asked, as kindly as possible, if he was looking for a place to stay, he nodded, held out his hand for shaking, said, "Yes. Yes, I am. I don't know where I should go from here. Just arrived. Name's Aleksander."

I grinned as the Trueblood came to a halt ten feet from us, his pearly smile fading as he realized I'd beaten him to his meal. "No," I told Aleksander, warning him not to give away his true name so easily here. "No, your name is Mouse."

I put my arm around his shoulders and walked him away from the Trueblood, who wrinkled his pasty white nose and tugged at a silver ring looped through one of his pointed ears. As we followed Third Street up to the canal, I told Mouse about Oberon House and why he should steer clear of it.

"They really keep human children in there?" he asked. "They make them...make them—"

"Yes," I said. "It's not much more than a brothel. A brothel for human storytellers."

I'd learned that the hard way, but I didn't tell Mouse that. I hadn't told anyone, ever, about my first few weeks in Bordertown. I'd managed to get out of there before I'd lost too much of my dignity. A girl who was in there with me had shown us all the way. She and some of the others still told stories on the streets of Soho. They call themselves the Bards. I hadn't seen her in a while.

"But I thought," said Mouse. "I thought..."

"All that glitters, Mouse," I said, but I didn't finish that either.

"What you said about not giving my true name to strangers?" said Mouse. "I just...I thought it would be different here." Wasn't everyone here for the same reasons, he wondered: peace, love, happiness, equality, fraternity, et cetera, et cetera?

"If that was true," I said, "everyone would be leaving the World to live here, now wouldn't they?"

Mouse nodded, looked down at the black-gummed stains on the sidewalk as we trudged toward my neighborhood. He was naïve but not stupid. A good chance he'd survive here, then.

We crossed the canal and headed west into the quiet streets of Letterville, where I rented a small apartment only slightly better than a Soho squat. The electricity was off again. Probably would be until the landlord could get someone to come by to repair or recast. So we lit the candles I keep for that kind of emergency, which happens so often it doesn't really count as one.

"Thank you," Alek said after we'd set the place glowing. "For helping me out."

I lifted his chin with the tip of a finger, trying to make him smile. But when he turned his face up to me, I saw from his glassy eyes that he was holding back tears.

"Where do you want me to sleep?" he asked steadily. He glanced over at my bed, then back at me. Without the tears in his eyes, I'd never have known how scared he was.

"No worries," I said. Realizing he thought I wanted him to sleep with me as some sort of exchange, I pulled my hand away. "You don't have to do anything, if that's what you're thinking." I started making up a bed from an old mattress I'd found in the street and had used for a year before I'd been able to save up for a new bed of my own. "You'll catch on to things soon," I told Mouse. "I'll show you the ropes."

There are so many things to learn if a person truly intends to live on the Border. Nothing much is what you expect, nothing much is what it seems. Even when you hear your native tongue on the lips of others, rarely will the words mean what they did in the world you came from.

An object lesson: There once was an elf who often stopped by my corner to listen to me playing. He came for three days straight, then a whole week. He never spoke, only smiled, clapped his hands after every song, and threw coins into my violin case like they were roses. Whenever he stood there watching me play, it was almost as if I could feel his eyes traveling down the length of my bow, over my body, under my clothes, as if they were his delicate, long fingers. Eventually one night he did speak to me, at the end of a long evening. I couldn't help myself. The way he looked at me, I wanted to be seen like that even more.

So he took me to his splendid home on Dragon's Tooth Hill, where the streets are awash with the sheen of gold and the sparkle of diamonds, and there he covered me in kisses and told me he had never loved anyone as much as he loved me. My skin burned at his touch. The next morning, I woke beneath his silken sheets, alone, like someone in a bad romance novel. I wasn't sure if I should be happy or sad. After locating the various pieces of my clothing and dressing myself, I wandered around until I found the dining room, where he was sipping coffee at the other end of a table as long as a corporate building's hallway. When I cleared my throat, he looked up from his book, tucked his silver hair behind the spade-points of his ears, and said, "Good morning. Would you like some coffee before you leave?"

They are like that, the Fair Ones. In the midst of passion, their love burns. In the light of day, the flame falters. His withdrawal could only be because of two things: I was human, and thus beneath him; and I lived on the coins others threw me, and thus was even further beneath him. So it goes.

He was the son of a businessman-turned-councilman who wanted to make a bid for the position of High Councilor. I discovered this only after his driver dropped me on the corner where the elf had picked me up the night before. The driver pressed a bag of coins into my hands before he gave his horses a secret word, and off they went into the traffic of bicycles, cars, and floating rickshaws pulled behind the strong legs of street runners.

Stitched upon the velvet of the bag was the elf's family crest. It was easy to recognize. It appeared on the side of a reconstructed skyscraper in the business district. Until that moment, I hadn't realized that the night before had been a transaction.

And when I complained about it a few days later at Danceland, where I'd gone to drink away my idiocy, the bartender, Valda, said, "I know exactly who you're talking about. He likes his humans, he does, that one. The sillier, the better." She laughed and poured me another drink. "This one's on the house, love," she said. "Go ahead. You earned it."

WE DO NOT COME IN PEACE

"Don't let my mistakes be yours," I told Mouse, giving him this story a few weeks after he'd settled in. I didn't tell him that I was paying our rent each month with a coin from that bag, that I was buying our food with the coins from that bag. I kept it under a floorboard beneath my bed, like buried treasure—hiding it not just for its value, but because it shamed me to see it, to be reminded.

"It doesn't make any sense." Mouse shook his head.

"What doesn't?"

"The stories about this place—back home, I mean—made Bordertown sound wonderful. People who were here before the Way closed off for all those years. I've read this one blog—"

"Blog?" I furrowed my eyebrows.

"Yeah, a journal someone keeps on the Internet."

He was endlessly educating me about things that had occurred in the World since I last saw it. Planes had crashed into buildings, new wars had started. People kept private things like journals out in the open, for all to read on the Internet.

"Their stories made this place sound like heaven," he said. "But really, it seems like it's hard to live here without joining a gang or turning tricks or thieving."

"I suppose it *is* wonderful here," I said. "For some."

"Yes," he said. "For some. And that's the thing that doesn't make any sense. It seems silly to run away from one world only to set up the same rotten systems all over again in a new one."

"I don't make the rules, Mouse," I said. "I just live here."

"But you're wrong," he said. "You *do* make the rules here. *Because* you live here. Don't you see?"

I ruffled his hair and laughed as I told him it looked like he was growing it long enough to pose as an elf. He shrugged my hand off as if I were a troublesome parent. "Sorry," I said, and looked out the window over my kitchen table.

From my grime-streaked window, I could see clouds of smoke rising from the mill stacks down by the canal. That view was the reason I rented that apartment. Back home, where I'd come from, there'd been smokestacks I could see from my kitchen window, too. So when I looked through this one, I could pretend for a moment that I'd gone home a year ago, when I still could have, before the Way between the World and the

Borderlands closed for those mysterious thirteen days, before enough time passed to make me a stranger to my old friends and family. Time has a funny way of bending here on the Border. Thirteen days here had been thirteen *years* back in the World, as we discovered when people like Mouse started coming through with their new toys and new ways of thinking. By now, back home, nobody's heard a word from me for thirteen years. I'd probably been declared officially dead. And if I'm not dead on paper, in the hearts of my old friends and family, I must be.

"Sorry," I said again, wishing things could be different for both of us.

"Don't be sorry, Marius," said Aleksander. "Be angry."

Over the short days of that winter, I showed him the city's darkest corners, its best angles, and the wild Nevernever that surrounded it. I pointed out the neutral territories, encouraged him to stick to those. And by his fifth month in the city, when spring returned and washed the streets down, he said, "I think I've decided to stay."

"Where?" I said. "In town? Or with me?"

That got a smile, a rare thing from Mouse, who had been carrying a frown around like an anchor.

But disappointment is an odd emotion to witness in others. It comes and goes as it pleases, returns after you think you've beaten it. For weeks—even after Mouse decided to stay, even after that glint of a smile he'd offered—it seemed he wouldn't speak unless I asked him a question. It was as if he lived inside the space of his own skull, and only occasionally would he come out, eyes blinking in the new light, mouth slowly opening to say, "I've taken a job as a bike messenger." That was in his sixth month.

"Where did you get a bike?" I asked, and Alek replied that he and a friend had gone in together on buying one. The friend paid for it, but Alek was paying his half off little by little with the job. Fair enough, I thought, hoping the work would be good for him.

Or, a month later, when summer was starting to heat up: "I met this guy who says the elves want to push the humans and halfies out of the Bordertown High Council. Said they've been up to something. Said he could smell bad magic brewing."

"And was this guy staggering around?" I asked. "That would explain a lot."

"He was perfectly sober," said Mouse.

I shrugged. "Just don't go getting caught up with anyone who worries about stuff like that too much." Gang wars sometimes break out because an elf looks at a human the wrong way, or a halfie tries to pass for a Trueblood and gets caught. Already the streets were heating up early that summer with random spats of violence. "Don't take any of that on yourself."

"Oh, Marius," he said, shaking his head, his mop of brown hair rolled into dreadlocks by that point. "I wish you weren't so afraid."

"Afraid?" I said.

"You're exactly the sort of human they desire."

"Who's they?" I asked. "And what sort is that?"

"The self-policing sort," said Mouse. "The sort that, in the back of their minds, really do believe the pointy-eared bastards are somehow better."

"You're a very rude boy," I said.

"I know you've been here longer than me, Marius," he said, "but don't do what they do. Don't try to pretend you're better than me just because you're a few years older."

"Do you hate me that much?"

He shook his head. "I don't hate you, Marius. I feel bad for you. I want to help you."

"And how are you going to do that?"

"By convincing you to believe you're worth something."

"I don't know what you're talking about," I said.

"You're just not ready to hear the truth," said Alek.

"Why are you still here?" I asked.

He looked shocked at the question. "Here with you?"

"Here in Bordertown," I said. "I mean, you seem to not like it here very much. So I don't understand. Why are you staying? The Way back to the World is there for you if you want it."

We looked at each other, then awkwardly away. He put his hand over mine on the table. Finally he said, "I do like you, Marius. I do. You're so very good. You're much kinder than I am. Thank you for everything. I don't say that enough. And there are things I like here. There are. And that's why I talk the way I've been doing. There are good things here. But they're threatened."

"It's almost evening," I said, looking out the window. The sky was tending toward violet poured over a red horizon of buildings. "I need to get ready to go down to Ho Street and stake my corner. Coins are waiting to be tossed."

"I may still be out when you get back," he said as I got up from the table.

"Where are you going?" I asked.

"Down to Soho, too, with some friends from work. We're going to the Magic Lantern to see a movie. Hopefully one will be playing." He laughed. The Magic Lantern wasn't a very reliable theater. Sometimes they would put on a live show so that if the movie cut out, you could keep watching. Other times, you couldn't tell if the projector would show the intended film or some nonsensical silent movie that was a cross between watching a stranger's family videos from the middle of the twentieth century and a surrealist experiment in green dogs and unopened umbrellas during winter. I sometimes went hoping for the stranger's home videos, especially now that the twentieth century was so far behind me, sealed away, impossible to go back to. I was relieved to hear Mouse make a noise like that, though—a laugh—and also relieved he'd recently been saying words like *friends* and *hopefully*.

"Have fun," I said, tucking my case under my arm to leave.

"Wait," said Mouse. I waited with my hand on the knob as he stood there searching for the words to tell me something. After a while, he seemed to give up and settled for: "Be safe while you're out there. I worry about you sometimes."

I smiled. I didn't know if he was somehow saying he loved me. And though I saw a possibility of love in him, I couldn't help but feel he was too young, that I'd be no better than the Trueblood who'd spotted him when Mouse had first arrived. I couldn't help remembering that Mouse had been a baby when I was already a teenager back in the World, thanks to the Way closing and screwing up time.

"No worries," I said, my voice low in my throat, holding it in as if it might escape me. I was a master of self-restraint. It was my new art form. "I'm a big boy," I told Mouse. "I'll be careful."

I've said that the music had left me. Although I didn't know it then, I realize now it was right around the time the Way between Borderland

and the World closed that it began to slip away. First for a night, as if it were just flaking out on me, not showing up where we'd arranged to meet. Then a week went by, and no matter how many times I placed myself on my corner across from Danceland, no matter how many times I put bow to string, I couldn't catch a song. I could play my old music, but nothing new would come, and the songs felt funny all of a sudden, as if they were too old-fashioned. A change was in the air around that time, a big one—you could see it by the banners of shining lights that stretched over the city like the aurora borealis—but I had the strongest feeling that I was somehow being left behind. As if the bus I needed to catch had stopped while I'd fallen asleep on the bench, then continued on without me.

I started to toss in my sleep during those long nights, and inevitably my thoughts would return to the world I'd left behind. I'd think of all the good things first. My mother's voice in the morning, waking me for school. My father's hand on my head like a hat, after I'd brought home straight A's. My friends in the school orchestra. My teacher, Mr. Humphrey, who told me I had talent and that I should go to college, that I'd get a scholarship for playing the violin the way I could. *Did.* Then I thought of all the bad things. A heart broken by a boy who didn't love me. The way my parents' faces fell when I told them who I really was, how all they could do was blink. Their silence. Their retreat from me. Thinking back on it, the things that had made me unhappy might have faded over time if I'd stayed. When I realized I was playing the game of regrets, though, I made myself stop and do other things.

I'd pace my apartment by candlelight, trying to think of something—anything—to make the music come back. That elf who had smiled and applauded and threw coins, who had taken me home and used me, I wondered if what he'd done had been the killing blow, because I'd already been bleeding confidence for a while.

And even after Mouse arrived—an event I'd hoped meant my fortunes were changing—I played my old-fashioned music on the streets only to keep the apartment and to keep us fed, to make the money from that elf last a little longer. Mouse's arrival hadn't changed things, not in the way I wanted. It didn't bring the music back. I'd been closed off from it, the way the World had been closed off from Borderland—but it didn't return after the Way was clear again.

For most of that summer, Mouse was gone during the day more and more. Delivering messages, I figured, on his shared bicycle. In the evenings he'd come back for a few hours, for dinner, some conversation, to ask how I was doing, to give me things he'd gotten on the job: a bag of coffee beans, a bar of dark chocolate, a package of cigarettes, though I never smoked as a rule. "You can trade them, then," he said when I rejected his offerings, and I realized he was, in his own way, paying me for room and board.

"You don't owe me anything, Alek," I said. "I've got the place covered. Do for yourself instead."

"No," he said. "We do for each other." He smiled, happier than I'd seen him since he'd arrived. I nodded and offered a smile of my own. That was our currency. No teeth. Just upturned corners.

I was happy for those offerings, but I was worried about where they'd come from. I wasn't stupid. I knew he must have been running something illegal on that bike of his—messages or drugs or black-market items from the World or the fair lands—but I traded his offerings anyway on the streets of Soho, for food and clothes and to keep the roof over our heads.

After Mouse started giving me things, I stopped playing my violin altogether. The *must* had gone out of me. Instead of playing on my corner, I started walking with my case under my arm, my collar up and my chin tucked against my chest. Rarely would I meet the eyes of a stranger, rarely would I do more than say hello to an acquaintance who stopped me to ask how I'd been doing. "Fine," I'd say, and keep moving. I didn't want to trap myself in a situation where I needed to explain why people no longer saw me out playing. I didn't want to admit I could still eke out a song but they all sounded labored now, awkward, as if I were a beginner all over again.

So I stopped trying, avoided my old haunts for a while, walked in other directions, my violin case tucked under my arm like a bunch of useless flowers. I looked like I was going somewhere, but I was hiding out in the open. And months later, in the summer, when I finally got up the nerve to go back to Ho Street—to what had been *my* corner—I found a girl with green spiky hair standing behind a table with a strange machine hooked up to two tiny speakers. She sang a song I'd never heard—the streets were full of them now more than ever—into a microphone attached to the machine. Her voice drifted down the block easily. I stood there listening, until she brought her tune to a close. And then I went up to her and said, "I'm sorry, but...what is all of this?" I waved my hands at the equipment on her table.

"This?" She pointed at the main piece of machinery. "It's a laptop." When I didn't respond, she said, "You know, a mobile computer? I can play downloaded karaoke songs on it? Well, as long as it's been spelled. Live and learn. This place rocks, but it has its downsides."

"Downloaded?" I said, vaguely recalling a word like this that Mouse had used.

The girl nodded but didn't explain. Instead, she tapped the keyboard and stroked her fingertip across its bottom edge, tapped a few more keys, and soon a new song was playing and she was singing it. Another song I didn't recognize. She smiled around the words. It wasn't my idea of music, but I placed a few coins on her table before leaving.

On my way home, bemused and a bit melancholy, I stopped in a café, hoping a strong cup of coffee might change my mood. But when I sat at a communal table, where a halfie with a long coat and scraggly teeth poured tea from a pot into his cup, he looked me up and down before asking, "What's wrong? Someone murder your sister?"

"Excuse me?" I said after swallowing a bitter sip.

"You look like you need a beer."

"I don't drink," I told him.

"Name's Billy Buttons," the halfie said. I didn't offer him mine. "New arrival, are you?"

"No. I've been around for a while. Why?"

"You look like you haven't got a clue what's going on," he said. "That's why."

"I just saw a girl singing karaoke songs from a miniature computer. When I left the World, computers took up an entire desk."

"Now they sit pleasantly on your lap like a cat," said the guy. "Some in the palm of your hand. Must be one of the new kids. They're bringing all sorts of nifty things with them from the World these days, aren't they?"

"Seems so."

"Well, you roll with the punches," said Billy. "Otherwise, you get knocked down. I've been around B-town long enough to learn to make adjustments when the World changes. Of course, it's worse for you younglings who were here before the Pinching Off. You've got all these kids coming through now who look like you but don't think or act like you. Makes you old before your time. It's a shame."

I nodded but didn't say anything. Quickly I drank the last of my coffee, then excused myself. The weird halfie said to keep my chin up, said that things change in ways we can't expect, and didn't I know that, after living in Bordertown as long as I have? He laughed loud and long, and was still laughing as the door of the café closed behind me.

I decided to take the long way home, to walk off my bad mood. So I turned down empty streets and abandoned alleys that took me around the perimeter of my neighborhood. But as I turned down one of those alleys, I found a crowd farther in, clogging the path. The people had their backs to me, so I couldn't see what they had gathered around. Suddenly their arms went up and they let out a collective cry and shook their fists in the air. I'd seen plenty of odd gatherings during my years in Bordertown, but not in a back alley with a crowd who raised fists and cheered in unison.

The alley was lit with lanterns people carried, and several bespelled fire globes hung in the air above, casting an orange glow over faces and shoulders. When I reached the back of the crowd, I stood on tiptoe, but I still couldn't see beyond their heads. And as the cheers began to fade, a lone voice remained at the center. A familiar voice—I knew it as soon as I heard it—and this is what the voice said:

"They take the goods we bring from our World, those are fine enough for them, and they take your rent and they'll take your children in trade. They take and take and take, that's what they know how to do. And yet we are beneath them. And yet our World is a garbage pit compared to their One True Realm. Why, then, are they so interested in our World? Why, then, do they want what our World produces? And why have we allowed them to take possession of our streets while we cannot even *tour* their precious Realm beyond Elfhaeme Gate?"

"They're liars!" someone from the crowd shouted.

"They're cheats!" another sent up like a rocket.

Then the voice at the center resumed speaking.

"We will send them a message, my friends. We will make them know that we will no longer grovel like worms at their perfectly molded ivory feet. And when we come for them, my friends," said the voice at the center, "what will we tell them?"

A hush fell over the crowd for only an instant, allowing them to collect enough breath to shout, "We do not come in peace! We do not come in peace! We do not come in peace!"

I pushed myself into the mass of people and threaded through the bodies until I reached the front of the crowd. I put my hands on the shoulders of two men to lift myself up and look beyond them, to put a face to the voice—the Voice of the Nameless, I would learn some people called him. Alek, Aleksander, Mouse.

Our eyes met briefly, and in that moment, he recognized the shock on my face, and I recognized how much we were strangers despite living together, despite taking care of each other.

He said, "Marius..."

I turned away.

I don't think of myself as stupid or naïve. After all, I was the one who saw Mouse and the danger he was in when he first arrived. After all, it was I who taught him how to survive on the Border. But I must have been under a spell for at least one of these conditions when it came to Mouse. Stupidity, naïveté, it doesn't matter; both lead to the same result: blindness to what's happening right in front of you.

I was blind, then. Blind most likely because I'd fallen into some kind of love with Mouse despite my efforts not to. Maybe it was because he reminded me of myself when I first spotted him. And in caring for him, I believed I was somehow protecting that younger version of myself that no one had taken the time to protect when I first arrived. Maybe it was because I thought I could make him into a little brother. But despite all my efforts to box him into some other kind of relationship, I had failed. Now the jury had returned with a verdict: clearly I was guilty of perjury. I had lied to myself, over and over again.

When he returned later that night, clicking the door shut quietly, he scuttled over to where I lay in bed pretending to sleep. He nudged my shoulder and whispered, "Marius? Marius, are you awake?"

I rolled over, sighing. "It's late, Mouse," I said. "What do you want?"

"I'm sorry." He sat down beside me, the mattress dipping. He put a hand near mine, but I didn't take it.

"Sorry for what?"

"For not telling you what I've been doing. For keeping secrets."

"You mean forming another gang? The streets are full of them. Do you really think another one is going to solve any problems? They just make more."

"It's not a gang," said Mouse.

"Then what is it?"

"A group," he said. "A group of freedom fighters."

"You're not free here?"

"Not necessarily that," said Mouse. "But it is unfair."

"Welcome to the world," I said, and moved to turn over on my side again.

"No," said Mouse. "I left the World for a reason. It doesn't have to be like that here."

"It's like this everywhere, Mouse," I said into my pillow. "Grow up. I had to."

"Only because people like you allow for it."

I felt his weight lift from the bed. And a moment later: the sound of the door clicking shut quietly.

Only so much truth can exist between two people until it becomes too much, and then they can't bear to be around each other. I didn't hold it against Mouse that he'd been keeping secrets from me. I had secrets of my own. When he'd been gone for a few weeks after that midsummer night when I'd discovered *his* secret, I decided I couldn't go on living as I was. *This apartment is too small,* I told myself. *And the music has gone to wherever it wants to be. And anyway, isn't it time to move on to something different, something real?*

Also, when I took out that bag of elf money from beneath its floorboard, it no longer rattled.

An object lesson I never shared with Mouse: I stood on my old corner later that day, holding that empty bag with the crest of a powerful True-blood family embroidered on it, and had a terrible idea. It was terrible because as soon as I had it, I knew it was bad. But it was strong, and grew so quickly that it took hold of my mind and conducted me, as if I were its puppet, to return to that elf's crystal mansion on Dragon's Tooth Hill, where I'd once spent a night thinking I was in love with someone, and once there I waited outside until that elf finally appeared and came to meet me.

"What do you want, Marius?" he asked with no hint of emotion.

"What I'm worth," I told him. I held the bag up and he looked away, embarrassed. I knew he would be. They have no scruples about doing shameful things, the Fair Ones. They only wish not to be reminded.

"You cannot blackmail me, Marius," he said, stiffening his back, lifting his chin, looking down his nose at me. "I've done no wrong here."

But an election was on the horizon, and his father's name had been on the tongue of every elf, human, and halfie all summer. Even Mouse had mentioned their family name once, when he'd come home with another bit of gossip he'd heard about the elves trying to edge humans out of the High Council. His father couldn't afford to have a reckless son paying street rats like me for a night of lust. It would be so…*tasteless*.

I reminded the elf of this and of the occasional bursts of violence that had flared in the streets once people realized the Way had closed. It made people nervous, even after it reopened, as if the entire city had been under a spell of magic. "And we all know where magic comes from, don't we?" I said. I stared hard until he looked away.

"You humans," he said, but didn't finish. Instead, he sighed and said, "If the money wasn't enough for you, what is it you want?"

I looked back at the gleaming façade of his father's mansion beyond his shoulder, smiled—no teeth, just upturned corners—and made my proposal.

A*rt and Lies*. That's what I got out of a night spent as an unwitting prostitute. I'd meant to save my dignity, go my own way, but after Mouse left I couldn't save anything. No Mouse to bring home coffee and chocolate from his mysterious delivery service. No music to play for coins on a corner. Nothing left to trade for a roof and clothes and meals. It was either I collect on that spell-promised favor, or I join the wharf rats and start drinking from the Mad River.

The elf sealed our deal with magic this time: I got what I wanted, and he got a spellbound promise that I would never return, never bother him or his family again.

It was only after I'd walked away from Dragon's Tooth Hill and back into Soho that I felt like I could release the breath I'd been holding.

When I moved from my apartment, I took the things Mouse had left behind and boxed them up. I stuck them in a corner of the crumbling Soho building the elf had restored for me. It was on Carmine Street, where I knew people, and I put up flyers advertising what I intended the place to be. People responded by bringing me paperbacks with dog-eared pages, CDs in plastic cases, vinyl records lurking in the corners of their attics, VHS tapes, VCRs covered in dust, flimsy comic books, paintings and sculptures from local artists. I paid for the used items and arranged for the art to be sold on consignment. A bit for me, a bit for the makers. Then I hung my sign in the window and pretended to be proud when people who knew me as a street violinist rang the bell over the door as they entered for the first time, smiling, congratulating me on my new venture.

And then, three weeks ago, I turned at the sound of that bell to see him come in, looking around cautiously as he stepped up to the counter, where I'd been pricing a set of semitattered books about teenaged love-crazed vampires someone had brought in. Alek, Aleksander, Mouse.

I didn't waste any time asking how he'd been or what he'd been up to. I just went to the back room to collect his box of left-behind things. When I pushed it across the counter, he said, "It's good to see you doing so well, Marius. Your place, it's really impressive."

"Thanks," I said, and tapped my finger against the counter.

"Don't you want to know how I've been?" he asked.

I could only shake my head.

"Then you don't want to know what's going to happen soon? Not far from here?" he asked.

I looked up, frowning. "Please say what you came to say."

"We're going to take it," he said. "We're going to take that bleeding Oberon House by storm, and then burn it to the ground."

"You've been drinking Mad River water," I told him. "You have no idea what you're saying. There are *children* in there," I added through clenched teeth.

"I know what I'm saying," he said. "I know what I'm doing, Marius. We have a plan. We're going to take the building first, then burn it down after we get the kids out, so those bastards know they can't abuse us any longer."

"You'll be killed," I said. "It's not possible. They're too powerful."

"We're powerful, too, Marius. You've always underestimated us. Underestimated yourself."

"I could turn you in to one of the elf gangs," I said, hoping that the threat would scare him off his plans. "I could warn the Silver Suits."

"You won't, though," said Mouse. "I know you, Marius."

"No," I said, "you don't, actually." Then: "Why are you telling me all this?"

"So you can tell others," he said. "Afterward, when it's over, we'll need a song, like all important battles and revolutions have. So people will know what was meant by it. You should be the person who does that."

"You shouldn't count on me for that," I said. "I don't want anything to do with your schemes."

"They're not schemes," said Mouse. "They're acts of justice. It was you who first taught me I couldn't trust them. Why are you trying to defend them? They wouldn't do the same for you."

My mouth dropped open for a long moment. Now I was at the root of his crazed revolution. "Stop," I said. "I don't want to hear any more."

He stood in the doorway holding his box of things, looking around the place with a squint in his eye. "It speaks volumes about you, Marius, this place. But I'm not sure you know that, do you?"

"Please leave," I said.

And he did leave, as soon as I turned away. I knew by the sound of the bell.

Tonight I waited in a doorway across the street from that shabby building his group had holed themselves up in, watching their silhouettes pass by windows, Mouse and his new friends. I couldn't help myself, I couldn't make myself go home. And later, after nearly two hours had passed, I watched the lights in the building go off, floor by floor. Then the door they'd gone through opened, and the same group of kids spilled out again. I pressed myself into the shadows of my alcove and gasped when I saw the full backpacks slung over their shoulders, cans of gasoline in their hands, bricks clenched in their fists, baseball bats, trash can lids buckled across their arms like shields. They were going to do it after all. They were going to do what he'd said.

I stood there, unable to move. What could I say? What could I do? I couldn't bring myself to go to the Silver Suits about it. It wasn't just elves

I distrusted. And anyway, I reasoned, they'll be caught. Surely they can't walk into Oberon House, take out the Truebloods running the place, and burn the place down. It would never happen.

I thought about going home, doing my best to pretend I hadn't seen anything. But even after I was halfway home, I found myself turning around, going back the way I'd come, back to Hell Street, then north to Ho, the street I'd seen Mouse and his gang go down. There were my feet, taking me to him as usual.

By the time I was a block from Oberon House, I knew I was already late to their party. Shouts and screams filled the air. Gunshots and spell-blasts sounded off at random intervals. The scent of smoke reached me before I walked into a fine cloud of ash and found a mob moving down the street toward me; and at their backs, Oberon House loomed, smoking, creaking, tufts of fire eating the windows. Sirens wailed. Silver Suits were arriving. Truebloods and humans and halfies stood in the streets, some fighting, some looking up at Oberon House as it burned. The voice of the mob boomed above the smoke and fire: "We do not come in peace! We do not come in peace! We do not come in peace!" as they marched toward me, fists pumping in the air.

I put my face in my hands. *What have you done, Mouse?* I thought. And then: *What did I do by letting you?*

I looked out at the mob through the spaces between my fingers and dropped my hands. There he was, at the head of the pack, his face smudged with ash, a bloody gash across his forehead. *He's done it,* I thought, and for some reason I laughed, only a little at first, then full on, like someone whose life has been changed by a tremendous tragedy or a miracle in an instant.

As the mob approached, I heard a faint whistling come from above me, as if a bird were perched somewhere overhead. No bird flew by when I looked up, though. Only the music. Only the music flew overhead, sifting through the smoke, waiting for me to take it, to shape it, if I would.

I'm not sure I've ever moved so fast as I did right then, taking my case from under my arm to release my violin. I stood there for a second and listened to what the music was trying to tell me, then I tried to play it—no, *let* myself play it—a song for Mouse, for Aleksander, the Voice of the Nameless, who stopped when he saw me and ran across the street to join me, while the mob marched on without him.

WE DO NOT COME IN PEACE

"Thank you," he said, after I finished my song for him, after I took the violin down and looked at his soot-smudged face and laughed at him, shaking my head.

"You're crazy," I said.

He only smiled and shrugged. "Seems like I have to go to extremes to get your attention. I knew you would come through for me, Marius."

"Well, I certainly didn't."

"I knew," he said, and put his hand on my shoulder where the violin had rested, pulled me down so he could kiss me.

I could turn you in to one of the elf gangs, I'd told him that day in the shop.

You won't, though, he'd said. *I know you, Marius.*

No, I'd said, *you don't, actually.*

But perhaps, to my surprise, he did.

We're used to seeing them come and go, these young swordsmen.

THE DUKE OF RIVERSIDE

Ellen Kushner

That kid never belonged here. We all knew that from the moment he walked through the door, looking nervous and madder than hell. Bad combination. Everyone figured he had a weapon, because people like that usually do. The drinkers stopped drinking, the barmaids stopped serving, and the dicers held up their dice mid-roll. Sukey moved a little closer to Annie, as the girls like to protect each other when they can.

Rosalie stepped forward. It is her bar, after all. "What can I get you?" she asked.

"What can you get me?" His voice told everyone that was the stupidest question he'd been asked all year. "What can you get me?" All sneer. And that snooty Hill accent. Definitely not from around here. "Do you happen to have Ludlow's treatise, *On the Causes of Nature?* Oh no, they banned it. How about a roast peacock, then? Or a cup of really strong poison?"

Rosalie rolled her eyes. "I'll go see," she said. Like she'd already taken his measure, and decided he wasn't dangerous after all, just nuts. She turned her back on him, and the whole room relaxed.

He was a scholar, clearly. He had that long student hair, tied back with a piece of string. And that long black robe they all wear, hanging off his bony shoulders like laundry, only it hadn't been washed for awhile. But pissed-off scholars don't usually come down to Riverside. Hell, they don't even come here to get pissed. They know it's a place you're likely to get rolled; rolled, and then maybe killed. Nobody drinks here who doesn't have to.

Red Sukey sidled up to him. She'd been holding on to Annie, but when Rosalie turned her back, Sukey grabbed her chance. "Buy me a drink?"

He looked down at her. He was incredibly tall. "What for? Are you thirsty?"

She's not very old. Not much experience there. "No." She moved a little closer to him, to show him what she had. "I'd be nice to you."

He got it then. "For a drink? Are you serious?"

We all waited to see if he had any money. Most men, you mention money, their hand goes automatically to where they keep their purse, just for an instant. But his hand didn't even go to his belt. Nothing, then; or he was smarter than he looked. I, myself, was willing to wait and see.

And then Nimble Willie stuck his head in through the doorway gasping, "Fight! Fight!" and we forgot all about the bony scholar and headed for the street to see. Poor Archer Fink had finally gotten St Vier to take his challenge, god knows how. Richard St Vier was too good to fight a newbie like Archer, and if Archer didn't know it, we all did. Probably it was that girl of his, the blonde, egging Fink on to show his stuff. Maybe she even thought he really had a chance.

We're used to seeing them come and go, these young swordsmen. They fight like stags in autumn, to prove who's best. Only, being swordsmen, they tend to kill each other off. That's how you get good jobs in the city, not to mention respect here in Riverside.

That day my money was on St Vier, but so was everyone else's. I only won eighteen brass minnows.

It was done in a minute—barely time to make our bets. St Vier lunged quick and hard, Archer Fink grunted and wheezed, and it was all over, blood shooting up after the tip of the sword when St Vier pulled it out.

The student was right there. He was standing very still; he didn't even put up his hand to keep the blood from hitting him. His black robe was spattered with shiny black drops. He stared at the body like he'd never seen one before.

St Vier walked away from the fight, and into the tavern. Rosalie brought him a drink. She loved that he drank at her place. It brought her custom. When the nobles from the Hill were looking for a swordsman to hire, they sent their servants down to Rosalie's to find him. She loved that, too.

The scholar followed him in. "I'll have one, too," he said to Rosalie.

She said, "First, let me see your money."

"You didn't ask *him* for money."

Rosalie snorted. "St Vier, I know. Who the hell are you?"

"I'm no one," he said fiercely. "Forget it."

"Who are you?" Rosalie said again in that tone of voice that always gets her cash on the barrel.

He turned his head and looked down at her. It was a long damn way. "Alec," he said.

"Is that all?"

"Just Alec."

The swordsman was ignoring the whole thing. He was leaning on the bar, knocking down his thirst with his back to them both—though one hand never left the sword at his side.

"St Vier," the kid said aloud. He pushed loose hair back from his face, not even noticing the smear of blood he left there. The air around him started to feel dangerous again. Maybe it was his voice, the way he said the name. "St Vier," he said again, long and low. I've heard nobles use that voice, up on the Hill when they're telling a servant they want something done. Yeah. I did some work up there once. But just once. They talk real slow, like they have all the time in the world. Which they do.

The swordsman heard it, too. He turned his head. "Yes?"

"You're Richard St Vier?"

The swordsman nodded.

"And you kill people."

St Vier looked him up and down. It stretched his neck some; the kid was a real beanpole. He must've seen what we all saw: young, skinny, hungry, poor, bad-tempered and out of place.

"Sometimes I do."

"Do you ever kill them just because they're no earthly use to anyone at all?"

"No. No, I don't think I've ever done that."

"Well." The kid stepped back, putting a sword's length between them. "That is disappointing. What do you do it for, then?"

"Sometimes just for practice."

"Like now, for instance? Was that just for practice?"

St Vier's eyes darted over to where Archer's girl had begun a horrible racket in the corner, weeping and wailing. Sukey and Annie were trying to keep her quiet her with cheap brandy. For a swordsman, St Vier is pretty easy-going. But he never likes a lot of noise.

"In a way."

"It must be very tiring, killing all those people."

"Not very."

"You'll do it again, then. Soon."

The swordsman looked at him again. St Vier was popular on the Hill, those days, fighting for the nobles at their parties and stuff. Demo matches only: First Blood, hardly ever to the Death. No wonder he liked to practice in Riverside. Nobles can be pretty squeamish. But it's a good bet St Vier would know that voice pretty well by now, the low, purring voice this ragged guy was using. "Look," St Vier said; "do you have a job for me? Is that what this is about?"

The student tugged his frayed cuff down. "A job? Me? I don't even have the price of a beer."

"Then what do you want?"

"I don't suppose you'd kill me for free."

A smile snuck its way onto the swordsman's face. "No."

"For practice, then?"

"Can you fight?"

The scholar opened his robe to show nothing hung on his belt, not even a knife. "Not particularly, no."

"That's no good then. I like a challenge."

"Oh." The young scholar turned away. "Maybe later, then. But remember," he said over his shoulder; "you had your chance."

Richard St Vier watched the tall man walk out of the bar alone. Sometimes nobles came down to Riverside in disguise, looking for kicks or for connection. Some disguise. He wasn't just ragged, he was dirty. His face was young, but thin and hollow like hunger. A starving nobleman? A jumped-up servant? A tutor in disgrace?

Richard shook his head. Poor guy. Whatever he was doing in Riverside, he was going to have an interesting time while he lasted. Maybe he should have bought him a beer, for a sort of welcome. The first day was always hard, here.

I, myself, did not expect to see that Alec again.

But then I kept hearing about him. Wandering Riverside like a lost soul, trying not to get laid but to get killed, near as I could tell. It should have been easy. He was going about it exactly the right way: insulting people, asking stupid questions.... The thing is, he was unarmed. He had no money. Sometimes he made people laugh, saying things no one else would dare to. No one really wanted to be the one to off him. He was probably crazy. That's a different kind of dangerous.

I saw him again at Rosalie's a few days later. I was looking over some very fine silver spoons that Hal had managed to find in a house uptown, and in walks the skinny kid, right up to where Rosalie is ladling out stew for Fabian Greenspan.

"Is that food?" he says to her. "Or are you trying to get rid of the old wash water?"

"You could use a little of both," Rosalie retorted.

Fabian sniggered. Some of the soup he was eating came out his nose.

"Oh, look," the kid said says. "It's medicinal, too."

Fabian had the shakes. It was early in the day for him—just past noon—and Rosalie wanted to feed him before he started drinking and she'd have to throw him out. He couldn't handle it at either end.

"Hungry?" Rosalie asked Alec.

"Hardly. I *like* rotten pears and cast-off cheese mold. And I've found the best place for getting them. You should try it. Slenderizing."

"Hey," Fabian protested. He had a soft spot for Rosalie.

The boy looked down his long nose. "Well, you do get thicker as you get older, don't you?"

"Hey!" Fabian roared feebly, and went for the kid.

"Hey," said another voice, a calmer voice. The swordsman St Vier was peeling Fabian off that Alec character.

"Hey, Richard," Rosalie said calmly. "Want some stew?" If she doesn't like you, she just ignores you.

The young scholar was standing very stiff. I guess he'd never been attacked by a guy with the shakes before. Or he wasn't used to being ignored.

"Richard St Vier," he drawled. "You're off your game."

"No," St Vier said; "I ate already." He was always polite, even to drunks.

"You're a disappointment," the scholar went on.

The swordsman turned to him, giving him his full attention. "How so?"

A swordsman's full attention is not something you really want on you. It gave me a chill. The tall kid's eyes glittered hard, like he was fevered, but his skin was pale, like he was casting his final throw.

"It's been three days, now. You haven't killed a soul. Don't think I haven't noticed. You haven't even stepped on a bug. I think you're vastly overrated. What's the matter, have you lost your nerve?

The swordsman stood up. "Come with me."

This is it, we thought. *Goodbye, scholar.*

The scholar's hands were shaking; I was close enough to see that. But he thrust his pale face forward and followed St Vier out of the tavern.

It wasn't going to be a pretty death. St Vier wouldn't waste good swordsmanship on an unarmed man. But I had a bet on with Hal, so we followed them out there.

The scholar was standing against a wall, very white in the face against his black robe and the crummy stone. "Remember," he was saying, fast and breathy; "one blow to the heart. They say you're quick."

Young men can be real fools. Not just the scholar, but the young swordsman we all called Dapper Dan, who must have taken a bad notion to impress St Vier. Guys like that think being a swordsman's all about risks and big gestures, and he made one now.

"Allow me," I heard him say, as he drew his blade.

St Vier was St Vier. Dan should never have shown cold steel around him. Someone with slower reflexes might have taken the time to notice that the blade wasn't coming in his direction. But Richard St Vier moved fast.

You have to love the guy. He drew and slashed right across Dan from the side, a gorgeous twist nobody else could have made in time. Dan squawked and fell, and St Vier said, "Damn," when he realized what he'd done.

The scholar hadn't even had time to move out of the way. He stared down at poor Dan.

"You should have let him," he said.

"It wasn't his business," said St Vier. But I was out there, and I saw: he hadn't drawn until Dan did. Whatever he was planning to do with the scholar, it wasn't the long, cold kiss of steel, as the poets say. "Would you like a drink?"

They walked back into Rosalie's tavern together, and that was that. From then on, you never saw them apart.

Nobody bet on when they started sleeping together, because there was no way of finding out for sure. Their landlady, Marie the whore and laundress, who lets out rooms above the courtyard of the old place with the well where she washes, is usually a pretty good egg, but she got all prissy with, "Master St Vier's business is his own and at least he pays his rent on time most months, not like some...." But why else did St Vier make it clear over and over that anyone who laid a finger on his crazy student would have him to answer to? More than one bully, pimp and bravo fell that year when they tried it anyway. As far as St Vier was concerned, there was one rule: Don't Mess with Alec, no matter what.

I guess Lord Horn didn't know about St Vier's Alec rule. How could he, when he lived way up on the Hill with the rest of them? What some old noble wanted Alec for was anybody's guess, but not everyone was sorry when Alec disappeared for awhile. It made the swordsman jumpy as hell, though. He made some inquiries, killed a few hired toughs who should have known not to mess with Riversiders, got Alec back, all right—and then he went after Lord Horn and took care of him, too.

Well, what else could he do? He had his point to make. But the city didn't see it that way. Brought St Vier up on murder charges, threw him in the Chop. Nobody liked it, but what could we do? We don't ask anyone in the city to do us any favors. We look after our own, no squealers—but if you're taken, good luck to you.

Alec broke that rule. For St Vier, see. Of course we didn't know it at the time. We thought Alec had left again because he was bored, or lonely, or scared shitless. Fabian Greenspan swore he'd seen him lying with his throat slit off Fuller's Way. But Fabian doesn't always see so clearly. Red Sukey said he'd thrown himself from the Bridge because of the tragedy of his eternal love. But Sukey likes theatre. Then Nimble Willie came back from plying his trade over by the Council Hall claiming Alec had passed him riding in a carriage with the Duchess Tremontaine's crest on it, all decked out in green velvet and gold lace. That was a little startling, because Willie's pretty reliable, but not nearly as startling as when St Vier turns up again the next day, and Alec a day or so later, hair cut short but wearing the same old black robe, rattier than ever. So we couldn't help ragging on Willie with, "So where's the gold and velvet, Willie?"

No velvet—and no money, either. Maybe he spent it all to spring St Vier. I know that Alec is broke again because I try touching him for five in silver against my next lucky job uptown and he gives me one of those speeches that basically translates as, *Get away from me or I'll get St Vier to rip your balls off.* Nice to know they're still such excellent friends. Everything back to normal. Except word trickles down from people with legitimate jobs up in the city (meaning Riversiders who just couldn't hack it any more, gone up there to scrub floors and dishes) that Alec is in fact a very close relative of the Duchess. So maybe he's lying about the money. But, then, why doesn't he buy himself some decent clothes?

Alec came storming out of the bedroom in their rooms at Marie's, shoving his hair back behind his ears. Richard stopped practicing long enough to get out of his way. Alec never really knew where his body was in relation to anything around him.

"Have you seen my boots?" Alec demanded. "I took them off last night, and they've vanished. I think someone ate them. I'm going to the market. Please don't consume anything else useful while I'm gone. The shad are in, and they sell out fast. I'll bring some home. Where are my boots?"

"Behind the bed."

"I've looked there."

"Look again."

Alec emerged fully-shod, clutching his robe to his throat. "I've lost my cloak-pin."

"It's here." Richard picked it up off the mantel, careful not to dislodge Alec's small collection of precious books. "Do you want me to come with you?"

"To protect me from murderous fishwives?"

Alec shoved his hair back behind his ears again, and shook his head with annoyance as it fell forward.

"There's nothing you can do about it," Richard said. "Just wait. It grows when it grows."

"How philosophical," Alec drawled sarcastically. "How very like the wise old farmer in the tutelary readers for young people."

"How long did it take you to grow it out the first time?"

"Years," Alec growled. "And everyone still laughed at me when I got to University, because I looked like a new boy. It had just gotten good and long when I left. The one thing I finally got right. And then I had to go and cut it, just to make a nice impression on the Council for the Duchess."

"Well, it worked," Richard said.

"Not that it wasn't worth it," Alec added. "She nearly died when she saw me all cleaned up."

The hair would grow long again; meanwhile, there was still enough for Richard to sink his fingers into, and he did.

Nobody knows who owns most of Riverside, but it's probably Alec's relatives, and they've probably buried the deeds, because who really wants their very own piece of this crumbling rabbit warren? Like there's that crazy cat-lady at the top of that old pile on Ferrian Alley. You'd pay *not* to own that house.

Young guys always believe in luck. Most of them never get old. And some, like that Alec, have it all, even if they may not look it at first.

Richard wasn't looking for the letters, but the swordsman had a very good sense for what was around him. He always knew where things stood in a room, and he knew when anything changed. The letters were hidden all over the place: under the mattress, behind Alec's books on the mantel piece, even in an old pair of winter boots gathering dust in the corner because they needed re-soling but no one could ever remember to take them out.

Richard knew Alec would never burn the letters, because there was writing only on one side, and Alec was terrifically cheap. Richard could see that it was good paper: thick and heavy-laid, the ink on it crisp and clean. He had no idea what the writing spelt out. But he did recognize the seals, heavy with wax that Alec would probably melt down sooner or later to reuse:

Tremontaine

I was there at Rosalie's the day the news came.

"Tremontaine!" Willie called, breathless, across the tavern. But Alec wouldn't look up from his dice. He was losing, as usual, but as usual refusing to quit and cut his losses.

"Hey, Alec, listen up!" Nimble Willie finally reached the table where Alec was dicing with Hal and Fat Rodge. "Hey!" he panted. Really, he could hardly breathe. "Didn't you hear me calling you?"

"I heard you calling *someone*. What is it, Willie? You're dripping like a cheap candle, and you stink worse than my luck."

"I've got news."

Alec's fingers tightened on the side of the table, and could you blame him? News could always be St Vier lying somewhere bleeding his guts out. "Well, spit it out. We're in the middle of a game, here."

"Your granny's gone."

"My 'granny'? Which 'granny' would that be, Willie?"

"You know what I mean. It's the duchess. The Duchess Tremontaine. She's dead. Last night. I came to tell you."

"Oh, re-ally?"

He lifted the dice, and looked at them for a long time.

"Snake eyes," he said, and threw.

We all stared at the two perfect spots there in the middle of the table. Then Alec got up and left the tavern. No one saw him again for days. But Hal kept his money for him, down to the last brass minnow, tied up in a handkerchief. You didn't want to piss off St Vier. And clearly, Alec's luck had turned.

"Aren't you going to see her off?" Richard asked. He was practicing in their rooms with a blunt-tipped sword, stretching and exercising against the wall, which was pitted with the marks of other practice bouts. Alec had steel of his own, a darning needle he'd learned to use in his time at University. It, too, was blunt-tipped, which was good, considering the uses to which Alec put sharp objects.

"I avoided her while she was alive. It seems hypocritical to pursue her now."

"I heard there might be fireworks. You love fireworks."

"They had fireworks last year for Lord Galing. It cheered everyone up. I'm sure the late Duchess Tremontaine would want us all to be as miserable as possible. There will probably be a choir."

Richard knew he was treading on dangerous ground, but he was genuinely curious. "They're not expecting you, then?"

Alec stabbed at the sock. "Oh, they're expecting me, Richard. The show won't be complete without the idiot grandson parading with his savage swordsman."

"Wear your scholar's robe," Richard said cheerfully. "It's black. It will give them fits."

"Shall I put a silver chain around your neck, and lead you in the procession?"

Richard winced. "That bad, eh?"

The needle fell still in Alec's hands. "Bad? Oh, so you'd actually mind? I was beginning to think you liked the idea."

Alec hated people knowing anything about him. Even Richard. And now it was out. All over the city. All over Riverside.

"If you wanted to go, I'd come with you, that's all."

Richard went back to practicing, striking his sword rhythmically against the wall, careful not to look at Alec, but hearing his acid, honey voice:

"By all means, let's go to the Tremontaine funeral, and join the solemn procession of important people showing of just how important they really are. They're expecting us, after all. We wouldn't want to disappoint them. And then we can poke holes in a few. That, they will not be expecting. Think what a thrill it will give the assembled mourners. It will be the talk of the town. The duchess will be utterly forgotten." Alec jabbed at the sock's hole, which was not getting any smaller. "Not that she won't be forgotten soon, anyway. She's got no power any more, has she? These people are no longer interested. They'll pay their respects, because everyone's watching, and then they'll go right back to trying to figure out who's giving the most important dinner parties now that she's gone. She never liked me, you know. I'm rotten at dinner parties. No conversation. And I slouch. She likes people who are good at things. You impressed her. She'd like it if you went. Did you ever work for her?"

"Never. You know that."

"Go now, then. Go up to the Hill, and show everyone you know how to behave properly. Just because I'm a disgrace doesn't mean you have to be."

"Why would I want to go there without you?"

"Why would you want to go there *with* me?"

Richard put his hands on Alec's shoulders. "Let's not," he said, "go anywhere at all." He could feel the tension radiating along his arms.

"How blissful," Alec drawled. "How domestic."

Richard reached down to uncover Alec's palm. The marks that scored it were vivid red, but the skin unbroken. It was only a darning needle. Richard raised the hand to his lips. The palm was hot and burning.

So it looked like everybody was going to the Duchess Tremontaine's funeral except Alec. And he was probably the only one actually invited. The rest of Riverside was just going to turn up along the route, which would run from her big house on the Hill to the Stone City outside of town. The nobles would ride in procession behind, and everyone would line up to watch them, which was just fine with us. Nothing better for pickpockets than a good, colorful procession—and nothing makes a man want a whore faster than being reminded of mortality.

If Alec wanted to hide the letters that kept coming, Richard wasn't going to say anything. If Alec wanted to stop crossing the river into the city, wanted to give up excursions to the booksellers and the theater, well, he got that way sometimes. The books were all too old, Alec claimed, and the theater played nothing but comedies. He detested comedies. Alec was drinking all the time. It made him loose-limbed and clumsy, quarrelsome and fanciful. It didn't mean anything, Richard thought.

Then, on their way home from the market, there was a strange swordsman fixed at the end of the alley, blocking their way. The stranger's sword was sheathed, but loudly and clearly he spoke: "I bear challenge to David Alexander Tielman Campion, Duke Tremontaine—"

For a moment, Richard didn't even understand the words. "What the hell?"

"Just kill him," Alec said.

Richard drew his sword. "I'll take the challenge."

The other man drew, and saluted.

The Duke of Riverside

"Is it to the Death?"

"I hope so," said Alec. "They can hardly expect me to give up the Duchy of Tremontaine for First Blood."

It was all over town. Alec was heir to Tremontaine. And on either side of the river, people were waiting to kill him before they'd let him into Tremontaine House. Lucky for him he had the greatest swordsman in the city at his side day and night to defend him. The rules were the rules. As long as St Vier was there to take the challenge, honor was satisfied. The nobles had laid out those rules themselves, to keep them from killing each other off when there were better men to die for them. All St Vier had to do was always be there, and never lose.

By the third challenge, Richard was getting curious.

"Is this usual when people inherit?" he asked, stepping around the dead man in the street to clean his sword.

Alec wiped his sleeve across his face. He'd barely had time to register the challenge before Richard struck the final blow. "No, it's my goddamned relatives. Contesting the succession."

"What's to contest? Weren't you always her heir?"

Alec scraped something off the sole of his boot against a corner of a wall. "No, Richard. Did you think I was holding out on you all this time?"

He had, actually.

What everyone wanted to know was, *Why?* Why this crazy guy, who didn't have enough sense to get out of Riverside when he could, and take his famous boyfriend with him? Was it some kind of a joke? If he didn't want to be a Duke, couldn't he just say so?

Not that we didn't enjoy the challenges. Nervous swordsmen from the Hill paid good money to find out where his young lordship might be. We told them where he might be. But never where he really was.

"So who was it, then?" Richard sheathed his sword, but kept his hand on the pommel as he walked.

"No one. She wouldn't name an heir while she lived. Maybe she thought it would make her immortal. Maybe she just couldn't decide."

Climbing the dark, narrow stairs to their rooms, Richard watched with extra caution for signs of intruders. He opened the door first, and waited until it was shut behind them to say, "So she died without naming an heir, and it automatically goes to you?"

"No, Richard." Alec flung his robe down on their only chair, and said with entirely unjustified elaborate patience, "Haven't you been listening? She did name me. Finally. At the end."

He fished behind *On Human Understanding* and pulled out a letter, heavy with seals.

"See? It's all very official. Chosen, chosen, chosen. Like a prize rosebush at the fair. By a dying woman they probably nagged to death until she just gave them a name to shut them up."

Richard admired the elaborate writing, heavy and black, looped and angled. "So you are now the Duke Tremontaine?"

It was the first time he'd said it aloud. It sounded very strange.

Alec snapped the paper shut, using the seals as ballast.

"Well, that depends, doesn't it?"

"On what?"

"On whether I live to the end of the trial period."

"There's a trial period?"

"Oh, yes. It's open season on me until the thirty days of mourning have passed."

"And then?" he dared to ask.

"It's over. We're safe. I just have to last that long. Then it's not my problem any more. Or yours."

"But if you don't want the duchy—"

"Who says I don't want it?"

"*Do* you?"

"I want," Alec said, untying Richard's shirt, "to make them sweat. Don't you?"

It was a little harder when they started sending down guys we knew. Steffi's kid, Luxe, who'd been so proud when that fancy uptown swordmaster took him on, and then Steffi never shut up about how her kid had finally gotten himself an important job as some noble's own house swordsman, and that's why her boy never came to see her anymore. When Luxe showed up at Rosalie's, she was thrilled. I have to admit he looked good, well-fed and strong, dressed in new clothes. They were not any noble's colors, though. We thought he was off-duty, but he wasn't. He bought a round for everyone, and then he said, "So what's new?" or "What's happening around here?" or something.

We all looked at each other. He had to know.

"Looking for St Vier?" Rosalie said bluntly. She'd never liked Luxe that much.

Luxe grinned. He had good teeth. "Why shouldn't I?"

"No reason. Everyone else is. But you just got lucky."

In they came, St Vier and Alec, walking close together. Alec's head was up, and he was laughing. St Vier had that half-smile, listening to him.

Everyone got quiet, not even trying to pretend they hadn't been talking about them.

St Vier's polite. He nodded to the room. Actually, he was checking it out – and as Alec stepped up to the counter and ordered a beer, St Vier grabbed him by the elbow and steered him back.

"Again?" said Alec.

"Again," his friend said.

Luxe smiled. "St Vier."

Steffi moved in, all tits and curls. "You remember my boy Luxe, Richard, right? Here he is, come to pay us a visit—"

Luxe didn't even do her the courtesy of telling her to shut up. He just kept on talking. "Will you take my challenge?"

"On behalf of his lordship, here?" St Vier asked. "Because if you're just showing off, I'd rather not."

Luxe straightened up, and you saw the nobleman's house servant that he'd learned to be. "I bear challenge. To the Tremontaine heir." He nodded at Alec, who was busy picking at a loose thread on his cuff. "That him?"

St Vier shifted his weight, cutting Luxe off from Alec just a little more. "Don't try."

"Guard, then." Luxe drew. There was sweat on his upper lip already. He had good form, though. People spread out, and the bets got going. I was taking as many as I could, so I missed some of the action. Then Steffi was moaning, "No no no no no no no," and Rosalie had her arms wrapped around her. St Vier had Luxe pinned to the floor, sweating, his blade at his throat. The throat, not the heart.

St Vier said, "Alec?"

Alec was sweating, too, pushing hair back from his face. "What?"

"Ask him. Ask him who sent him."

We couldn't believe it. If there's one thing swordsmen don't do, it's ask that question. The patron pays, the patron calls the shots, and protects whoever's working for him, so you keep your mouth shut. That's the rules.

"I don't care who sent him! They can all go to hell."

"So do I kill him, then?"

Steffi screamed.

"Hell, no," Alec said. "What for?" And turned away.

He walked on out of the tavern, and St Vier followed him. We all stood staring at the man on the floor.

"Shit," Luxe said. He was shaking, and he wouldn't get up. "Oh, shit."

The next day, I had my great idea. I waited for Alec on the street, not in Rosalie's where everyone would see us. I waited til I saw him out with his basket to do his marketing, and I went up to him and I said, "Look, here's the thing."

He looked down his long nose at me. Way down. I can't help if I'm short. "Yes," he said; "I can see that."

I ignored the dig. You just have to. I said, "You want a message to someone? Someone up on the Hill, maybe? Something you want to say, but not write down?"

He just looked at me. But not in that sneery way. His chin went down a little, listening. He had the weirdest eyes.

"You can trust me." I tried not to talk too fast, which is something people say I sometimes do. But it was hard with those eyes, and him not saying anything back. "Say you make them an offer. A hundred royals, a thousand, I dunno, what's it worth to them?" He snorted. "Look, you don't want it; they do. So why not benefit? You save everyone a lot of grief, and make a profit. Good for them, good for you, and everyone gets what they want."

He said slowly, "I hadn't thought of that."

Well of course he hadn't.

"Just say the word," I told him. "I'm your man."

"Are you?"

The way he looked at me then.... If I'd ever doubted he was really one of them, I didn't anymore. It wasn't just his eyes, it was his voice. Something curious and measuring, like he was checking me out for position of third footman on the left or something. *I'm your man.*

That's not how I'd meant it, either. I just meant it the regular way.

"I know you're a fair-minded guy so I won't even name a price. I just—well, you know where to find me."

He nodded, turned, and walked away.

Richard met Alec on the stairs coming up. It was too dark for Alec to see how bloody the swordsman's shirt was, but he could smell it.

"Don't go up," Richard said. "There's a dead man in there."

"In *there?*" Alec pointed with his chin to their door at the top of the stairs. He was carrying a basket of fruit. The first cherries were in from the country, and he'd spent far too much on them.

"It's a mess," Richard said. He walked Alec back down the narrow stairs. "I'll tell Marie to clean it up."

Down in the courtyard, Alec could see the corners of the swordsman's mouth were white. "I'll tell her."

Marie was white, too. "I didn't," she said. "I swear."

"Didn't let the poor bastard in? I should think not."

"We know you hate cleaning up blood, Marie, it's all right."

"But who?" she said. "Who told them where you live?"

"Everyone knows where we live," Alec drawled. "It's a wonder they didn't try it before. Maybe they did, and got sick of waiting, last time. Don't worry about it."

"How much longer?" Richard asked, when she'd gone upstairs with her pail and some rags, and sent a boy to find someone to remove the body.

"Seven days," Alec said. "And then they'll stop sending you new toys to play with."

"I don't like them messing up the house."

"Neither does Marie. I'll draw her another bucket of water. She appreciates these little gestures."

"I think," St Vier said, "we'll sleep at Rosalie's tonight."

What was I doing out that night? Trying to earn a living, same as everyone else. The job finished early, and I was headed to Rosalie's for a drink. I wasn't trying to spy on anybody. But I saw that guy Alec come out Rosalie's back door, the one nobody uses, alone. He had a lantern. The moon was good enough for me. Alec was moving fast, but a moment later I saw St Vier come out the same door. He didn't have a light, and I thought he'd catch up to Alec soon enough. But he didn't. St Vier wasn't really dressed, either: shirt unlaced, jacket unbuttoned, though he did have his sword in his hand. He strapped it on as he walked, slowly and quietly, following the man with the lantern.

It didn't take a wizard to know something was up. I should've turned around and gone straight into the tavern, maybe. But I thought, Who knows? Maybe they'll need backup. So I followed them.

Alec went to the river, across from the University. Good, I thought. He's finally going back to where he came from! But he just stood on the bank, looking over. St Vier stayed in the shadows, looking at Alec. When Alec moved closer to the water St Vier got tense, like he was thinking the beanpole might throw himself in. But then Alec moved on, walking along the embankment, trailing his hand along the low wall like it was some giant pet.

When the wall petered out he swung back into Riverside, passing through the old market, which was pretty much empty except for a few people who'd built themselves a fire to keep out the chill and the spooks til dawn. They glanced up when Alec passed, trying to make themselves small, not to be noticed. He didn't even look. St Vier walked right by them, too, a moment later. I figured it wouldn't hurt to say hello and see if it was anyone I knew, but they weren't too friendly.

It was harder in the little streets to keep behind them. Alec was moving slower. Like it was a bright spring day, and he had all the time in the world to get from Rosalie's tavern to his own lodgings. I heard St Vier had killed a man there today.

They didn't go in. Alec leaned his head against the crumbling stone archway to the courtyard. His arm was up over his head, and his fist was clenched. He spread his fingers out slowly, ran them down the outer wall. He backed away slowly from the house, like he didn't want to let go. Even slower he walked down the street, where it was so dark we both would have lost him without the lantern.

Did he know St Vier was following him? How could he not? How could he think he'd get so far in the night alone? And did St Vier know it was me behind him? He must have. Or maybe not. Maybe everyone was out taking a little midnight walk that just happened to go all around Riverside. All around the places the two of them liked to eat and drink and buy things, make trouble and get out of it, kill and get talked about. All of them. Like a farewell tour.

Alec crossed Riverside, all the way to the Bridge—the good bridge, the big stone one that takes you to the side of the city with all the nice stuff: the excellent shops and pretty little houses, the wide paths by the River where people go walking under the trees, until you climb all the way up to the Hill, where the nobles in their mansions can enjoy fresh breezes and a really good view. There are some nasty bits, too, with nasty people in them who don't care who your boyfriend is, or codes of honor or anything. If Alec was planning to sneak up to Tremontaine House with his lantern in the dark, he'd better be careful.

But the dark was a little less dark now. You could see his bony, ragged form against the sky behind him. He went up the Bridge, but didn't cross it—didn't even set one foot on it. He just stood there, staring at the city. Then he held his lantern up high, high over his head, like he was showing it to the River, or showing the whole world where he stood. And he goes and throws the whole thing far out into the water.

Alec turned around, then, back to Riverside, back to us. I couldn't see his face, but I heard his voice. "Richard?" he asked, into the graying light.

The funny thing was, he was looking in the wrong direction.

St Vier stepped out of the shadows. "Let's go home."

They walked right past me.

Most people in Riverside lock their doors if they own anything of value, but Richard St Vier had gotten out of the habit. This morning, though, he found the door to their rooms locked tight. They had to go back down to Marie's to get her key.

She handed them the cold old iron. "You'll want to keep this. I'll put a gate over the courtyard entry, too, maybe. Should I?"

"Not yet."

Their rooms were spotless, the old elmwood floor scrubbed almost white. "Like the pages of a book," said Alec. He took a burnt stick from the hearth, and wrote something on the floor with it, then scuffed it out with his foot, leaving a charcoal smear.

Richard stood in the middle of the room. The furniture was off. It had been knocked around during the fight, of course, and then Marie had moved it to do the floor, and not put it back exactly right. She'd missed a spot of blood on the wall. He pulled the chaise longue back to its place between the window and the fireplace. The inlaid table Alec had pawned his velvet coat for should be closer to the wall. He remembered the day Alec had re-appeared in Riverside, fresh from his last fight with the Duchess, groceries in hand and tiny shards of glass still glittering on the shoulders of that coat.

Alec flung himself into their ratty old chaise longue. Stuffing oozed. He twisted uncomfortably, got up, took a book from the pile on the mantelpiece—which Marie had dusted and straightened—and tried the chaise again.

Richard went into the next room, where his opponent had been hiding, waiting. It looked all right, but he hated knowing anyone had been in there. He opened his sword chest. Everything seemed in place. He took out a practice sword, and went back to the front room to work. For awhile, the room was quiet except for the rhythmic thud of his feet on the floor, the sword on the wall.

Then Alec looked up from the book he hadn't been reading. "Richard," he said. "Let's go to Tremontaine House."

"All right." Richard put the sword up. "When?"

"How long will it take you to change your shirt?"

"And you? Are you going to change?"

Alec considered his own frayed cuffs. "No. No, I don't think so."

He pulled on his scholar's robe, and then went out the door and down the stairs without looking back.

Richard did not stop to change his shirt; he grabbed the nearest decent sword and followed Alec down the narrow stairs, catching up with him on the landing. Alec didn't say anything; he just kept walking. Walking toward the Bridge. He walked down the narrow lanes where the old houses practically touched each other in perpetual twilight. He walked along the streets where the gutters overflowed, past the lion fountain with the broken nose where women were washing linens.

And then it turned into a story. That's the only way he could describe it.

THE DUKE OF RIVERSIDE

"Where are you going?" asked Lucy Diver, and when Alec answered "Tremontaine House," Lucy put down her washing and said, "Oh, yeah? Mind if I come, too?" Alec shrugged, *Why not?* and Lucy did.

They walked through the Market Square, and people looked up from their trading in fresh-caught fish and stolen watches.

"Hey, Alec!" Toothless John called out. "I got good trout for you today!"

But Alec didn't stop.

"Where are you going?" John asked, and Lucy answered, "Tremontaine House!" and John fell in with them.

They came upon Fat Rodge, and Hal, and "Where are you going?" they asked, and John answered, "Up the Hill," and they came along, too.

They picked up three or four more this way, and after that people just started joining because it was a crowd, and it was a nice day to be going somewhere new.

I was one of the ones who marched that day, the day that funny kid, Alec, became the Duke Tremontaine.

A whole big bunch of us parading through Riverside, drunk and sober, some at the end of their day and some just starting out, because everyone likes to be in on the action. The girls were waving ribbons in the air, and everyone was singing something different. St Vier was guarding all of us, like some crazy wedding procession, and other swordsmen joined in, too, making a very nice appearance.

For a guy with a mouth like that on him, Alec was awful quiet. In fact, I don't think he ever said a word. Just kept on walking, a beanpole in black, paying no attention to anyone around him, just walking like he knew if he stopped the whole thing would fall apart. Sometimes we even had to run to keep up with him.

When we got to the Bridge, we kept right on going. We marched through the city, past all the shops and the fancy houses, singing and carrying on, laughing as people fell back out of our way, and we heard them shouting and screaming and calling to each other to run away or to come and see. Some even lined up, cheering. I heard "Riverside!" and "Tremontaine!" and a whole lot else, besides. But we didn't stop. We marched all the way up the broad streets to the Hill, past all those high walls and gold-and-iron gates, until we came to the biggest and fanciest, the one that was Alec's, and they had to let him in.

We lifted him up on our shoulders and carried him all the way there—over the Bridge, all the way up the Hill to Tremontaine House.

After all, he was one of ours.

The Contributors

Chris Barzak has published many short stories. His debut novel, *One for Sorrow,* won the Crawford Award. His second novel, *The Love We Share Without Knowing,* was placed on the 2008 James Tiptree Jr. Award Honor List. He holds an MFA in Creative Writing from Chatham University and currently teaches fiction writing at Youngstown State University.

Richard Bowes is a multi-award winning author: his story "Streetcar Dreams" won the World Fantasy Award for Best Novella in 1998; his novel *Minions of the Moon* earned the Lambda Literary Award in 2000 (and will be reprinted by Lethe Press in late 2012); a short story addressing the impact of 9/11 on Manhattanites, "There's a Hole in the City" won the Million Writers Award for Fiction; and his novella "If Angels Fight" won his second World Fantasy Award.

Tom Cardamone writes queer speculative fiction. He is the editor of *The Lost Library: Gay Fiction Rediscovered.* His short story collection, *Pumpkin Teeth,* was a finalist for the Lambda Literary Award. This fall his surrealist novella *Green Thumb* will be published by the BrazenHead imprint of Lethe Press.

K. M. Ferebee was bred, born, and raised in Texas. Currently she lives, more or less, in New York City. Her work has appeared or is forthcoming in *Shimmer* and *The Brooklyn Rail*. She has a strange obsession with the geography of London, and no great gift for gardening.

RICHARD E. GROPP lives on a mountain outside of Seattle with his partner of fifteen years. It is a small mountain. This is his first published story, but his novel *Bad Glass* won the Suvudu Writing Contest and will be released by DelRey in late 2012.

NABIL HIJAZI evolved from a sophisticated mass-mailing advertising algorithm. Problematic source control and inconsistent naming conventions have created confusion as to Nabil's gender, location, and species; but it is rumored that version 5.0 (Flying Squirrel) travels regularly between Silicon Valley and Betelgeuse.

TED INFINITY comes from a very long line of Infinities, all pseudonymous. He is a technical writer who lives in the San Francisco Bay Area.

ALEX JEFFERS dislikes the cold of New England but that is where he lives. His recent short fiction has appeared online at GigaNotoSaurus.org, in print in *Icarus*, and is forthcoming in two anthologies, *Boys of Summer* and *The Touch of the Sea*. Lethe Press will release Jeffers's collection of wonder stories *You Will Meet a Stranger Far from Home* in July. He can be found on the web at sentenceandparagraph.com.

MAT JOINER lives in Birmingham with his partner. His dark short fiction has been published in *Never Again*.

ELLEN KUSHNER for many years was the host of the radio program Sound & Spirit. She is arguably best known for the Riverside series which includes *Swordspoint, The Privilege of the Sword, The Fall of the Kings* (co-written with her wife, Delia Sherman), and several short stories. She won the World Fantasy Award and the Mythopoeic Award for her novel *Thomas the Rhymer*.

Joel Lane is a British novelist, short story writer, poet, critic and anthology editor. He has twice received the British Fantasy Award. Nine Arches Press recently released a chapbook, *Do Not Pass Go*.

Kristopher Reisz grew up in Decatur, Alabama, which had three miniature golf courses and not much else. While still in high school, he decided his life's ambition was to make as much money as possible without having to get up before noon. Thus, he set out to become a writer. He sold his first story to a small horror magazine for five dollars. The check bounced. Some might have taken that as a sign, but he remembered his motto, Carpe Afternoon, and soldiered on. His young adult novel, *Tripping to Somewhere*, is an acclaimed book of queer speculative fiction.

Sam Sommer is a playwright, accomplished designer and author of several short stories. He is the recipient of two Off-Off Broadway Review awards for Scenic Design for the shows *Cowboys* and *Tango Masculino*.

Lee Thomas is the Lambda Literary Award and Bram Stoker Award-winning author of *Stained, The Dust of Wonderland, In the Closet, Under the Bed,* and *The German*. Recent and forthcoming releases include *Torn* and *Like Light for Flies*. He resides in Austin, Texas.

Stellan Thorne is a writer, mostly of speculative fiction. When he's not writing, he can usually be spotted sunning himself gently by the light of a monitor or rolling polyhedral dice behind a cardboard screen. On rare occasions he has been spotted going outdoors. He lives in Manchester, which is possibly the best city in the world, where he does various queer and geeky things.

Justin Torres grew up in upstate New York. His work has appeared in *The New Yorker, Granta, Tin House, Glimmer Train,* and other publications. A graduate of the Iowa Writers' Workshop, he is a recipient of the Rolón United States Artist Fellowship in Literature, and is now a Wallace Stegner Fellow at Stanford. He has worked as a farmhand, a dog-walker, a creative writing teacher, and a bookseller.

THE EDITOR

STEVE BERMAN writes way too little fiction but does manage to edit at least one anthology every year so his feline companion, Daulton, can be kept content with daily meals of rotisserie chicken. The *Wilde Stories* annual series has twice been a finalist for the Lambda Literary Award, which pleases Steve because he does have a great love for queer speculative fiction. He resides in southern New Jersey, the only state in the Union with an official devil.

Lightning Source UK Ltd.
Milton Keynes UK
UKHW03f1128260418
321691UK00001B/356/P

9 781590 213988